Castaway on Temurlone

a space opera

By David Wesley Hill

Published by
Temurlone Press
www.temurlonepress.com

ISBN: 978-0983611714

Cover art by Vincent Di Fate
Cover design by Gail Dubov

For Gail Pamela Dubov

.

Table of Contents

CHAPTER ONE

The Old Alien and the Cee

Our long-term corporate strategy relied upon a simple concept: If we increased the size of our market, sales would grow proportionally. Thus we hired the best and the brightest—poets, philosophers, physicists, cosmologists, mathematicians, and comics. We set them a single challenge:

Prove the existence of God.

Seventeen years later, it is my pleasure to bring you the good news that they have succeeded.

Vassily X. Hardcourt: *Good News for Our Stockholders: The 2602 Annual Report of the Icon Corporation*

A rough hand grabbed my shoulder and shook me awake and I found myself looking into the yellow eyes of Jo Feringel, my mother's man. It was well before dawn and only a hint of light entered the room through the salt crusted lattices of the window. But this was enough to allow me to make out the nose as protuberant as a muzzle, the nostrils fringed with a mustache of cilia. His fingers were connected to one another by a webbing of loose skin. I shook myself free, unable to endure his touch.

"Get yourself dressed, boy," Jo Feringel said. "Be quick about it."

"Why?"

"Never mind why. Just do as I say, hear? And make a good job of it. Shirt and pants and shoes and all that. I want you looking decent."

He left the room without further words. My mother's other

children, both sons of Jo Feringel and not of my own father, peered at me through the darkness from the bed next to mine. They were years younger than me and took after him, having the same elongated noses and bristles of mustache, which expanded underwater into gills. We got along well enough but there was a distance between us not entirely due to the difference in our ages. They were his children, only partly my brothers. Quill, who was two[1], hissed from under the blanket hiding their heads:

"What is happening, Pim?"

"You know as much as I do," I answered while pulling on my pants and tucking my good white shirt into the waist.

"What have you done?" This was from the other boy, Venn, who was three. "Bet you did something bad."

"No, not that I recall, I don't think," I replied, searching my memory for any occasion when I might have caused greater trouble than usual. Nothing came to mind. So I slid my feet into socks and laced my shoes. Then I punched my brothers for luck, causing protests and fits of quiet giggling, and joined Jo Feringel and my mother in the main area of the house.

---

1   In keeping with millennia of tradition, The Bureau of Interstellar Standards based temporal measurement upon the metric second, defined as the interval taken to complete 10,000,000,000 oscillations of the hydrogen atom (this was almost, but not quite equal to the old, astronomically-determined second). The standard metric minute was defined as 100 seconds; the metric hour as 100 minutes. With thousands of inhabited planets having varying periods of rotation and revolution, however, it was impractical to standardize such units as the day, the week, or the month, and these intervals were defined uniquely on different worlds, if they were indeed measured at all. On the other hand, The Bureau recognized the utility of a standard year, its interval independent of the revolution of any particular celestial body. Thus the metric year was defined as 10,000 metric hours (roughly equivalent to three terrestrial years), and the year A.D. 2602 (*anno domini*) became A.I. 1 (*anno infinitum*).

My mother was heavy with another child. Her time was near and her belly was unwieldy. She was standing beside the stove, tending a pot of rice porridge, stirring the bubbling gruel with a wood spoon. Her eyes were red and she refused to look at me.

Jo Feringel was at the table in the center of the room, a cup of tea steaming in his fist. The nictitating membranes covering his eyes slid upward under his true lids, then down again. He indicated a chair.

"Seat yourself," he told me.

I sat. My mother brought over a bowl of porridge, a spoon carved from pink shell, and smaller dishes of minced leeks and cockles. She stroked my cheek with the back of her hand, then returned to the kitchen alcove. I ignored the food and faced Jo Feringel.

"What's going on?" I asked.

"Well, I'll tell you, no problem. We have an appointment, you and I."

"An appointment?"

"That's right, boy. There's a freighter in orbit, the *Miraculous Abernathy*—you might have noticed her tenders coming in to port yesterday. I asked around. Turns out she's short a man or two, and looking to hire. The pay's not bad, even for unskilled labor, which is where you fit in, sure enough. I spoke with one of the mates and he agreed to look you over. We're meeting him in an hour."

"Are we."

"Mind your tone, boy—we are, that's a fact." Feringel sipped the tea and set the mug deliberately on the table between us. "I want you to understand I've done you a good turn. Have no doubt about it. It's three months now since you've been finished with schooling, isn't that right?"

"Something like that," I admitted.

"And what have you done with yourself? Nothing much."

"I've been looking for work," I said.

"I know you have. I also know you've been made no offers. No mystery there! Mollusk and crustacean prices are down. No one's hiring. Not the canneries and freezers, not the warehouses. And you can't work the water, not that there's much doing out in the farms—you just aren't designed for it. No, there is nothing for you here, boy."

The town we lived in was the only one in the entire world. Three centuries before, the planet had been a hunk of rock covered with mold and lichen and not much else. Then a commercial consortium seeded the ocean with terrestrial oysters, clams, mussels, and other bivalves, as well as with periwinkles, abalone, conches, lobsters, and crabs. When the shellfish had established themselves, the consortium set up a colony at a suitable headland, built freezing facilities and canneries, and populated the town with an indentured workforce genetically tailored to harvest the ocean with a minimum of mechanical assistance. Jo Feringel and the others like him could remain underwater indefinitely, absorbing oxygen through their gills, their skin protected from cold and salt by an oily secretion produced by dermal glands, the webbing between their fingers and toes propelling them easily through the coastal bays.

During the hundred years of its franchise, the consortium made a fair profit on its investment. In the centuries after that, the town—now an independent subscriber to The Standard Interstellar Catalog—continued exporting shellfish throughout the stellar neighborhood. Unfortunately, trade suffered whenever the economies of nearby planets went into recession, which had been the case now for several years.

"No," Feringel repeated. "There's nothing here for you, boy."

I didn't disagree. We'd had the same conversation a dozen times, and he wasn't telling me anything I didn't know. Most of my class-mates—except those few who could afford to continue their educa-tion off world—were already working beside their families in the shellfish beds and crustacean farms. But this was an option closed to me, as Feringel pointed out, because I lacked their amphibious adap-tations. Ashore, unfortunately, my prospects were equally bleak. For months I had gone from warehouse to warehouse along Port Road, from cannery to cannery, and revisited each more than once, until the foremen and administrators all knew my name. They treated me politely but no one had a position to offer, however menial. I had long since come to the same conclusion as Feringel, that my future lay elsewhere, away from this place, from this small town and its gray world, only I hadn't figured out how to go about leaving. Now that I considered the idea, seriously instead of as an idle daydream, shipping out aboard a freighter made a lot of sense. I couldn't quite own up to it, but the thought of going into space excited me, too. Perhaps this was my father's heritage. According to my mother, he'd been a restless man.

Yet I couldn't bring myself to agree out loud with Jo Feringel. Instead I said: "What if I don't want to sign on?"

"Then you'd be a damn fool. You have a real chance here to earn decent money while learning a trade, that's my opinion. I wouldn't turn down the opportunity myself." Feringel studied his clasped hands a moment, the webbing bunched between the fingers like the folds of an umbrella, and fixed his eyes on me. His under-lids blinked twice before he continued: "Maybe I've been hasty. Maybe you have a better idea. If you do, boy, let me hear it." He paused long enough for me to answer but no matter how much I wanted to disagree with him, I couldn't find anything to say, and the silence stretched on. Finally, he said:

"I didn't think so. Well, then, that's settled. Get your jacket. It's a brisk walk to the port and we've little enough time as it is."

Now my mother began crying in earnest, her tears spilling into the pot of rice gruel. Rising from the table, Jo Feringel put his arms around her, cradling her belly with his webbed fingers. He wasn't unkind, I gave him that, although I had disliked him for years. Maybe it was simply he wasn't my father, a man I barely remembered but loved fiercely anyway. He'd been a commercial rep—a salesman—never what you would call successful, traveling from place to place in search of the big deal but finding only small ones, earning just enough to remain solvent. Until he reached this forsaken town and contracted a respiratory infection that proved resistant to medical treatment. His death had stranded my mother and me among strangers with little money and fewer prospects. For a while she supported us by taking in laundry and working at domestic chores but she never earned much, and we'd been barely getting by when she met Jo Feringel.

Shoving my chair back from the table, I got to my feet and went outside and waited on the porch until he joined me. Without further conversation, we set off together for the landing field.

The road was paved with crushed shell and our feet made crackling sounds as we walked, as if something was cooking in a pan. From a distance came the grumble of surf. Soon Feringel and I were among warehouses, these mostly silent, the loading docks vacant except for drowsy watchmen. Past them was the expanse of blackened concrete that was the spaceport, where three small ships were parked—the tenders belonging to the freighter in orbit. Beside them were refrigerated trucks from which men were unloading bags of mussels, living soft-shell crabs packed in straw, cases of frozen crab meat, and portable aquariums stocked with lobsters, their claws secured by elastic bands.

Jo Feringel led me to the nearest tender, a squat tube forty meters in length. Before the entrance to the cargo hold stood an off worlder—a lean man with fingers as long as Feringel's although without webbing. He wore a loose blouse and baggy pantaloons secured at the waist by a crimson sash. In his hands was a personal assistant and he was checking off items on an inventory list as the longshoremen loaded the vessel, some manhandling crates, others operating fork lifts to move pallets into the hold.

Jo Feringel tapped my arm. "That's the fellow I spoke to," he said, indicating the man directing the operation. "Marval Wirthy, the seventeenth mate. Mind your tongue and your manners and all will go well, or so I guess. He strikes me as a stern taskmaster with little humor in him. You'll be under his eye. That's just the natural way of things."

I nodded reluctantly, recognizing good advice when I heard it, no matter the source.

Placing the assistant in a pouch, Marval Wirthy turned his attention on us. His face was as pale as chalk, the nose a snub, the lips a line with creases at each corner. I did not doubt Marval Wirthy was as humorless as Jo Feringel warned.

"Ah, Mr. Feringel. Is this the boy you mentioned?"

"It is, sir. Pimsol Anderts, or just Pim."

"He seems taller than you led me to believe."

"I don't know how that could be possible. The boy is as tall as he is, no more, no less."

7

"I will accept your word on the matter, Mr. Feringel. The good thing is he's thin. That's important. He'll have to squeeze through many tight corners while at his duties." Marval Wirthy now addressed me directly. "Are you ready to follow instructions, Mister Anderts? I won't mislead you, the work is difficult and not at all entertaining. You'll start out as an apprentice environmental specialist. It is not a glamorous position but where you go from there is up to you. The future is wide open for a determined young man. We're offering a standard five-year indenture contract. The salary is one thousand hhours per annum[2], paid in quarterly installments or deposited to your account in the financial institution of your choice. There's also a sign-on bonus of five hundred hhours, payable immediately in cash. Is this acceptable, Mr. Anderts?"

"It does seem attractive, sir."

"I am so very relieved you agree. The *Miraculous Abernathy* has need of hardy crew. Men unafraid of honest labor. Men committed to excellence. Will you be one of them?"

"Absolutely, sir."

"Excellent. Simply press your thumb here and you'll be signed

---

2   Worlds participating in the interstellar economy used currencies based upon the value of units of basic labor: mminutes and hhours. (Ddays, wweeks, mmonths, yyears, etc., were also in use, but these denominations were defined differently by their issuing banks.) This, of course, gave rise to the common expression: "Time is money." However, since intelligent species performed varying amounts of useful work during a given period, the currencies could not be of equal value. Thus an hour of human toil (hhour[h]) was worth one and a half hours of kelocca labor (hhour[k]) but only half an hour of Visgooth exertion (hhour[v]). Exchange rates fluctuated according to investor confidence in the physical and intellectual characteristics of each race. Twice each century The Bureau of Interstellar Standards issued *A Comparative Analysis of the Relative Efficiency of Discrete Non-entropic Systems*, a report highly regarded by currency speculators.

aboard, that's a good lad." Marval Wirthy held out the personal assistant. For a moment I hesitated. Five years was a serious commit-
ment, almost the length of my entire life lived over again. Nor was a
thousand hhours much more than the poorest laborer earned. And
it galled me to be taking Jo Feringel's advice in any matter. But I
couldn't argue with him—there was no place for me, not here. Perhaps there never had been. Perhaps I had always known it. Maybe
that was why I found it so easy to put my finger on the screen.

Marval Wirthy snapped the assistant shut with a loud click.
"The *Abernathy* departs orbit noon tomorrow. You have leave for the
rest of today. Settle your affairs and return at half past thirteen in
the morning." Now Marval Wirthy's voice became flat with warning
and all pretense of politeness disappeared. "Punctuality is a virtue,
Mister Anderts. Be so much as a minute tardy and I will dispatch a
shore party to fetch you under restraint, not a dignified experience,
to be sure. You belong to the *Abernathy* now. Am I understood?"

"Completely, sir."

"I certainly hope so, Mister Anderts. Welcome aboard."

With this pleasantry Marval Wirthy returned his attention to
the loading operation while Jo Feringel and I returned to town and
parted ways, he to his daily work, I to take a last look at the place
that had been my home. For a while I wandered along Harbor Street,
the main commercial area, its storefronts tilted at separate angles, as
crooked as bad teeth. Already I felt nostalgic, which was strange
since I would be carrying away few happy memories. Nor were there
many besides my mother and my brothers to whom I wanted to say
good-bye. My only real friend was not even human. Aaa was a huge
old bivalve from a world a hundred parsecs toward the galactic center. He lived in the shallows south of town and resembled nothing so

much as another clam except he was larger than I was. His shell was white with striations of red. As always, he was partly submerged in the breakers, his shell ajar, allowing waves to push water through the membranes that served as his mouth. Aaa was a filtration feeder.

From between the lips of the shell extruded two stalks, each topped with an eyeball the size of my fist. A third stalk, tipped with a flexible sphincter of muscle, wormed into the air and sprayed me with tepid fluid—Aaa's version, I had learned, of a cough.

"What brings you visiting, Pimsol Anderts?" Aaa asked, his voice a low rumble, intelligible despite his unique method of speaking.

"I have come to say good-bye," I explained.

"Ah, glad news! The scholarship was granted?"

I laughed. "That's not it. Just the opposite, in fact. Not that I figured I had much of a chance, what with my grades. No, Feringel's got me work on a freighter, the *Miraculous Abernathy*. She sails tomorrow."

A groan jetted from Aaa's sphincter and his eyeballs drooped.

"I will miss your companionship," confessed the mollusk. "Still, I delight in your good fortune."

"Hardly that," I snapped. "God knows what the ship's like— some decrepit old hulk, I'll bet. No, Feringel's just tired of seeing me around. As far as he's concerned, I'm only another mouth to feed, particularly since I'm none of his own blood. He isn't doing me a favor."

"To the contrary, my friend," exclaimed Aaa. "I envy you with all my intestines. If only I were younger! To sail space again, as I once did with my Bee. She was a correspondent for The Bureau and less sessile than I am."

Then another thought occurred to the bivalve, perhaps some un- wanted memory. Despite his thick accent, I could hear melancholy in Aaa's voice. Giving forth a sad sigh, which vented water meters into the air in a plume of froth, he polished his eyeballs against his interior membrane and said:

"I have never told you, have I, what brought me to this charming beach on this lovely planet so far from my own spawning place?"

Charming and *lovely* were not the words I would have chosen to describe my home world. Much, I realized, depended on your point of view. "No, you've never said."

"That is because the truth does not reflect well on me. However, as your friend, I owe you a parting gift and the best gift I can give you is the gift of good advice. I will tell you my story and it may be that you will learn from the mistakes I have made." The tendrils lining the mouth of Aaa's shell began pulsing. "Ah, Pimsol Anderts," he went on, "looking at me, you may think you see a fine specimen of a mollusk, stout of shell and bright of gill. Unfortunately, the very opposite is true! What I really am is a fugitive, a coward, a moral bankrupt who betrayed his own true love, the most beautiful Bee there ever was."

Aaa's species was divided into three sexes instead of two. He was male; the Bee was female; and the Cee—as best as I could gather from Aaa's roundabout explanation—was a combination of both genders. "Our biology allows us to mate once only," Aaa explained. "Thus, as you may imagine, we attach great importance to the event."

"Stands to reason," I agreed, nodding sagely, not that I had much experience with biology, alien or human. The local girls preferred boys with gills.

"Typically," Aaa went on, "we perform the act to culminate a relationship instead of to begin a romance, as you mammals do, and so it went with my Bee and myself. Not until after a lifetime together were we ready to consummate our love. Then we gave up our journeying and returned to the planet that spawned us. But hesitation assailed me when the moment approached. A thousand uncertainties filled my thoughts, a thousand questions. Perhaps we had become betrothed too soon. Perhaps there was another Bee more suitable for me, another Aaa for her. Mostly, though, I was afraid. You see, Pimsol Anderts, among my kind, to mate is to die—"

"Why, that doesn't seem right or fair," I exclaimed.

"It is indeed one of God's crueler jests," the old mollusk agreed. "The reproductive act begins an inescapable metabolic process in both the Aaa and the Bee, resulting in their physical dissolution. Most consider this a joyous event, the ultimate proof of love, when an Aaa and Bee surrender life itself to create a new generation together. To the contrary, I discovered I loved living my life more than I loved my Bee. On the very morning of our ceremony, with all our friends and family gathered in the shallows to witness our union, I stole away to the spaceport and departed forever."

Aaa fell silent. When it became obvious he had finished speaking, I said, "I'm sorry, Aaa, but I don't get your point."

"It is simple, Pimsol Anderts. Not a single day has gone by that I haven't missed my Bee and regretted my cowardice. Profit from the example of a stupid mollusk, young mammal. Seize the moment, as God intended. Never pass up a chance for love or for adventure. Fear no evil except your own lack of courage, else you will end up as I have, old and alone, wondering what might have been."

As Aaa fell quiet, I heard the whine of a car passing overhead.

At first I thought it a van ferrying workers out to the lobster herds at the edge of the continental shelf. Then the car began circling. It descended toward the sea and came to a halt ten meters above the surface. A hatch opened and a container fell from the opening. It hit the water with a great splash, a featureless silver orb, oval as an egg. As the disturbance caused by its landing died away, the thing split apart, revealing a nightmare.

The creature was as large as Aaa but all tentacles, in the middle of which was a bulbous head with protruding orange eyes.

Its beak was orange, too, and serrated like a saw.

At the tips of the tentacles were pincers the size of hands. All were snapping open and shut while the tentacles whipped the surface of the sea to a froth. Suddenly I was deafened by a piercing whistle close to my ear. A stream of water jetted from Aaa's vocal tube straight up. The tendrils lining his shell stood out stiff with shock.

"It is impossible," whispered the ancient mollusk. "Impossible."

"What is?" I asked him. "What is that ugly thing?"

Aaa's voice was a whisper, a dribble of liquid issuing from the sphincter.

"It is my beautiful Bee," he replied.

"Ten years—" the Bee's voice was strangely gentle—"for ten years I have searched for you from world to world, never surrendering hope, never despairing, following a trail that grew ever fainter. Countless were the nights I cried myself to dormancy, wondering what had become of my own true love. But now I have found you and we are reunited. Universe of miracles! Let me come in unto you, Aaa, and we will share together the pleasure of the flesh, as it was meant to be."

"Stay away!" There was no mistaking the old mollusk's panic.

"Only if you tell me you do not love me." The Bee stretched forth a tentacle in an endearing gesture.

"I cannot. Even now, I cannot deny it. I love—I have always

loved you."

"Then put aside your fear, which has caused so much mischief. Let me come in unto you, my dearest, and we will become one soul."

For a moment I thought Aaa would agree. Even I, of another species entirely, could feel his yearning to be embraced by the Bee, to sacrifice his life to their love.

Somehow, however, the bivalve found the nerve to resist. In a voice scarcely louder than a croak, he said: "No."

From the interior of Aaa's shell emerged a tube thicker than my waist. He began forcing water through it, stirring up clouds of sand and grit as he freed himself from the place he'd rested in for so long. Slowly the huge mollusk lifted from the sea bottom and began lurching through the shallows in clumsy wallops of spray. I did not know what good he thought this would do—the Bee was obviously faster. She stretched her tentacles out and began slithering through the water after him. Without thinking, I leaped sideways, interposing myself between Aaa and the Bee. She braked in a flurry of limbs and regarded me with round orange eyes.

"Who are you and why are you interfering?"

"I am Pim Anderts, to answer your first question. As for why I'm interfering, well, Aaa's my friend. If he doesn't—if he doesn't want to do this thing with you, I don't think it's right for you to make him."

"This is a private affair. You know nothing of our relationship."

"I know it means his death. Your death, too, for that matter."

"Is that what he said?" The Bee's beak moved from side to side as she spoke, causing her words to be accompanied by a wet grinding sound. "The silly old fool! Sometimes I wonder why I love him as much as I do. Pim Anderts, I tell you once more—move aside. I have waited too long for this moment. We were meant to be together. It is our destiny."

I didn't know where I found the resolution to remain between the Bee's pincers and the fleeing mollusk.

Not that it made much difference. The Bee darted around me and hurled herself through the water after Aaa.

Somehow I managed to catch a tentacle as it whipped past. My weight slowed the Bee only a little and I was carried through the shallows in a rush, salt water foaming in my nostrils and in my eyes. Then she slapped the tentacle back and forth against the sea bed in an effort to break my hold. Finally the Bee sent other tentacles after me, wrapped them around my chest and shoulders, and lifted me into the air.

The Bee's head was a glistening dome more or less my size. Immobilized by the coils, I was carried directly before her huge lidless orange eyes and held suspended. I couldn't miss the exasperation in her voice despite the alien articulation of her beak.

"However misguided, your loyalty is touching," said the Bee. "Promise to interfere no further. I wouldn't wish to harm my love's true friend."

The pressure of the tentacles around my chest made breathing hard but even so I inhaled enough of the Bee's iodine reek to set me coughing.

"I can't promise that," I managed to say eventually.

"Oh, males!" There was no mistaking the Bee's petulance. Her tentacles tensed around me and I feared I would be mangled between them but they only carried me nearer. "What must I do with you?" asked the Bee, perhaps rhetorically. "You are a brave nuisance but a nuisance nonetheless. Forgive me, Pim Anderts, you leave me no choice. We will not meet again."

The Bee opened her beak, revealing a cavity studded with wicked spikes, from which wafted a fetid odor.

I struggled against the coils but they were as firm as metal. The Bee was inhaling deeply, as if preparing for exercise. Then she began swinging me in a circle around the gray bulb of her dome. Perhaps I completed two revolutions, or three—I was too nauseated to keep count. At some point the Bee released me and sent me skimming over the waves until I slammed into the water twenty meters away. Trying not to drown and coming up for air and getting my breath back required all my attention during the next frantic seconds. When I was able to look around, the Bee was almost upon Aaa and closing fast. I began scrambling through the shallows toward them but had covered less than a quarter of the distance when the Bee caught up with Aaa and wrapped her tentacles around his shell.

The mollusk let out a despairing scream and, as bivalves do in the face of danger, clamped his shell shut, withdrawing his append-ages to the safety of his insides.

I would have guessed it would require industrial machinery to pry the two halves apart but the Bee accomplished this on her own, her tentacles becoming taut with strain as she levered open Aaa's shell, exposing the pink membrane lining his interior.

Keeping the two sides wedged ajar with a pair of tentacles, the Bee put others inside Aaa. I couldn't tell what they were doing but they were moving and poking around, and that was enough to make me sick and angry.

What I was witnessing, I knew, was the physical act of repro-duction as performed by Aaa's species. An act that would result in his death as well as in the death of the Bee. An act that was being performed upon my friend without his consent.

"Stop that right now," I yelled as I waded toward them through the surf. "Just quit it, you hear me?"

The Bee made no sign that she did. Instead she slipped her cranium through the gap in Aaa's shell and then pulled the rest of herself inside, first her beak, last the tips of the tentacles holding apart the two halves, which snapped shut with a smack just as I returned upon the scene.

Despite Aaa's size, I did not guess there was room enough inside him to comfortably accommodate the Bee. This assumption was proved correct when the shell began rocking back and forth, as if an invisible struggle was going on inside. Then it tipped sideways, rolled a couple meters, and gave another lurch. Finally the mollusk quivered violently, causing the surrounding water to become murky. This was Aaa's last spasm.

His shell fell open with a moist sucking sound. What I could see of his interior looked morbid instead of healthy pink. The stuff was so curdled, I couldn't tell which parts had belonged to the Bee and which parts to Aaa.

Aaa had spoken less than the truth. He was dead, sure enough—but more, he was decaying with phenomenal speed, his organs melting into an organic slurry as I watched.

The stink of his rotting was so foul that I couldn't stay at Aaa's side. I retreated to shore and sat there on the beach as the afternoon faded, keeping a sort of gloomy vigil long after I should have returned home.

Aaa's shell began collapsing in on itself, as if it were being eaten away from within. This, I supposed, was further example of the accelerated decay process I had noticed.

The hard material of the shell liquefied, revealing a ball of organic debris. I figured the waves would wash this detritus away but instead it remained whole—and began to twitch. I waded back into the water and peered cautiously at the thing. Mainly it seemed composed of a webbing of arteries around a curtain of leathery tissue. Could it be an egg? I wondered. The act that had murdered Aaa, after all, had been the act of reproduction. That would explain the scraping noise coming from beneath the skin.

Something wanted out.

There was a ripping sound and I stumbled back as the globe tore down the middle.

An appendage pushed upward into the open air. It struggled furiously against an elastic cocoon of membrane, which stretched and then broke apart. First a head, then shoulders, then glorious iridescent wings emerged from the egg. As they dried, the wings became even more brilliant, glowing with bioluminescence in the twilight, scarlet and umber and a purple so intense that it made your heart ache. As the wings began beating, the creature lifted skyward and hovered above the egg from which it had come.

It had tentacles identical to the Bee's. The pattern of light tracing its wings was identical to the pattern of Aaa's shell. Yet despite being so obviously the child of its parents, this was no newborn. The look in its lambent orange eyes was too knowing and wise. No, it was something else.

"What—who are you?" I asked.

"Is it not obvious, Pimsol Anderts?" answered the creature in a voice as silken as the Bee's but as good-natured as Aaa's voice had always been. "I am, of course, the Cee."

Once again Aaa had spoken less than the truth. The wise old mollusk I had known was dead, no question. But he lived on in the Cee.

It turned out the process I had witnessed was less one of reproduction than one of metamorphosis. As Aaa and the Bee joined together, their neural tissue was incorporated into the new creature, into the Cee, so there was no loss of personal identity but rather an augmentation of consciousness, as the lovers were connected thought to thought within one body.

"How could I have feared what is so wonderful?" mused the Cee, its wings rippling outlines of living light. "The intimacy, Pimsol Anderts. I cannot begin to describe it."

"But that's you in there, isn't it, Aaa?" I asked.

"Yes, I am here. But I am also the Bee. Together we are the Cee."

This third gender was hermaphroditic. Sexual reproduction, combining the genetic material of Aaa and the Bee, would take place internally. Then the Cee would release fertilized spores by the trillions into the ocean. An insignificant percentage of these spores would hatch into animalcules, of which an even smaller percentage would survive to adulthood, some to become mollusks, some to become tentacled horrors.

"That's a relief, Cee," I said. "For awhile there I thought I had lost you. It is not good watching a friend die."

"But I am here still, only more so, for a moment longer. Never forget, Pimsol Anderts, this is a universe of miracles."

"So everyone says. Sometimes it's hard to believe, though, particularly after a day like today. But do you know something strange, Cee? Remember what you said when you were Aaa?"

"Certainly I remember what I said since it was I who spoke. Not that you appreciated my advice, I don't think."

"You're right, I didn't. My life wasn't an adventure, however you looked at it. It was just going from bad to worse. Now, though, well, if you could die and be reborn, who knows what else might happen? At the least I will be away from here, which is no small accomplishment by itself."

"Precisely, young mammal. Seize each day as if it were your last, just as this is mine, and you will have no regrets for a life misspent."

Something in what the Cee said did not sound right. "What do you mean, this is your last day?" I asked.

"I mean exactly that," replied the Cee, alighting on the sand and stepping daintily on the ends of its tentacles. "This is my first day and my last day. I live now for one reason only, to take my mating flight and to scatter my seed upon the water. Afterward I will die of old age. The sequence is genetically predetermined. It is both painless and inescapable."

"But the Bee—but you told me Aaa was wrong."

"Did I?"

"You said there was nothing to fear."

"There isn't. Far worse than death is living poorly. And I—we— have an entire day in which to live well."

"But that's just it," I protested. "A day's not much."

"Trust me," said the Cee, patting my shoulder with a pincer. "A day can be eternity. It is God's gift to all of us, each and every one."

Then its wings picked up tempo, scattering sand about as they stroked the air. Soon all to be seen of the Cee was a pretty pattern of light against the night, an iridescent ember growing ever fainter as it soared skyward. I watched until the spark disappeared from sight altogether and then trudged back along the beach toward home.

CHAPTER TWO
An Inauspicious Departure

It was both impossible and undesirable to impose a single code of governance upon human beings, much less upon thousands of sentient species, each with its own outlook! Yet interstellar civilization vitally required a standard structure of conduct. Creating one was a challenge The Bureau was uniquely prepared to meet!

First The Bureau conducted 15 million focus groups among 8,204 human and nonhuman cultures. During the next twenty years the data was compiled, parsed, and analyzed. In A.I. 94 the lessons learned were released as *The Standard Interstellar Catalog of Sentient Rights*, a two-page codicil detailing minimum individual, corporate, and civic safeguards and responsibilities.

Does The Bureau enforce the terms of *The Standard Interstellar Catalog?* Absolutely not! Subscribers—from independent townships of a dozen beings to empires of a dozen solar systems—pay a fee to The Bureau, which then dispatches a highly-trained correspondent to perform an on-site inspection. Results are published annually.

Merchants, investors, financial organizations, importers and exporters, vacationers, tourists, and other travelers wisely patronize those locales that receive high ratings and prudently avoid the rest, which suffer economic hardship as a result.

Employee Guide to The Bureau of Interstellar Standards
27th Edition, A.I. 139

I gave most of my sign-on bonus to my mother, keeping only what I hoped would be sufficient to tide me over until the first quarterly pay-out. Packing did not take long. All my belongings fit in a duffel bag. There was not much besides my clothing that I cared to bring, anyway, just a jar of pearls the size of grains of sand, a couple books, a traveler's watch that had belonged to my father, which could be adjusted to the diurnal cycle of whatever world you happened to be on, some other knick knacks.

The translucent yellow light of daybreak, filtering through the salt crusting the narrow windowpanes, allowed my brothers to follow what I was doing. Their nictitating under lids were shiny with interest as they peered at me from their bed.

"What you up to, Pim?" asked Venn.

"Where you going?" asked Quill.

"I'm packing," I said, answering one question. "I'm leaving," I said, answering the second. "I'm shipping out on a freighter."

"For space?" This from Venn.

"For space."

"Can I have your bed?" This from Quill.

"I don't see why not," I replied. "It's not as if I'm taking it with me."

This answer raised a whine of protest from Venn, who immediately claimed the bed for himself, perhaps just because Quill had asked for it first, and soon the boys were rolling across the floor in a flurry of blankets, fists, and immense noses. I watched them a moment, for some reason amused and not, as usual, irritated by their antics. Then I hefted the duffel bag and stepped over them and went into the kitchen. My mother was setting down mugs of tea on the dining table. The shine on her cheeks told me she'd been crying again, or had never stopped. Despite her pregnancy, she was a thin woman and for the first time I realized her hair, always a rich brown, had become threaded with white, the corners of her eyes lined with wrinkles. How could I not have noticed how old she was getting?

Suddenly I had to blink to clear my own eyes. "Don't worry," I told her as she turned off the element under the skillet in which she'd made my favorite breakfast, an omelet of crab roe and melted cheese. "Don't worry about me," I repeated. "I'll be all right, see if it isn't so."

A wan smile lit my mother's face. "I know you'll do fine, Pim. Someday you'll come back home and you'll be the captain of your own ship. You'll tell us of all the places you've been, and of all the sights you've seen in this universe of miracles, and your brothers will die of envy, won't they just."

"I'll miss the kids," I said. "I never thought I would but I will, I can tell. Isn't that something."

My mother reached beneath the collar of her dress and removed a locket, which contained a hologram of her and my father when they were young and life had stretched ahead of them, bright as a dream. She pressed it to my palm and closed my fingers around it.

"Take this to remember us," she whispered. "Now sit down and eat. There's no guessing when your next meal will be, nor what it will be like."

"It won't be as good as this, that's for certain," I said, inhaling deeply as my mother took a tray of muffins from the oven. It was just as well that I had no idea how prophetic this prediction would turn out to be.

Jo Feringel accompanied me to the landing field. Our footsteps crackling on the crushed shell of the road, we kept up a brisk pace most of the way but as we approached our destination, Feringel slowed and gave me an odd look. "Pim," he said, tugging his nose, "you and I haven't always seen eye to eye. No mystery there, the young and the old rarely do. Nor do most kin, by blood or marriage. But I want you to understand I think you have a fine opportunity here. I don't want you to go off believing otherwise."

"It is an opportunity, no question," I said. "What kind of opportunity is another matter."

"It is the only one you have, boy. That's the fact that counts. What you make of it is up to you and to no one else. Sulking and surliness will profit you nothing while alacrity and a pleasant smile will get you many places. That's my opinion, take it or leave it."

I knew he meant well. As I've said, Jo Feringel wasn't a cruel man. But there was too much history behind us for me to be little more than civil to him even at this juncture. In any case I had been given so much advice recently, I was not inclined to listen to any of it, good or bad. Instead I said:

"You'll look after my mother?"

"I always have. No one can say different."

"Just keep on, then, and it's all right between us."

"That will have to suffice. I wish you luck, boy. And God's good humor, whatever it's worth."

This was a blessing I would rather have done without, as I would rather not have clasped Jo Feringel's hand in parting. But I returned the gesture with a firm grip of my own and then went over to Marval Wirthy. A single tender remained on the landing field, the other two having already departed for the *Miraculous Abernathy* in geo-synchronous orbit three hundred kilometers overhead. The seventeenth mate was standing at the foot of the ramp leading into the hold of the small ship. He acknowledged my arrival by ticking off an item on his personal assistant and instructed me to go aboard and keep out from underfoot.

The passenger cabin, just forward of the hold, held six rows of acceleration couches. I pushed my duffel bag into an overhead locker and strapped myself into a seat toward the back of the compartment. During the next hour the other passengers assembled—several men remarkably like Marval Wirthy, as well as a gang of nondescripts in plain work clothes. Some tipped their couches upright and became busy with datawork; a few slept; the rest stared with bored expressions at the exterior screens that paneled the walls of the cabin. No one spared me more than an incurious glance. Marval Wirthy was last to come aboard. An acceleration warning sounded as he finished locking himself into his own couch.

I had been in space, traveling with my parents, but it had been long before and I had been very young. The experience felt new to me now, as if it were my first time—the pressure of lift-off; vertigo as the tender clawed free of the planetary gravity well; then the relief of weightlessness as the vessel rose above the atmosphere and the engines quieted. I had forgotten how dark space was, and how hard the stars were, and how zero-g made the tears drift from your eyes before you could catch them.

Soon the *Miraculous Abernathy* appeared in the forward screens. She was an ancient ship, more than a kilometer long, and seemed to have been put together of random components instead of being constructed according to a formal plan. Since she was an interstellar vessel and would never enter a planetary atmosphere, her design was free of aerodynamic constraints. The *Abernathy* sprouted in all directions, a hodgepodge of environmental blisters, machine shops, factories, fusion plants, and other, less readily identifiable, modules.

Most of the ship was ablaze with light but some sections, scattered randomly here and there, seemed to be derelict, the portals dark, equipment abandoned. I began to wonder if my original suspicions had been correct. Perhaps, as I had worried to Aaa, the *Abernathy* was a decrepit old hulk after all.[1]

The landing ledge we docked on was an architectural structure several hectares square. As we jockeyed into place beside the other two tenders, massive airlocks descended and the hangar flooded with atmosphere. Then gravity came on.

A dozen vessels—maintenance scooters, winged scouts, defensive fighters bristling with missiles, personnel and cargo ferries—were berthed in slots along the sides of the hangar. Forklifts and industrial scooters converged on the tender as I followed Marval Wirthy and the other passengers out of the main lock and trailed behind the seventeenth mate while he conferred with various subordinates and made arrangements for the tender to be unloaded. When he finally remembered me, he made a curt gesture and led the way into a network of corridors lit by phosphorescent paneling. All the doorways were labeled in a cursive lettering I couldn't read, probably a commercial code. Most of the doors were shut. In the few that were open, I glimpsed men and women tending banks of circuitry or hunched over data terminals or engaged in other important tasks. Most were noticeably like Marvel Wirthy, with the same pale

---

1   Interstellar merchant clans intentionally allowed areas of residential space aboard their vessels to remain unoccupied, much as a field is allowed to lie fallow, in order to provide their crews with the necessary human psychological experience of a frontier. Over generations, in an erratic process, the population of a ship would leave their homes behind and migrate into new neighborhoods. The effort of pioneering, renovating, and re-engineering the new quarters served as an outlet for energy that might otherwise be directed into less wholesome channels.

complexion and long face and fingers, although there were scattered examples of other racial types among them, as well as a few non-humans.

We descended along four escalators and proceeded through another snarl of corridors, these different from the ones on the upper decks in that the lighting was poor and the walls were streaky with grime. Then we emerged into a cavernous chamber, which seemed to be a barracks—the forecastle. Rows of bunks reached from one end of the room to the other. Each had a privacy screen that could be closed around it and a locker beneath the mattress. There was also a communal area with divans and lounge chairs arranged around low tables. Perhaps fifty people were present, some boys and girls about my age, some older men and women—non-human laborers, I learned, had separate accommodations elsewhere. A few were sleeping but the rest were eating, playing cards, watching entertainment screens, or chatting desultorily.

Conversation died off as I followed Marval Wirthy across the barracks to a recessed window in the far wall. He rapped on it, summoning a man paler than he was, whose peevish expression put me on edge although I tried not to show what I felt.

"Oh, it's you, coz,[2]" said the newcomer as he lifted the partition.

"Clarege, this is Pimsol Anderts, newly signed aboard. Mister Anderts, Chief Clarege here will be your immediate supervisor from this point forward. His word is your *Script*ure, do you hear? Follow his instructions in all respects, great and small, without hesitation. Is that understood?"

"Yes, sir."

Chief Clarege gave me a lengthy study and evidently disliked

2   *Standard Dictionary of Interstellar Vernacular*: coz noun 1. (Colloquial) Cousin

what he saw, for his lips pursed in a thinner line. Ultimately arriving at an unpleasant decision, he handed me a key, a bundle of coveralls and shirts, a sturdy set of knee-high boots, and an equally heavy pair of gloves. "Bunk fifty-six," he told me reluctantly. "Keep your belongings in the locker under the bed, every article, or I confiscate it. Any fighting, so much as an unkind word, and you're both fined, it doesn't matter who was the instigator. Maintain your person in an acceptable condition of physical hygiene or face fiscal penalty. I tolerate neither slackards nor slovens, Mister Anderts. And trouble-makers not at all. Am I clear? Perfectly clear?"

"As clear as the day is long, sir."

Clarege Wirthy screwed his eyes together in disapproving scrutiny. "What is that supposed to mean, Anderts?"

"It is a common expression, sir."

"Not one I have heard before. Allow me to warn you. I dislike novelty as much as I dislike hyperbole."

"Sorry, sir. In the future I will try my best to anticipate your predilections. What am I to do next?"

Chief Clarege paused before answering, as if examining my response for symptoms of eccentricity or insubordination. "You'll partner with bunk fifty-seven," he said at last. "Smit will explain what you need to know."

Each bunk was numbered in standard numerals and I found my place without difficulty. I unpacked the duffel bag into the locker below the mattress, putting away my clothes and putting on the uniform I'd been given.

The boy in the next bunk had his cheek propped on one elbow as he watched me settle in. He was as dark as I was but his hair was the color of amber, a deep reddish-orange with startling yellow

28

highlights. I hunched forward on my bunk so I wouldn't hit my head against the privacy screen, and introduced myself. "You're in fifty-seven?" I went on. "We're partners, that's what Chief Clarege said."

My neighbor gave me a look very like the one I had just received from the ship's officer. "The evil bastard has it out for me, that's plain," he observed. "Well, there is nothing to do about it, never mind the inconvenience. How did you say you're called?"

"Pimsol Anderts. Pim."

"I am Every Smit. Listen to what I say, and obey my instructions, and we'll get along just fine."

"I've heard similar advice, and not long ago."

"Then you won't forget it, not if you have any sense. The work's aggravating enough with someone who knows what he's about, and that isn't you. Just don't slow me down, Anderts, that's all I can say."

"I'll try not to."

Smit grunted noncommittally "We'll see," he replied just as a buzzer sounded. Smit swung himself into a sitting position and fit his feet into boots. As I followed his example, he explained: "Watch change. Each shift is six hours. We work one on, two off. That's the routine and it doesn't vary, not by a second, so get used to it. Bring the gloves. You'll need them."

Chief Clarege's office also served as an equipment locker. We joined the line of men assembling in front of the recessed window. One after another those ahead of us shuffled up to the partition. To some, Clarege gave cleaning materials; to others, maintenance tools. When Smit and I arrived at the partition, Clarege handed each of us a trident, a net, a sack, and some other small items. The nets were woven of wire mesh, flexible as quicksilver. The tridents were metal spears as tall as I was. Mine had tines that were razor sharp, as I learned after I touched its edge with a fingertip.

"What are we hunting?" I asked.

Every Smit's pale blue eyes widened in surprise. "You really don't have a clue what we're about," he observed sourly. "Well, I will enlighten you, Anderts. If you haven't noticed, the *Abernathy*'s an old ship. She was built in the Phobos shipyards, that's right next door to Old Earth, back in the second century, almost a hundred and fifty years ago, in A.I. 162 to be precise. There's no telling how many ports of call she's visited since. Hundreds, thousands, who can say?

"Consider it, Anderts! At each world there has been traffic back and forth, freight coming up from the planet and cargo going down, that's just the nature of the business. Decontamination procedures are standard, but vermin always manage to hitch a ride and something or other, usually nasty or disgusting, manages to survive the extermination protocol. That's where we come in. We're on rat detail."

I shouldn't have been surprised. What had Marval Wirthy told me my position would be? Apprentice environmental specialist?

Exactly. Rat specialist.

I knew of rats. There were rats at home, living in burrows in the sand and feeding on clams and crabs on the beach. I had read there were rats everywhere throughout the galaxy where humanity had settled.

"That's what we're after?" I asked. "Rats?"

"Rats and other things. Most are carbon-based life forms, however ugly, although I have run into some damn strange beasties, Anderts, a couple with silicon metabolisms. They find their way into the air and heating ducts, power conduits, and unused personnel quarters and storerooms. The ship's big, you don't know the half of it—1.24 kilometers from stem to stern and a third of that at her widest. We're talking cubic volume. Which means there are many places to hide.

And reproduce. Our duty is to trim the population down by hand. Usually the work's routine, aggravating, as I said, but not particularly dangerous. Except when there's a bloom."

"A bloom?" I asked.

Every Smit nodded. "An explosive population increase. Mainly caused by the introduction of some new kind of vermin although there are exceptions. Like when the Purvs learned how to screw open the glucose vats on Level 81 with their tails. Can you believe it? I discovered one of the slimy little thugs showing others how it was done, nonchalant as you please, as if it were a damned classroom and he himself the damned headmaster. Had to fumigate the deck with poison gas before the knowledge was transferred to other levels. Not a nice job, Anderts. The buggers screamed like girls."

I followed Every Smit along several anonymous hallways until we came to a small portal. This admitted us into the network of ventilation tunnels running throughout the ship, as complex a system as the capillaries of the human body. The tunnels were scarcely wider than we were, and I now understood why Marval Wirthy had been concerned about my size. If I had been much larger, I wouldn't have been able to squeeze through. Every ten meters there was a luminescent ceiling panel, but in-between were pockets of shadow in which anything could be hiding. Smit halted at the entrance to a chamber housing a giant slowly-spinning fan. He pointed to something crouched by its base.

"See that?"

I nodded. "What is it?"

"A schvee. Comes from a place called Holbrook's World. Nasty, real nasty. The venom's toxic. Faster than it looks, too. Gets into everything. Watch carefully. I will show you how it's done. Next time it's up to you."

The schvee had six legs, an iridescent blue carapace, four round

31

eyes, and mandibles on either side of its jaws. I estimated its weight at five kilos, large enough to cause trouble if you weren't careful. It hissed furiously as Every Smit approached, and clicked its mandibles. Smit shook his net at the thing, engaging its attention in the wrong direction. When all four eyes were following the net, he slid the trident forward until it was almost touching the schvee. Then he jabbed. The tines cracked the schvee's shell and pinned it against the floor, where it twitched awhile before expiring. Every Smit shook the carcass off the trident into the bag.

"One down. Four to go. That's the quota. And they're not all so nice and gentle as this one, take my word for it. We have to account for a minimum of five each per shift—schvees, rats, purvs, it doesn't matter what kind of vermin, just so as we bring back proof. Clarege isn't a trusting man. He wants to be certain we're working and not larking about. God would have a good laugh if some Wirthy nabob were to discover droppings in his soup. We would be sure to suffer."

"What happens if we don't meet the quota?" I asked.

"Clarege imposes a monetary penalty."

For the remainder of the shift I followed Every Smit through the tunnels and began to learn my way around the immense old ship. Its core, constructed in the Phobos shipyards during the heyday of terrestrial expansion in the first century, had been added to and retrofitted until its original lines were lost under layers of storage tanks, machine shops, hangars, and environmental units. The engineering section was a vast, bright chamber. In the center of the huge space were the Avatar™ engines that supplied the *Abernathy* with gravity and propelled the ship between the stars—a surreal knot of gleaming metal studded with industrial crystals the size of fists. In the heart of the machine, captured behind invisible curtains of force, was the singularity powering the whole thing, a point impossible to make out except as an absence of light in the middle of an inferno. Only the fact that the force field absorbed most of the visible spectrum allowed Smit and me to look directly at the Avatars™ without being blinded.

We were levels below the one on which we'd started, in a tunnel parallel to the interior hull of the ship, when Smit held up a finger. Bands of light and dark stretched into the distance. He knelt and placed an ear against the corridor deck. I followed his example. Soon I became aware of a whisper, as if sand was rubbing together.

Smit said: "Spread your net open and lie on top of it. The edges join together. Bring them up around yourself and seal them closely."

I was about to ask why but he was already following his own instructions, so I did as I had been told. Once sealed, the net surrounded me in a flexible cocoon of metal mesh. Despite the closeness of the weave, I had a good view of what was going on outside the bag. Which was nothing, although the scratching was becoming louder. I twisted around, trying to get a better view of whatever was approaching, but did not see anything out of the ordinary. Every Smit noticed my curiosity and said:

"Vhoulls are harmless. Most of the time. So small and stupid you wouldn't worry about them. Other times, Anderts, the only thing to do is get out of their way."

Rats interrupted him—a dozen gray terrestrial rats with bald tails running fast along the corridor and right over us. Then came a schvee, hissing indignantly. Then several animals that resembled rodents except they had scales instead of fur and feathery antennas instead of eyes. These and the others ignored us and fled without stopping. The scrabbling sound had become loud enough to make conversation impossible. Suddenly, however, there was silence.

I felt a weight upon my leg. Slowly I peered through the mesh down the length of my body.

Perched on my thigh was what could only be a vhoull.

It was no taller than my thumb and covered by a thicket of greenish-brown fur.

It skittered forward, hidden claws scratching against the net. Reaching a position midway between my chest and my chin, the vhoull twitched the hair out of the way of its single eye and peered at the mesh beneath its feet. The little animal seemed innocuous, as innocent as a clam—right until the moment its torso split in half, revealing a mouth too large for such a small creature and filled to the throat with rows of sharp teeth. Launching itself onto the net, the vhoull began trying to chew through it with single-minded desperation. As if that was a cue, hundreds of vhoulls appeared, carpeting the tunnel in a writhing mat of hungry furry things. Soon both Smit and I were blanketed with vhoulls, all attempting to gnaw through the mesh protecting us in order to sink their teeth into our flesh. The sound of their chewing against the wire was unnerving.

Five minutes passed. Finally even the dullest vhoull figured out that it couldn't penetrate the net and reluctantly went off with the rest of the horde in search of easier prey.

Every Smit regained his feet.

"I see what you meant about blooms," I said. "I wouldn't want to run into those vhoulls unprotected. They're small but they're nasty."

He shrugged. "That was not much, Anderts. Vhoulls don't swarm for long. There's never enough food for their needs, that's the problem. Soon they turn upon each other, or starve, and when their numbers fall below a certain point, they revert to their normal behavior and go their separate ways, meek and as friendly as can be. No, Anderts, with vhoulls it isn't the bloom you have to be concerned about. It is the die off."

"Of course—the die off."

"Exactly. Come on. It is too good an opportunity to pass up. If we're nimble, we'll make quota quick."

He set off briskly after the vhoulls. We did not go far before we came across tiny corpses. The first few had been chewed upon or dismembered, presumably by the others. With increasing frequency, however, the vhoulls appeared whole but emaciated and their glossy fur was white where it had not fallen away entirely, as if they had died of starvation or old age. A little further on, in a chamber created by a three-way intersection, we discovered what remained of the swarm.

Most of the creatures were dead. Their bodies covered the deck so thickly that we couldn't go forward without trampling a half dozen underfoot with each step. The few vhoulls left alive were moving with only a fraction of their former energy, grazing listlessly on their fellows and uttering disconsolate peeps.

Smit held up a hand. "We are not the only ones that know about the vhoull's life cycle," he whispered, pointing across the intersection, where a schvee was sucking up mouthfuls of small corpses while clacking its mandibles with relish. "Soon this place will be crawling with all sorts of scavengers and opportunists. Come on, Anderts. Bag the schvee. I will take the next one. We'll be out of here in no time."

"All right," I muttered and, as Smit had demonstrated, approached the schvee with my trident off to one side and with the net held ahead of me. While its four glittering insectile eyes followed the net, I slid the trident forward until it was nearly touching the thing's carapace. But as I stabbed it, my foot skidded sideways out from under me.

I had stepped on a vhoull corpse. Instead of penetrating, the trident slid along the carapace, leaving behind only a shallow scratch in the schvee's chitin. This was, however, more than enough to enrage the creature, which lunged at me as I fell to the deck.

Hissing malevolently, it locked its mandibles around my boot and tried earnestly to chew through the tough material. I kicked out with my other foot but the schvee refused to let go.

"Yes, that's the way to do it, Anderts," said Smit, doubled over with laughter. "Choke the damned beast with your boot. Go on, shove your whole leg down its throat!"

I dropped the trident. I also squashed another gross of vhoulls under me, so that much of my uniform was coated with their circulatory fluid, blood as green as their fur. My ears burning, I tried not to listen to Smit as I scrambled after the trident, dragging the schvee behind me. This further enraged the thing, and its hissing grew louder and it shook its head back and forth furiously as it tried to worry its mandibles through my boot. Finally my fingers closed around the haft of the trident. All thoughts of proper technique forgotten, I struck out again and again, until a last thrust cracked the animal's bright blue carapace, spilling coils of gut and strange internal organs onto the deck. With a peculiar tortured hiss, the schvee relaxed its grip, its four eyes filmed over, and the thing expired. Pulling myself to my feet, I glanced reproachfully at Smit.

"Thanks for all your help," I told him. "I don't know what I would have done without you."

"Think nothing of it, Anderts," he replied without apology.

"Right." I looked down sourly at the filthy mess I had made of myself while wrestling with the schvee.

Spatters of aquamarine blood daubed me from head to toe, and bits of dead vhoull adhered to my overalls like tufts of beard. But it was impossible to remain irritated at Smit—there was no malice in him, as far as I could see, only a sort of sardonic humor, more good-natured than otherwise. While I began plucking myself clean of squashed vhoull, he said:

"Put the schvee in your sack, Anderts. Remember what I told you, we have a quota, and Clarege is a right suspicious bastard. Get moving now. It won't be long before we have more visitors."

Gingerly lifting the schvee, I deposited the corpse into my bag just as the next scavenger arrived, a slithering thing with lobster claws and a thousand tiny legs. Smit killed it, as he did the next—a rotund animal with a snout longer than its body. As he'd predicted, we made our quotas of vermin inside of an hour. Just then, however, a flock of uglybirds flew in.

These avians are so remarkably repulsive that it is impossible for humans to look at them. Just glimpsing the birds sideways was enough to make my stomach churn. This gave the birds a sort of practical invisibility. The flock was smart enough to take full advantage of the situation.

I couldn't decide which was worse—the insane gleam in their demented eyes or the vile black slobber seeping from their gaping orifices.

Smit and I flailed blindly at them but our blows went wide since we couldn't focus on the things long enough to aim. Cawing raucously, the uglybirds stole the dead vermin from our game bags. Then they flew off two-by-two into the labyrinth below decks, each pair clutching a trophy in their claws.

My eyes were hurting from being squeezed shut when Smit

glumly told me I could open them again. We'd been robbed clean. The uglybirds had also gobbled up most of the vhoull corpses.

Smit shook his fist after the uglybirds. "That's it, Anderts, we're in for trouble," he predicted. "No chance of making quota, that's for sure. Not now. Everything with any sense has made itself scarce. Clarege won't be pleased. No, he won't." Smit nodded slowly. "This isn't going to be pleasant."

Unfortunately, Smit's pessimism was borne out. We had to return to Chief Clarege empty-handed.

First he inspected our equipment for damage, clucking and frowning each time he discovered the slightest scratch. After all the gear was accounted for, he peered into Smit's bag. When Clarege lifted his long face, it was evident he was not happy. My bag did not impress him, either.

"Just one schvee between the two of you," Clarege complained, "and a runt at that. Is this acceptable? Is this anywhere near what is required? I hold Anderts harmless since he's new to the *Abernathy* and must be educated, although I fear the effort will be wasted. But Smit, in you I am disappointed! A veteran rat-catcher such as yourself should do far better. What do you have to say? I am listening."

"There was a vhoull swarming."

"Of course there was a vhoull swarming. The little horrors are always swarming. Come to the point, Smit!"

"And a feeding frenzy."

"Is this supposed to be news? There's always a feeding frenzy after a vhoull swarming. One leads to another without fail, as surely as one watch ends in another. I am a patient man, Smit, but even I can tolerate only so much prevarication. Get on with it."

"Then we ran into a flock of uglybirds. The disgusting buggers stole everything we had. You know what they're like, chief. Just a glimpse is enough to make you puke."

"And why didn't you put on the filtering lenses designed to protect against just such an eventuality?"

"They weren't issued to us, chief."

"Then why didn't you request them? Smit, you must learn responsibility. Your rash and hasty behavior jeopardized not only your own safety, and the safety of Anderts here, but also the safety of the expensive equipment in your custody. Remember what the *Script*ures say. Be prepared. Ignorance is no excuse. Count on God to make it difficult."

"Sorry, sir."

Smit's apology seemed to offend Chief Clarege. "Don't be sorry, Smit. Be efficient. Do you understand me?"

"Yes, sir."

"No, I don't think so. In fact, I suspect what we have here is not ignorance but willful sloth. Isn't that correct, Smit?"

"I don't know what you mean, chief."

"I mean you were slacking off, pure and simple. Larking about with not a thought as to your duties until it was too late. Well, we cannot have it. I would command no respect if I overlooked such a glaring infraction of the regulations. Smit, you're fined thirty hhours. Six hhours for failing to meet quota and twenty-four hhours for mendacity. Be grateful it isn't more. Perhaps you'll be diligent in the future."

Clarege frowned at me peevishly. "Is there something you want to say, Anderts?" he snapped. "Are you experiencing intestinal difficulty?"

"No, sir—I mean, yes, I do want to say something, Chief Clarege. There was a vhoull swarming. Just as Smit said. And we both made our quotas, until the uglybirds came."

"Ah, now I understand completely, Anderts. You rehearsed this story together, isn't that the stem and stern of it? Fortunately, I am not easily taken in, not Clarege Wirthy. I have seen through a thousand more convincing perjuries. Anderts, I was intending to overlook your role in this affair. You're new, and, I suspect, simple. But it is obvious you collaborated with Smit and are equally guilty of his offense. You also are fined thirty hhours. I will debit the sum from your account."

It took all my willpower not to argue against this unfair penalty. But it was obvious any more discussion would only further irritate Clarege Wirthy and so I remained silent.

Every Smit threw himself onto his bunk and began cursing in a low monotone as I settled down less precipitously on my own cot. "Didn't I tell you, Anderts? Didn't I? The bastard has it out for me. Thirty hhours! Can you imagine?"

I did not like the situation any better than Smit. My first shift aboard the *Miraculous Abernathy*, and already I had been labeled a troublemaker by my supervisor. "Don't forget I was fined, too," I reminded Smit. "I had better be careful or else I will end up owing the ship more than I earn."

The innocence in my voice caused Every Smit to forget his own problems and give me a sharp look. "Don't be stupid, Anderts," he told me. "Of course, you'll end up owing the ship. That's the set-up. We'll hunt rats and shovel crap until the day we die, that's just the way things are. We're not Wirthys, you and I. We're cheap labor, doing what no Wirthy cares to. The cheapest kind of labor, Anderts."

I shook my head at Smit's revelation. "I don't know about you," I told him, "but I have a contract. It runs long enough, but not forever."

My naiveté appalled him. "We all have contracts," Smit said. "So what? None of us will get off this damn ship alive."

CHAPTER THREE
Painful Lessons Aboard
The *Miraculous Abernathy*

Those were heady times! Sales of religious artifacts, accoutrements, and gewgaws increased exponentially on every planet settled by humanity and on thousands of planets belonging to non-human races. Our corporate profits were staggering. Although we issued dividend after dividend and invested heavily in retooling and infrastructure improvement, we still had more surplus cash than we knew what to do with. I don't recall whether I thought of it first, or whether Ralph Singh, our CFO, came up with the idea.

Why rest on our laurels? Imagine what would happen to sales when the Icon Corporation opened a direct communications channel with the Lord and brought back answers to the basic questions of existence.

Practically, it was an excellent way to employ our surplus capital and to avoid the tax consequences of wealth beyond the dreams of avarice.

God, of course, does watch over the fall of every sparrow, but the Lord historically has remained aloof from daily material events. The task before us was to demand our deity's attention.

The galaxy knows what happened. We primed 512 stars with nova mines and exploded them, asking three questions in binary language:

1.   Why did you create the universe?
2.   What is the meaning of life?
3.   Is there personal survival after death?

The reply came a week later and our sales went straight into the toilet.

Vassily X. Hardcourt, quoted in: *Bankruptcy Proceedings of The Icon Corporation, Volume 549, A.D. 2612 27th Edition, A.I. 139*

S mit was exaggerating, but not by much.

Speaking with elaborate slowness, as if to a child or lack wit, he explained the set-up, obviously enjoying the opportunity to play the pedant. "It is not your contract, Anderts," he said, ticking one finger with the tip of another to make the point. "I expect it conforms pretty damn closely to the *Standard Catalog*. Or at least to the *Plain Text Abridged Version*. The *Abernathy*'s a subscriber to The Bureau, of course."

I nodded slowly. Who would deal with a ship that wasn't? What corporation, government, or individual of any species would do business with a vessel that did not publicly guarantee respect for private property and personal liberty? Subscribing to The Bureau was a requirement in order to engage in interstellar commerce.

"I read it, Smit," I told him. "Not thoroughly, and I skimmed a lot. But the contract seemed legal."

Smit wagged an admonitory finger in my direction and shook his head, setting the cowry shells in his locks clacking together. "Oh, it's legal. That isn't in question. Listen to what I say, Anderts. All Wirthys are sly bastards, from Clarege on up. Tell me, what do you know of Imogene Wirthy?"

The question did not seem to have much to do with the rest of our conversation.

"Nothing at all," I replied.

By his expression it was apparent Smit had expected no other response. "Well, then," he said, "allow me to educate you in certain facts of history. Have you noticed how most of the crew, saving you and me and the rest of our lowly acquaintances down here in the forecastle, all share a certain disagreeable similarity? Which is to say, pale complexions, noses that are stretched too long for proper breathing, and eyes the color of mud."

Despite its severity, the description easily accommodated both Chief Clarege and Marval Wirthy.

"And I am sure it hasn't escaped you, either, Anderts," Smit went on, "that most share the same secondary appellation, which is to say they're all Wirthys. They all descend from Imogene Wirthy, who founded the clan back in the second century. She was a right canny bitch from what I have heard, and determined to establish her own merchant dynasty. In A.I. 160 she sank every mminute she owned into commissioning and launching the *Abernathy*, and crewed the ship with her own kids and kin and with clones of her own self. I have been told there are still one or two walking around that are direct copies of the old woman but I don't believe it personally."

"What is the point of all this, Smit?" His patronizing attitude was beginning to irritate me.

"The point, Anderts, is that your contract is legitimate. To the letter. But you're looking in the wrong direction. Just like the schvee, remember? It didn't see the trident coming. Neither do you." Smit sighed theatrically. "Amazing you've survived as long as you have," he mused. "Back home, you'd have been put out of your misery long ago."

"Enlighten me," I snapped. "What am I missing?"

Smit swung his feet over the side of the bunk. "What you're

missing is the fact that Wirthys have rigged the set up aboard ship. Sure, Anderts, our bunks, our food and water, our uniforms, and other basic necessities are supplied free of charge. That much is according to agreement. But what you haven't figured on is how much everything else costs. And let me tell you, after a couple basic meals, you'll be lining up at the luxury dispensers like the rest of us."

"I don't think so, Smit."

"That's what you say now. Anyway, even if you don't spend, it doesn't matter. One way or the other you end up owing the Wirthys money. I've seen it happen. Clarege keeps an eye out and the bastard squeezes it from you somehow. You're never allowed to get far enough ahead to pay off your score and you have to keep on working. That's how it is here."

Still I shook my head stubbornly, swearing to myself that I would live within my means, ignore luxuries, and refuse credit. I would beat the system and leave the ship at the end of five years of service, avoiding debt and servitude aboard the *Miraculous Abernathy*.

I was, of course, unaware of the full dimensions of the situation. Although I learned soon enough.

As Smit had warned, our basic provisions consisted of a single dish, a brick of tasteless fiber. It sustained life but that was all that could be said for it. Inside of a week I was sick of the stuff and glancing hungrily at the dispensers, where true meals could be purchased at prices approximately twice their real value. Even the water cost. Not cold water for drinking—that would have violated the letter of the contract. But the hot water was metered. By my second frigid shower, I had to resist the temptation to put my thumb to the plate beside the nozzle and raise the temperature, cursing all the Wirthys but especially their foxy old clone grandmother, Imogene Wirthy, who had spawned the rest. Instead I remained under the cold water longer than necessary, perhaps to demonstrate to myself I could.

A dozen people were playing cards in the central area of the forecastle when I returned from showering. It was a game that never ended, one player taking another's seat as shifts and fortunes changed. Usually it was poker being played, according to ancient rules. I watched from the sidelines since I neither understood the principles nor wished to risk my money. I was, however, beginning to get a sense of the company I was among.

No two had the same history. Every Smit had been raised in the urban ghettos of Van Diver's World, where the population density approached one million persons per cubic kilometer. Forbes Takagi, less than half my height despite having several years on me, was the younger brother of a prince and had been sold into bondage as a matter of policy when his brother assumed leadership of their tribe. Perry Entwhistle, from far Ramoravar, had been raised for speculative purposes by a pack of shee, an intelligent non-human race, and he'd been put up for sale once his market value promised to yield the shee good return on their investment.

Canny Galdo, who had a broad flat face dusted with purplish freckles, folded her hand with an exaggerated display of disgust and pushed her chair from the table.

"That's it for me. I have had no luck. Who wants my seat? What of you, Anderts? Will you take my place?"

"No, thanks. I am just learning the game."

"Aren't we all? Come on now, put an ante in. What better way to study? And at a reasonable charge, too."

"That's what I am afraid of," I admitted. "Lessons might cost more than I can afford."

"To the contrary! You might win a fortune."

"Unlikely, not with my luck." Galdo's insistence began to puzzle me.

"What are you saving your money for, Anderts?" she went on, her tone becoming challenging. "You're putting it away for your old age? For your retirement, are you? For when you're on the beach, living off a fat pension courtesy of our generous Wirthy patrons?"

The way she put it, the idea seemed ridiculous.

Now I noticed that the purplish freckles on Canny Galdo's face were actually miniature malformed eyes the size of grains of rice.

The condition was called Gardener's Optic Syndrome. It was caused by a virus that had originated on a world far toward the galactic rim. There the virus lived within a population of shrew-like creatures, causing nothing more than an occasional flu. Somehow, however, it crossed not only from one species to another but from one biology to another, an event of statistical improbability. While not itself composed of DNA, the virus was able to insert itself into human genetic material, freakishly triggering the chemical sequences activating the growth of eyes, until the host was covered with tiny visual organs.

Medical technology had conquered Gardener's Optic Syndrome centuries before. The problem was that once having grown a certain number of eyes, many patients refused to allow themselves to be cured, having become addicted to the enhanced perceptual stimuli. I suspected Canny Galdo was nearing this threshold.

She grinned and glanced around at the other players. A couple laughed along with her at my expense, amused by my naiveté. Obviously no one believed in a future apart from indenture aboard the *Abernathy*.

"I don't know about that," I answered, trying to keep my voice level. "But I do know I have better use for my funds, what little I have, than squandering them in a game I haven't played."

Refusing to say anything further, I nodded to them all and returned to my bunk, managing to sleep for the remainder of the watch. We were working two off and one on, six hours per shift. Eventually Every Smit informed me I no longer required his tutoring and was sufficiently trained to go out on my own, and I did so after that. It was a dirty job, catching and killing rats and schvees and other vermin, dull except when it was dangerous, but I appreciated the time away from the forecastle.

I had descended toward the stern, passing through several great holds, mostly empty except for stacks of dusty cases, the odds and ends of forgotten cargoes. I left a trail of traps and poison behind me, as we were instructed to do every so often. Swinging back toward the barracks, I took a route through the upper decks, Clarege Wirthy having instructed us to pay particular attention to keeping this area free of vermin, since it was where the Wirthys congregated. I remained in the service corridors but once I had to cross a main interchange, where there was foot and scooter traffic.

I was half across when I came face to face with a young woman who was striding ahead firmly while carrying on an energetic conversation with someone on the phone. The dialog engaged her attention and she did not notice me. We would have collided if I hadn't stepped smartly aside.

"Careful there," she said, turning me an impersonal glance. "You need to watch where you're going."

Ordinarily I would have ignored the remark and gone on my way but something about her voice stopped me in my tracks. "Excuse me," I replied—

That was the moment I first took a good look at her. I had never imagined the existence of a woman—a girl—like her. She was a Wirthy but in her their features became beautiful, the wide mouth a miracle, the pale complexion fascinating. She had an air of complete self-possession, which intrigued me while at the same time making me aware of the gulf between us. She was a merchant scion possibly descended from Imogene Wirthy herself while I was an apprentice environmental engineer, a rat catcher. But it was not merely the difference in our stations that separated us. There was a challenge in her eyes that dared me to measure up to her standards.

"Yes?" she said impatiently. "What is it?"

I had meant to tell her that she was in the wrong, not I, and that she, not I, needed to mind her bearing. Yet not a word reached my lips, although plenty of blood reached my ears, and I felt them redden. As she regarded me, her expression softened and became quizzical, and I was certain she was adjusting her appraisal of my intelligence downward. I knew I had to answer but I was afraid that anything I said would sound foolish or that I might stammer. Finally I got out:

"Excuse me, but I think both of us were equally at fault. At least I wasn't on the phone."

"Which is all the more reason for you to pay diligent attention," she replied with a logic that escaped me. "If you have no sense of responsibility for your fellow passers-by, at least display common courtesy."

"I will keep your advice in mind," I answered, a far from gallant reply, yet all that I could come up with. The girl was already turning away, my presence forgotten as she resumed her conversation with someone more important, leaving me to stare dumbly at her retreating figure. I couldn't wrench my gaze off her, not that I tried, and I was almost bowled over by other pedestrians before she was out of sight. I never knew how I found my way back to my bunk, or how long I lay dreaming, before her spell faded.

"Anderts." It was Renny Blothridge. He was kneeling next to my bunk, peering in at me.

Renny was a dozen years my senior. His stiff curls of yellow hair were gathered in a topknot, while his cheeks and neck were painted with bars of black and jade green. He came from a world with gravity 25 percent higher than standard, and this accounted for his squat musculature and overall thickness. Early on his surly expression had warned me to keep a good distance from him.

"Anderts," he said. "I am hungry, and I am broke, and that's not fun. Maybe you don't understand the situation, maybe you haven't been told, but it's tradition that the new boys and girls take care of those who have been aboard longer. So why don't you go on over to that machine and bring me back a fine dinner, something hot and meaty, smothered in sauce *bordelaise* with thyme and laurel for flavor. And tap a pint of stout while you're at it since I am thirsty as well."

"That's not a healthy diet," I answered. "You would be better off following my example, Renny."

From my pocket I took one of the fiber and protein bars the Wirthys provided in fulfillment of the indenture contract, which was all I had eaten since I had arrived since I was being careful with my money. I took a bite and held the rest out. "The stuff may taste like crap but it's free."

"Renny Blothridge doesn't eat crap, Anderts. Get that straight." He swept the bar aside and pinched my chin between thumb and forefinger, a gesture intended to be intimidating. "Are you going to do what is right?"

I had thought about how I would act when this situation arose, and had concluded I had two choices. I could submit to Renny Blothridge and become a slave to him as well as to the Wirthys. Or I could resist.

The only fact I understood about fighting was you were supposed to hit hard. My punch took Renny in the abdomen and sent him back in a crouch as he struggled to draw breath. His stomach was as hard as shell and it hurt my fist but even so I sent a blow to his jaw and another to his nose. Renny only grimaced, shook his head, straightened, and embraced me with such strength that I couldn't free myself. His hands locked behind my neck and forced my chin into my chest.

I had never expected to win this fight but I had determined not to surrender. The pain in my shoulders and neck, however, was causing me to rethink this decision.

"What do you say, Anderts?" Renny asked. "Have you decided that generosity is a virtue to be applauded among comrades? Speak up. I cannot hear you."

"Buy your own dinner, Renny."

Somehow I broke his hold and wrenched away. The forecastle was silent except for the noise of my gasping. Renny Blothridge, showing no sign of exercise, started toward me. I backed off.

"Think of your reputation, Anderts," Renny went on. "It is not pleasant to be considered tightfisted. Everyone appreciates a generous fellow."

He launched himself upon me. I couldn't dodge and was brought to the floor. His thighs wrapped around my midsection, just below my rib cage, thighs strengthened to stone due to a lifetime in high gravity. They ground together and forced the air from my lungs and

I felt myself becoming light headed. I tried to pummel him but the angle was all wrong and my blows were weak and ineffective. Darkness began constricting my vision, swaddling my sight in shadow. I only had to do what Renny asked and the pain would go away. This option became more attractive the longer I struggled to withstand the grinding of his knees against my stomach and the small of my back. Still I refused to give in, determined to hold out one more second, and one more after that. As if from far away I heard:

"What precisely is going on here?"

Clarege Wirthy had emerged from his office behind the glass partition. Renny relaxed his grip and I tried to breathe. "Blothridge and Anderts," Clarege observed dolefully. "Engaged in a direct violation of regulations, which is to say, in fighting. Why am I not surprised?"

"No fighting, sir," Renny said. "Just a tussle among friends, isn't that the truth, Anderts?"

I nodded, which was a mistake, since my neck was a bar of pain. "We weren't fighting," I agreed.

Our assurances, however, proved unconvincing to Clarege Wirthy. "Experience has taught me to believe the evidence of my eyes," he replied, "and I know what I saw. You are both fined ten ddays, and it will be double that the next time, I promise. And for the next month you're on two, off one. Perhaps that will deter you from mischief."

Clarege Wirthy called up our accounts and entered the debits.

For the rest of the shift I tried to ignore the pain where bruises were forming. Every Smit, in his own bunk, remarked:

"That was entertaining, Anderts. You employ an unusual method of defense, against humans as well as schvees. If I understand correctly, your strategy is to allow the other fellow to hurt you until he grows bored and wanders away."

Ignoring the sarcasm, I said, "I may not have won but I did not lose, either. Blothridge has to buy his own meals. I won't be paying for them."

"Is that what you believe?" Smit asked. "Well, perhaps so. You've saved yourself the cost of a meal, Anderts, very well and good. And been fined the cost of a dozen feasts. That is victory of a sort, I will agree." Then Smit sobered. "You really don't get it?" he asked.

"Get what?"

"How things work."

Just in time I stopped myself from shaking my head. "Maybe not," I admitted.

"It is as I told you, Anderts. Clarege has an eye on what is going on. And there are a couple here who do as he tells them. You haven't been following the rules. You were setting a precedent, not parting with a ssecond, not even on trifles. From now on spend a little, lose a couple hhours at cards, and you won't be troubled. See if what I say isn't the truth."

"Blothridge was also fined," I protested.

"Of what consequence is that? Come on, Anderts, where's your common sense? What is entered in a spreadsheet can be deleted as easily, if you're the one keeping the books. And if you were to watch Renny, as I have, you'd learn he doesn't stint himself, either, no matter his protests about being broke and hungry."

My innocence continued to amaze Smit. In the overcrowded urban maze on Van Diver's World where he'd been raised, where two square meters of personal space was the usual allotment, you developed an acute political sense or were murdered by your neighbors. You also learned unarmed combat. "What is more, Anderts," Smit went on, "you understand nothing about handling yourself. My little brother could have done better."

"I never got into fights," I said. "I never had to learn."

"You do now. Tell you what, Anderts, I will make you a proposition. I will teach you a trick or two so you won't be quite the amateur. What do you say to that?"

"You'll teach me?" I asked, knowing that Smit was too canny to give anything away for free. Perhaps I was learning. "What do you want in return, Smit? What's the price?"

"No price, Anderts. If there were, you couldn't afford it, anyway, you're as broke as I am. No, all I want is a promise. Someday I will need a favor, there's no telling what it might be, so don't ask. Help me when I require help and we'll be quits, you and I."

"That's it, Smit? All you want is a promise?"

"You're the kind of simpleton who'll honor his word, Anderts. That could come in handy someday. You never know when you'll need someone at your back. This is truly a universe of miracles."

Every Smit, of course, would never think twice about reneging on his own word, as I discovered later on. He couldn't help it. Duplicity was just too much a part of his character. He'd been taught to lie by the example of his family, friends, and neighbors while growing up in the crowded ghettos of Van Diver's World. With such an extraordinary population density, survival in the warrens depended upon getting along. You learned never to say what you thought but instead to say what you thought was appropriate, what would ease the situation or turn it to your advantage. A promise to Every Smit was as ephemeral as the wind. He did, however, recognize that I had a different point of view and he made use of this fact.

Although I disliked committing myself to such a loose arrangement, it was common sense to deal with the present instead of worrying about what might or might not take place in the future. So I accepted his offer, and made my own promise in return.

Thus began the most painful month of my life.

During our free shifts we went to an empty storeroom two levels below the forecastle and well away from curious eyes, where Smit instructed me in the hand-to-hand martial technology in general use on Van Diver's World, a vicious and deadly sequence of routines that utilized not only your hands and feet, but your fingers, toes, elbows, and knees to destructive advantage. I came away from the first sessions dazed and aching, bruised in places I had never hurt before, muscles on fire from being stretched in unusual positions and from being asked to perform new tasks.

It was not until our eleventh engagement that I managed to land a return blow.

"Good, Anderts," Every Smit said. "Now do it again."

I couldn't, not then. Nor did I ever become Smit's equal. But neither was I as defenseless as before.

Stubbornly I continued to avoid spending cash or accepting credit or playing cards. I knew this course would lead to trouble and in order to escape notice I began remaining away from the barracks two shifts out of three even after the penalty duty imposed by Clarege Wirthy expired.

My wandering led me into an environmental module empty a century. Neglected furniture and appliances were cloaked in dust ten centimeters deep and I had to put on a respirator in order to breathe because of the clouds my passage stirred up. I was trailing a thing called a gossamer thief, a flat disc of silicon that walked on hundreds of tiny hands. Thieves were scavengers. Their habit of constructing nests with wire stolen from power nodes made them a continual nuisance.

The one I was after massed so little that it skittered ahead on top of the dust without falling through. Then it disappeared.

I was in a private sleeping chamber. In the center of the room stood the remains of a bed with brass posters. The mattress fell apart when I poked it with my trident, revealing a network of corroded springs and a seething mess of gossamer thieves, huge old ancients and fry no larger than fingers. Despite the respirator I could smell their musty stink and I began stabbing right and left, trying to account for as many as possible.

The nest itself was a tangle of copper, gold, and glass wire stripped of sheathing. I put on my gloves and began ripping it apart and stuffing the pieces into my bag. This caused a rain of objects to fall from the snarled wire: silica pellets of excrement; small pieces of metal and glass gathered for food; gaudy odds and ends, perhaps collected simply because of their shininess. Then there was a heavier clunk as something larger hit the floor. I poked around in the dust until I found what had dropped—a metal bracelet inlaid with hemispheres of crystal, each a different color.

This, I realized, was not simply an ornament but a personal device of some sort. It had such an air of antiquity that I couldn't begin to guess its age. The Tripartite Administration, which had controlled a measurable percentage of human space for several decades, had produced work with a similar style and feel. But so had the Kali Commune, a confederation more remote in history. I pressed the crystals one after the other. Nothing happened. Either the bracelet needed repair, or it was drained of power, or else it had to be worn in order to be activated.

I slipped it onto my wrist. The crystals flushed with light soft as mother of pearl. There was a sharp tingling where the bracelet touched my skin and I felt its diameter contract. I could no longer slide it back over my hand.

"Remain calm, sir. I am extracting a blood sample. It is a painless procedure and quickly over."

I heard this voice not with my ears but somewhere inside my head. "What are you?" I asked. "Who are you?"

"There is no need to speak out loud, sir. Simply address your thoughts to me and I will comprehend through neural induction. As for what I am, I am your personal attendant, aristocracy grade, manufactured in the year 160 by Bandar Bush Technologies of El Paso, Texas. As for who I am, why, my name is Alger, sir, and I am at your service."

This time I thought the question instead of using my voice. "Alger, why are you sampling my blood?"

"One of my standard duties is to monitor your physical condition, sir. And a good thing, too, if I may say so myself. Analysis has revealed that you are currently suffering from severe deficiencies of several vitamins, including C, B, and X. Evidently you have been subsisting for some time on an unbalanced diet. In fact, sir, within two weeks you would have begun displaying debilitating physical symptoms had I not just now injected you with an invigorating tonic rich in nutrients and anti-oxidants. Luckily, as your personal attendant, aristocracy grade, I come configured with a nano-molecular forge, which allows me to manufacture reasonable amounts of a broad range of compounds given a sufficient source of raw material."

"Debilitating physical symptoms," I muttered. I had, indeed, been subsisting for some time on an unbalanced diet, the ration bars provided by the Wirthy dispensers. They may have been tasteless but I had taken it for granted that they were healthy. Smit was right. I was naïve.

"I have also doused you with a viral antagonist, antibiotics, and a vermifuge," Alger went on. "You may suffer some intestinal distress, sir, but you did require purging."

It could only have been my imagination that made me feel a hesitant twinge in my stomach. "What are your other duties?" I asked Alger.

"Why, I am here to advise you, sir. I have in storage the entire *Human Library*, although much is certainly obsolete, since I have not been able to update my memory for 141 years due to the dust coating my data ports. I serve as a local communications link, and interface with the twenty-two major claves of intelligent systems. I also provide security services. I am able to sense threats to your person and either provide warning or take offensive action. In short, I am your assistant and will advise, serve, and protect you, sir, to the extent of my abilities."

"Tell me, Alger," I asked mildly, "and I hope you don't take offense, but how did a personal assistant as valuable as yourself come to be at the bottom of a thieves nest for 141 years?"

"Sir, allow me not to bore you with my personal history. It is a tedious story and of little interest to anyone. Shall we leave it at that?"

"I would bet the truth is more entertaining," I said. "But I will leave it alone on one condition. Do not medicate me again without permission or take any similar action without my consent. I don't care for it."

"Sir, your well being is my responsibility. Am I to trouble you with every particular? Miss Imogene never concerned herself with petty details."

"Imogene Wirthy?"

"The same. A decisive woman. As temperamental as she was brilliant. I am privileged having served her."

"Nevertheless, Alger, do not initiate any procedure without asking, no matter what understanding you had with Imogene Wirthy. I'm not her."

"What if you were incapacitated, sir?"

"All I can say is use your best judgment under the circumstances."

"Very well. Does this mean you do not care for unsolicited advice?"

"No, if it's good advice, I want to hear it."

"I understand, sir. In that case I advise you to have your weapon ready. We are being approached by an abattoir. By the spacing of its stride I estimate it is two meters long and masses fifty kilos. The abattoir is entering the next room. It is snarling."

"An abattoir?" I had never heard of one before. Given its name, I doubted the approaching creature would be friendly.

"The species evolved on a planet that had been dragged nearer its sun less than a million years ago due to the passage of a wandering moon," Alger elaborated. "The ecology struggled to adapt but there were massive extinctions and the biosphere was dying. Competition was ruthless. Abattoirs were the last carnivores alive when the planet was surveyed. They are wily predators with incredible stamina. Many notables of high net worth keep them as pets and bodyguards. A small percentage can be domesticated if they are raised from cubs."

"Is this one tame?"

"I do not know, sir."

"What does it look like—no, don't tell me. I can see for myself."

Through the door to the sleeping chamber came a long sleek head. The abattoir was as sinuous as a sheet of paper and almost as thin, an evolutionary adaptation allowing it to present the least surface area to the sun. It was covered by silver quills, which rippled as it moved. Its eyes were mere pinpricks, nothing more than vestiges, while its ears were fanlike organs embroidered with golden veins. The abattoir turned toward me and smiled, and I understood immediately why the species had been given its name. I had never imagined so many teeth could fill one mouth.

"Alger," I said quickly, "you said you have offensive capabilities."

"I do, sir. Regrettably, however, nothing I possess would be useful under the circumstances. Notice the abattoir's fur. It incorporates a high percentage of metal. This makes it impervious to electronic penetration as well as bulletproof, at least against micro-caliber ammunition. It will also resist modulated light."

The abattoir slid another meter into the room. "Alger," I snapped, "tell me something helpful!"

The abattoir was making a throaty, malevolent purr. Alger said thoughtfully, "Several references concur that abattoirs are social animals, sir, with complex kinship patterns and rituals. The sharing of food among pack members is stereotyped behavior. Perhaps if you—"

I was already fumbling in my pocket for a protein and fiber bar. It took forever to unwrap. I broke off a piece and tossed the food at the abattoir.

It swallowed the chunk in one gulp. Then it regarded me again and yawned, hundreds of needlelike teeth gaping apart. This time I aimed straight at its mouth. It snapped the morsel from the air without effort.

"Notice the collar," Alger went on. "The creature is indeed tame."

This observation provided me little comfort since I was worrying about what would happen after I ran out of food to give the beast. I was down to two pieces, then to just one, then to none. I held out my hand to demonstrate they were empty. The abattoir brought its muzzle to the tips of my fingers and scrutinized them until satisfied there was nothing more to eat. Then it lay down while spreading open its ears and peering upward, a gesture of unmistakable significance. I gingerly scratched it. The skin was warm but very hard and smooth. I examined its collar but the lettering was in the cursive commercial code I couldn't decipher. Alger, however, interpreted the inscription easily:

"'I am Silver. I belong to Mirable Wirthy.'"

Without hesitation, Silver, the abattoir, followed at my heels through a half kilometer of ducts and tunnels until we reached the forecastle. As we went along, Alger attempted to access the ship's information network, having been unable to do so for more than a century, but achieved only partial success. "It is astonishing how technology has evolved," Alger said, more to himself than to me. "I can interface with some older operating systems. These, however, were superseded long ago and delegated to tertiary roles. The newer command overlays are entirely opaque. It is frustrating."

Silence widened around us as I led Silver to the window behind which sat Clarege Wirthy. The chief started back before remembering a partition separated him from the abattoir.

"Anderts, why have you brought that vicious thing here?"

"It is tame enough, sir. It is wearing a collar."

"Of course, of course. Come to think of it, I believe I know just whom it belongs to. What is on the collar?"

I shrugged. It was only common sense but I thought it best not to let on I could now, with Alger's help, fathom Wirthy commercial code. In fact, it would be better not to make known any of Alger's capabilities. With a petulant expression, Clarege Wirthy came out of his office and approached the abattoir. Silver's purring became a warning mumble and his lips skinned back to reveal a thicket of metal incisors. Clarege jerked his hand away as if it had been singed. "Control your animal," he snapped.

"It's not mine," I protested but I resumed scratching the abattoir behind the ear and this time Silver permitted his collar to be inspected.

"Just as I thought," Clarege Wirthy said. "The thing belongs to Mirable."

"Who, sir?"

"Mirable Wirthy. The captain's daughter."

CHAPTER FOUR

The Pirate and the Captain's Daughter

1. An individual owns their body unless they mortgage or sell it.

2. Except in the above instances, an individual's body may not be imprisoned, injured, coerced, consumed, or caused to die by any other individual or group of individuals. Unless, of course, the individual deserved such treatment.

3. Communication is an inalienable privilege. The stifling of free speech cannot be condoned. Nor should zealots and loudmouths be endured.

4. An individual owns their possessions until it can be proven they are stolen.

5. Except in the above instance, an individual's possessions may not be taken from them by any other individual or group of individuals. Unless, however, there is good reason to do so.

6. An individual or group of individuals have the right to conduct themselves according to their own customs, no matter how bizarre. Neither should they impose their poor manners on other individuals or groups.

7. Unrestricted individual travel is a basic freedom. An individual or group of individuals may journey where they wish, as long as they pay their scores and do not become obstreperous, in which case it is permissible to speed them on their way.

8. Where applicable, an individual has the right to reproduce or not to reproduce with any other individual or group of individuals as long as such reproduction

(or failure to reproduce) is voluntary (except in the case of weebies and scrones and similar species, where the male or female sexes are rather stupid).

The Standard Interstellar Catalog of Sentient Rights,
The Plain Text Abridged Version, A.I. 97

Clarege Wirthy retreated into his office while Silver accompanied me to my bunk, slid onto the mattress, and curled up in a ball at my feet after finishing another ration bar. Every Smit remained cautiously on the far side of his own bunk and plied me with questions about the abattoir. Omitting any mention of Alger, I explained how I had met Silver. "Mirable Wirthy," I asked, "what do you know of her?"

"Nothing much and that at fifth hand—the captain's daughter doesn't associate with forecastle crew. A vain and pretty thing, that's all I have heard. Could even be true."

"Do you suppose she's missed this great beast?" Silver's pinpoint eyes were closed and his quills were flat against his body. Even so he was larger than I was, although impossibly thin. Without waiting for Smit to answer, carried on by my own imagination, I continued, "Of course she's missed him. Who wouldn't? She will be relieved to have him back."

"I hope so, for your sake." Every Smit had a poor opinion of human nature. "Wirthys are a peculiar folk, though," he added. "And women of any sort are unpredictable, that's been my experience."

I scrambled to my feet as Chief Clarege escorted Marval Wirthy to my bunk. This was the first time I had encountered the seventeenth mate since he'd handed me over to Clarege. There was much I wanted to say to him, none of it pleasant. But I held my tongue while Marval Wirthy looked from me to Silver and then back in my direction. It was obvious he did not remember who I was and Clarege had to supply my name. "Anderts," Marval Wirthy said, "why have you stolen this animal?"

Out of the corner of my eye I noticed Smit nodding. "I didn't steal him," I said. "I found him while at my duties. He found me, I should say."

It was as if I hadn't spoken. "Theft is a serious matter," Marval Wirthy continued. "A misdemeanor of this severity cannot be ignored. The truth now, or it will go even worse for you. Were you holding the animal for a reward, was that your plan?"

"Not at all. I am offended you would think so. Although I wouldn't refuse any small or large appreciation if it were offered."

"There will be no such appreciation. The real issue before us is your offense. We will discuss it after I return the pet to its owner, who has been concerned for its well-being."

Marval Wirthy made a motion as if to take hold of the abattoir's collar. That was a mistake. Displaying remarkable restraint, Silver left a red weal across the back of the officer's hand.

"Another thing you will have to answer for, Anderts," Marval Wirthy said, examining the scratch with displeasure. "Corrupting the animal. I cannot imagine the consequences if it has to be put down."

"You startled him," I explained. "That's all it was. Come on, Silver. Come along now."

I was only guessing the abattoir would obey my commands but he slid obediently from the bunk. "Maybe it would be best if I went with you, sir" I volunteered. "Just to make sure Silver isn't nervous."

Marval Wirthy acknowledged my suggestion by turning wordlessly for the exit. Soon we were far above the maintenance and cargo levels. There were mostly Wirthys here, all with a similar cast to them. Not for the first time I wondered how the clan avoided becoming inbred, whether through practicing exogamy with other vessels or through genetic editing.

Our destination was an environmental blister at the very bow of the ship, protected from space by a rigid transparent bubble, which allowed an uninterrupted view of the full dark expanse of space spangled with stars.

A girl sat on a wood bench under this dome of night. She had on the white blouse and pants the Wirthys wore, gathered at the waist by a black sash instead of a red one. Her legs were curled beneath her and she was leaning against the arm of the bench, her oval face illuminated by the back-lighting of the book she held before her. Hearing our approach, she glanced away from the screen.

"Silver!"

The abattoir sped to the girl. He ran rings around her, a continuous gleaming blur. When he finally slowed, it was to rest his head on her lap. "Marval," she said. "I had begun to worry. Last time he did not come back for five days. Once he gets a taste of schvee, there is no stopping him, the silly monster. Hunting is in his blood."

Finally she noticed me. "And who is this?"

I did not answer since I knew I would make an idiot of myself. This allowed Marval Wirthy to state:

"The miscreant who took off with your pet. He had some idea of a reward, I don't doubt. We will have a stern talk with him later, Clarege and I."

Still I couldn't speak. It was the same girl I had met so briefly. Mirable Wirthy. The captain's daughter. I knew Every Smit's pessimistic evaluation had to be accurate and I prepared myself to dislike her but in her face I saw nothing vain or foolish. Nor did I see any recognition in her regard, and it was apparent that she had forgotten our earlier meeting.

Nor was I the only one at a loss. In my mind I heard Alger saying:

"But it cannot be Miss Imogene, not after so many years. No, it is absolutely impossible."

"What is?" I thought.

He sounded calmer. "For an instant I was nonplussed, sir. This young woman is the very image of Imogene Wirthy and Imogene Wirthy is long deceased. Then I realized she must be a clone. Miss Imogene planned thoroughly for her succession. Undoubtedly there is a tissue sample in cryogenic storage. Every generation a cell is germinated, and Imogene Wirthy once again walks the halls of her ship. Her rationale was that no one would look after her business better than she would."

"But this is the captain's daughter."

"That was indeed what everyone called Miss Imogene. The Captain. She thought it rather amusing. No doubt the custom has continued to this day."

I forced myself to look at Mirable Wirthy straight on. It was hard accepting that here was the genetic embodiment of a wily and powerful matriarch who had been dead for a century. I wondered how much of the girl was the product of individual experience rather than of DNA but I couldn't begin to guess. I knew one fact for sure, though. It wouldn't do to underestimate her. Nor, I suspected, would it pay to keep quiet.

"The truth is Silver found me," I said aloud. "Any other story is a lie."

I think it surprised Mirable Wirthy that I addressed her directly. "Why should I believe you?" she asked.

I shrugged. "Do you suppose I could force Silver to do anything he did not want to? I wouldn't care to try."

Her laugh was easy. "The boy has a point, Marval."

"I agree he exerts an undue influence over the animal. I have yet to mention how he encouraged it to attack me." Marval had been holding his scratched hand to one side but now he brought it forward. "Only quick thinking prevented the injury from being more serious."

"You do so exaggerate, Marval," she said. "If Silver truly meant you harm, you would be lacking a hand." Then she asked me: "Whatever is your name, boy?"

"My name is Pimsol Anderts and I am not a boy."

"No, why, I suppose you're not. Well, then, Pimsol Anderts, who is not a boy, Marval says you expect a reward. But unlike Marval, I am convinced you are due one. Should you have a choice, what would you request?"

If Mirable Wirthy had been another girl, I might have asked for money or for some privilege. But she had a quality about her that dared me to speak honestly. Had he heard, Every Smit would have thought I was being rash and unworldly, not to mention stupid. Perhaps I was all three.

"A fair deal, that's what," I told her. "It is not right the way things are set up aboard this ship. Even the food's no good."

"Must we listen to nonsense?" Marval Wirthy interrupted. "I hear the same tripe below decks whenever the crew has time on their hands."

"No, Marval, let him continue. Tell me, Pimsol Anderts, what exactly are your complaints? You mentioned the food. What do you think is wrong with it? I want to understand."

Her gaze was so innocent I began to hope the innocence was real. I repeated what Alger had told me. "You would get sick if you ate it long enough," I finished.

"Marval, have you heard anything of this before?"

"Not more than a hundred times. It is a typical forecastle rumor and means nothing."

"Sir, it's not a rumor."

"What proof would you have, Anderts? Are you, unbeknownst to the ship at large, a molecular engineer?"

Too late I realized I would have to reveal Alger's capabilities in order to make my point. So I could only repeat:

"Well, it is not a rumor."

Marval Wirthy snorted. "Just as I thought. Mirable, we've wasted your time sufficiently. Anderts, come along. Consider yourself lucky Miss Mirable has seen fit to overlook your transgression. I would be far less sentimental, you may be sure of that."

Feeling awkward and foolish, I allowed the mate to lead me away. All I had managed was to make myself ridiculous, both to Marval Wirthy and, of more consequence, to Mirable Wirthy, the captain's daughter.

Every Smit released a whistle after I had explained what had happened.

"Everyone knows the crap's no good, Anderts," he said. "So what? No one eats it."

"Except me."

He shook his head with exasperation and continued plaiting his coppery hair in thin braids.

"Except those too ignorant to figure out what is best, I will agree."

"What is best?" I muttered. "What is best isn't necessarily what is right."

"What does *right* have to do with anything?" he asked, once again dumbfounded by my innocence. "What is important, Anderts, is what *is*. Take it from me, you are not going to change the situation aboard this damn ship. Now you've named yourself as even more of a trouble-maker. Clarege never forgets an injury or an irritation, no matter how slight."

The next watches, however, were uneventful. Then the *Abernathy* jockeyed into orbit around a dusky red world that was without any significant body of water. Instead of being dispatched on my usual duties, I was directed to the main cargo bay, where I joined the gang unloading freight from the tenders coming from the surface. This was hard, sweaty work. We were supervised by yet another Wirthy, Erasmus Wirthy, whose genial expression encouraged me to speak up:

"What planet is that, sir?" I asked while wrestling a crate onto a pallet.

"It has no name humans can pronounce, Anderts," Erasmus replied. "The chart designation is HH 5813(d)."

"Now that is interesting," Alger observed. "It was not one of our ports of call, not during my time, sir, but I have several references on file, including a lengthy entry in *Hoover's Handbook of Non-hominid Intelligent Species*, volume 28, page 9,210, paragraph 3. The edition to which I am referring was last updated in the year A.I. 149, but I doubt the situation on HH 5813(d) has changed significantly."

I was beginning to suspect I understood why Alger had become mislaid. Somehow I doubted Imogene Wirthy, financial magnate and merchant captain, had been a patient woman.

"Go on," I thought.

"Of course, sir. Would you care for the full article or for an abstract?"

"The abstract will do."

"As you wish." Before Alger could continue, however, a fork lift took a turn too narrowly, spilling its cargo to the floor of the hold. Several crates broke open, scattering pads of manure everywhere, and I became aware of an appalling reek. The stuff was alive with fat white worms the length of my forearm, which writhed blindly amid the detritus, groping upward with eyeless heads. Erasmus Wirthy detailed a crew to shovel up the mess. The rest of us were told to ring the area and prevent the worms from getting away. "Gentle with them," he instructed. "Take care with each and every one. I don't want harm done, not a nick nor a scratch."

"Why not?" someone asked.

"They're paying passengers, that's why, which is more than you need to know. Now get on with it."

According to Alger, the worms constituted a hive mind of sophisticated intelligence. As juveniles they lived in the digestive tracts of bovine arthropods that grazed upon the endless grasslands of HH 5813(d). Upon reaching maturity, they allowed themselves to be deposited from their hosts, burrowed underground, and joined the rest of their kind as components of a subterranean neural strata underlying the entire world.

"The hive mind can be instructed to filter pure elements from earth and rock," Alger went on, "and to deposit castings of refined ore at specific sites on the surface. As you may imagine, the worms are in high demand on worlds lacking industrial mining technology. What makes the process more profitable is that they subsidize the cost of their own transportation."

"The worms? Why?" Gingerly using the toe of my boot, I nudged one that had wriggled too close. It gaped eyelessly at the unexpected touch.

"Opinion is mixed, sir. There are conceptual and linguistic barriers to any real mutual understanding. However, as best as can be determined, the worms consider themselves tourists and insist on paying their own way."

From the red planet the *Abernathy* traveled fifteen light years outward along the galactic arm. Then we entered a node of stars packed as closely together as crab roe, all with settled planets, and we began loading and discharging goods at almost every solar system. I never learned the name of the place where the worms disembarked but I remember it had gold clouds and a single continent girding the equator. A dozen stops later we were orbiting a world much larger than normal for a world with an oxygen-nitrogen atmosphere although its gravity was less than standard due to the scarcity of heavy elements, primarily metals, in its composition.

"Temurlone," Alger said. "An unusual planet, sir. A profitable port of call."

Beyond the loading dock, Temurlone took up the entire sky, a glowing blue and tan orb obscured by great swathes of white cloud. A moon not much smaller than a world itself was visible against the bulk of the planet.

"There are human settlements, whose cultures have diverged in eccentric directions," Alger continued. "We would take on handcrafts, rugs, pottery, metalwork, gourmet comestibles, drugs and essences, and other items of unusual nature, leaving off manufactured goods. It was a good trade. There are also many nonhuman enclaves and occasionally one or another would supply us with merchandise.

"Unfortunately," Alger went on, "Temurlone is not altogether civilized. The very size of the planet mitigates against the development of any centralized authority. It would not be out of the question for dacoits to conceal themselves among the consignment and cause mischief. Miss Imogene always enforced the most strict precautions when taking on cargo."

That this custom had not fallen into abeyance was demonstrated by the fact Marval Wirthy himself led our crew to the loading dock. A squad of marines, all Wirthys, dressed alike in white uniforms, accompanied us. They ringed the tender with lasers at the ready while the flight crew filed out of the ship and then four marines went inside to search for stowaways. Only after they signaled all clear were the loading doors opened. Marval Wirthy waved a hand and we began maneuvering the cargo from the tender. As each crate was removed from the ship, a marine passed a wand over it, scanning for anomalies.

Canny Galdo and I were working together. We took on a load of crates from the tender and carried it far back in the stacks. Canny was operating the fork lift while I stood to one side and helped her position the load in the space allotted. As she backed the machine from the crate, a false door opened in its side, revealing a hidden compartment, the interior shiny with shielding insulation, which had prevented it from being discovered. Men scrambled out, pistols in their fists. Canny's thousand eyes stretched wide. She opened her mouth to speak—I never knew what she meant to do, whether to yell a warning or just ask their business—and was immediately shot dead.

I kept my mouth closed and raised my hands.

One after another, and then several at once, in no particular order, Canny's eyes were closing. The fork lift came to a stop as her fingers relaxed their hold on the controls. She slumped from her seat and sprawled on the deck.

"Do you wish to live, my boy?"

The question was asked in standard interstellar vernacular but in a dialect so thick that I had trouble understanding what was said. I nodded.

The man facing me appeared more machine than flesh. Both his arms were metal sheathed in clear material so you could see the interior workings; his eyes were digital lenses; and his cranium was studded with augmentation sockets.

From concealment in other crates emerged more of the boarding party. Most were human, at least relatively so. All were armed. And all had an air of menace that let me understand this was a seasoned crew, not an impromptu band of adventurers. They separated into smaller groups and dispersed through the hold. Soon I heard yells and the sound of a fire fight.

"Speak, my boy. The captain's locker, can you lead us to it?"

I did not doubt my life depended on an affirmative answer but I had no idea what the captain's locker was, nor any idea of its location. Alger, however, was familiar with the expression. "It is, sir, the vault where items of value are stored during transit. Gemstones, high-denomination currency, letters of credit, precious metals, drugs, artwork. That sort of thing."

I had to restrain myself from yelling out loud. "Do you know where it is?"

"Almost certainly."

"Almost certainly?"

"I still have not achieved an interface with the current operating systems," Alger explained. "The plans of the ship in my memory may not be entirely reliable."

It was not as if I had a choice. I answered the pirate in as confident a voice as I could manage: "The captain's locker? Sure, I know the way. What of it?"

His artificial hand closed around my shoulder with a grip far beyond my strength to break.

"Take us there. And you have my word that you may live."

He pushed me forward while beckoning the rest of the crew to follow. I stepped around the body of Canny Galdo and past those of Marval Wirthy and the marines who had accompanied him. For Marval I felt nothing for I had never liked him and he had treated me badly. Strangely I felt more for the other dead men although I did not know any of them except Canny. The rest of the work gang had fled. Alger's directions led us up several escalators into territory I had passed through when I had been brought before Mirable Wirthy.

"I believe I recognize where we are, sir," Alger said. "Yes, indeed. Take the second hallway on the left."

That was when sirens began sounding and the lights began flickering in an emergency pattern.

"Duck, sir."

I threw myself flat just as a laser burst scored the wall where I had been and then targeted the pirate behind me. At its touch his body became reflective, rendering the laser harmless. His grin revealed that his natural teeth had been replaced by composite ones, the front canines adapted into fangs capable of injecting venom as well as slicing flesh. He aimed his own weapon at the sniper. There was an oddly subdued noise, more like a loud slap than an explosion, and I was dampened by a spray of fluid and fine organic matter. The pirate lifted me upright by my shirt collar and shoved me forward.

"Get on with it, my boy. Be nimble. Time is money."

I risked a glance over my shoulder as I stumbled ahead. There were fifty or more men and things strung out in single file along the corridor.

My guess was this was to be a quick raid, in and out before serious opposition could be readied. It was impossible such a small number could hope to seize the *Miraculous Abernathy* against a crew of many hundred Wirthys.

"Thanks, Alger," I thought as I led the pirates toward the captain's locker.

"For what, sir?"

"For telling me to duck."

"Please, make nothing of it. It was my duty and my privilege."

"Even so, Alger, I owe you." Silently I instructed myself to have more patience with my personal attendant, aristocracy grade, in the future.

There was another ambush, which left two of the boarding party dead in addition to six Wirthy marines. Then we entered a wide chamber furnished with data terminals at which clerks had been working until just recently. In the center was a vault ten meters on a side. It was a cube of impervious metal, smooth except where interrupted by a single reinforced door, which was shut. At a gesture from my captor, two raiders sprinted to the door and applied electronic devices to the plate beside the handle. The rest positioned themselves at the entrances to the room.

That was when I realized my usefulness was over. The same thought occurred to the pirate leader. I could see it in his red eyes as the lenses focused on me, filling with bright sparks of green and gold. I knew he was weighing which was the better course, to let me go or to kill me. There was no possibility his decision would be swayed by human sentiment. I had decided to take the chance and run, when he said:

"You have done as you promised, my boy. I cannot do less myself, not if I value my honor, which I do—it is my single weakness. So be off."

"You've lost a couple men, captain," I answered.

"That I have and I do not care for it. God's good humor to them, one and all. Come to the point."

"My point is I would like to sign on. I'm no Wirthy, and I owe them nothing. Let me join you and be your man."

I would never have believed such an apparition as the pirate leader could laugh. It was fitting that his amusement was a horrible thing.

"I like your spirit, my boy," he said. "You have globes, however hairless. But we need men who know what they're about, not babes fresh from the womb with dew in their eyes. No, take off while time remains."

"I can learn, captain," I argued. "I will serve you well, see if I won't."

But he only dismissed me and turned to confer with the technicians, who had failed to open the vault. "It is as I feared," the captain muttered—Hartung, I heard the others call him. "Any weapon strong enough to scratch the thing would destroy the ship. There isn't a combination, of course. Nor a time delay. No, the door is keyed to the genetic sequence of one person. The question is who."

Alger observed, "A similar procedure was followed during my own time, sir. Miss Imogene was particular about restricting access to the locker. Her touch alone could free the door. I would suppose the same holds true today. Not Miss Imogene herself, of course, since she has long since passed. Someone else."

Hartung now returned his attention to me. "No way around it.

We'll have to take hostages. You'll do for a start, my boy. Sit down over there and make yourself useful."

"I am no hostage, captain," I protested. "I'm a recruit."

"You are what I say you are, and not another word. You should have listened to my advice and decamped when there was opportunity. Well, that is what comes of not seizing the moment, as the good God instructed."

"What of your honor, captain?" I asked. "You said you'd set me free."

"Which I did. That you chose to remain in harm's way is your own affair. New circumstances have precedence. I trust you can appreciate my point of view. Smartly now, my boy. Smartly."

Soon I was joined by other crew members, mostly Wirthys but also some people I knew, including Every Smit. We were all on the floor with our backs to the vault. Smit squatted next to me. He was bleeding from a gash below the hairline and his left eye was swollen. "The bastard did it on general principle," he said, spitting out a fragment of tooth. "I wasn't causing trouble and coming along sweetly. Say, what do you suppose they want of us? Nothing good, I don't imagine."

I explained what I had overheard. Smit laughed. "Maybe these others here—" he indicated the Wirthys—"have some value. But not you and I, Anderts, nor any of our like. Let us hope our worth isn't put to the test."

For a while there was intermittent gunfire in the nearby corridors. Then the pirates opened negotiations by choosing one of the hostages at random, a man I had never seen before, shooting him, and tossing his body from the room. A second man refused to go quietly and was bludgeoned unconscious before being dragged away and murdered. Still no response was received. For a third time a selection was made.

We all shrank back while a nonhuman with bulbous eyes and skin too loose for its body decided among us. He regarded Smit and me with equal dispassion. But I was the one he prodded forward. Captain Hartung once more uttered his terrible laugh.

"This is true irony," he said. "It seems you are to be of service after all, my boy."

"Small chance of that, captain. I don't mean spit to anyone here. Least of all to the Wirthys. Go ahead and do what you must but it will get you nothing."

Green and gold streaks shot through the red lighting of Hartung's eyes. "We are allowing five minutes for an answer to our requests to arrive. Is there any last thing you would care for?"

"I don't know as I would care for anything from you," I replied, angry less at my own fate than at what I had just witnessed. "You're all nothing but thugs. I should have realized it from what happened to Canny. But I told myself it was just bad luck on her part and nerves on yours. I guess I wanted off this ship too badly to see what was plain before my eyes."

"No, my boy," replied the pirate. "We're pragmatists, that's what we are, every man of us. We do what works under the circumstances. According to the historical data, the taking of hostages leads to the capitulation of a boarded vessel in 92 percent of such engagements. These merchant clans are all alike. Inbred, insular, and spiritless. It won't be long before they knuckle under. But the true question, though, the real issue in front of us, is will it be soon enough to do you any good? That's a marvelous rare puzzle. I envy you the opportunity to have such a fascinating dilemma to ponder."

To Alger I thought: "Your defensive capabilities—what are they?"

"Sir, I am capable of firing micro-caliber projectiles, tipped either with explosive charges or biological toxins, to a distance of ten meters."

Looking at Captain Hartung's metal skin and at the armor his men wore, I did not think this would be much help. But Alger hadn't finished.

"I can also increase your reaction speed through the administration of stimulants," he went on. "And lower your sensory threshold, so you may be more aware of danger."

That sounded useful. "Do it."

Aloud I said to Hartung, "Spare me the philosophy, captain. I am not interested."

"How unfortunate. This is the precise moment in a man's life when philosophy becomes important. Have you lived to the limit, as God instructed? Have you regrets about what you have done or what you have left undone? Will your death be an accident? Or is it part of some larger plan, some inscrutable or farcical subplot of our universe of miracles? Three minutes remain for you to answer these questions as best you may. Is this space enough in which to judge a lifetime? I tell you, I honestly don't know."

Hartung threw his head back and the chamber echoed with his terrible laughter. Then he took me by my collar and lifted me until my face was level with his. An earnest expression rested uneasily on his artificial features. "Do you have any idea how many men I have killed?" he asked.

"No, captain, I don't."

"No, well, why should you? Especially since I lost count myself when I was about your age. Not that it matters. One or a thousand, it's all the same. The point is no one, not a single one of the men or persons of sentience I have slain, either with my own hands or through proxies, has ever come back with news from beyond. To me that is a fact of grave significance. Perhaps there is ultimately nothing on the other side of death, no matter what God told us. In which case it's immaterial whether you strive your utmost or lead a life of boring dullness. It makes no difference one way or the other."

I couldn't decide whether Captain Hartung was appalled by this realization or elated by it.

The chemicals Alger was injecting into my bloodstream began to take effect and Hartung's voice seemed loud and slow, as if he was drawing out his words to twice their length.

Despite my anger and fear, I was troubled by the questions Hartung posed. The plain truth, if I looked at my life hard, was I hadn't accomplished much. For too long I had allowed myself to be controlled by the situations in which I had found myself instead of taking charge of events. That had to change, I swore it. I remembered what the Cee had told me, that it did not matter how long you lived as long as you lived well, if only for a day. Suddenly, if tardily, I understood what it had meant and I vowed I wouldn't submit quietly to execution. Live or die, it would be my choice and no one else's. And if I survived—but I couldn't plan that far ahead. I had to concentrate on the moment. I relaxed and allowed my posture to fall into the ready stance Smit had taught me, prepared to attack or defend as necessary. Captain Hartung said:

"Thirty-seven seconds, my boy. Have you any parting words? I doubt we'll be meeting again. At least if we accept the accuracy of past data."

I had to hold myself under strict control in order not to reveal my heightened reaction time. I focused my enhanced vision on Captain Hartung. Up close, he appeared invulnerable. Both his metal and his flesh bore scars that testified to his durability.

"No, captain, I don't have anything to say. Not to you. I won't waste my breath."

I was concentrating on what I had to do next. If I allowed myself to fall, I might be able to kick his legs out from under him and gain a chance to run.

"You disappoint me, my boy. I had thought you would be more articulate. This is, so to speak, your finest moment. It would be a shame to let it pass without comment and go silently into the long night."

He raised his pistol and put its muzzle to my head.

The noises of my breathing and heartbeat were so loud in my own ears it was amazing to me no one else heard them.

I would have to catch Hartung in the knees at an angle since the joints were probably reinforced against direct impact. Even so I did not expect the odds were in my favor.

"They are not, sir," Alger said. "I estimate the likelihood of your incapacitating the captain at 24 percent."

"That low?"

"That high, sir. I allowed a generous margin for luck."

I had to remind myself of my decision to be patient with Alger. Hartung was saying:

"Ten seconds, my boy. Eight."

I would have to move without thinking, kicking out fluidly as I dropped to the deck. Only Alger's chemical protocol gave this desperate plan any chance of success. Five seconds. Three—

CHAPTER FIVE
An Uneasy Stalemate

Temurlone—a world too grand to encompass in a single article, which is why 4,366 others follow this introduction. With its immense horizons, never-ending vistas, and magnificent geology—as well as a climate that is pleasant for humans and most oxygen-breathing sentient species—the planet has attracted visitors and settlers from the furthest reaches of space since its discovery in A.I. 65 by an itinerant commercial representative named Horace Witherell.

Witherell sold shares in the find as he continued along his usual marketing route, often providing several different purchasers with deeds to the same Temurlone property. These deceptions were not discovered until long after Witherell absconded with the money and departed the stage of history.

The first settlers, in A.I.72, belonged to an athletic cult and were firmly convinced of the salutary benefits of exercise.

The Human Library: Edition A.I. 300

"**Stop this immediately.** I will allow no more."

Escorted by armed pirates, a party of Wirthy officers came into the chamber—a negotiating team, all dressed alike in plain tunics and pants distinguished by sashes of different colors. The group was led by an imposing woman in her thirties with a mane of black hair that was beginning to turn gray. I was certain

I recognized her although I was equally sure I had never seen her before. Trailed by her retinue, she strode up to us and fixed Captain Hartung with a withering glare. "What is your name, dead man?" she asked imperiously.

"Are you addressing me, ma'am?" Hartung replied, unimpressed by her demeanor. "If so, let me assure you I am very much alive. Furthermore, I intend to remain alive far into old age and comfortable retirement on a generous annuity, even if I have to exterminate every last one of your crew in order to do so. Quickly or slowly, it does not matter. Must I provide another demonstration?"

Despite my augmented metabolism, Hartung grabbed me by the throat before I knew what was happening. With only a little extra pressure, his grip would snap my neck. It was just as well I hadn't tried to take him on.

Her stare never wavered. "There will be no further killing," she instructed him. "I am Vander Wirthy, captain of this vessel. Tell me what you want and it will be done, so we may be rid of you."

Hartung dropped his hand to my shoulder. Only then did I become aware of the ring of pain where he had held me.

"I am glad we understand one another, Captain Vander," Hartung said suavely. "As for what I want, why, that is simplicity itself. I desire access to your locker here. I will release half the hostages when it is open—"

"Three quarters."

"—the other quarter when we board the tender you will have waiting for us. The tender will be fueled and in flight-ready condition. We will give the boat a thorough inspection before setting free a single person."

The longer I regarded Vander Wirthy, the more certain I became that we had met. It was not simply that she had the typical look of the clan—the oval face, the wide mouth, the high forehead with a smooth hairline, the tapered fingers equally as long as Jo Feringel's. The feeling of recognition went deeper. Then, belatedly, I realized the truth. The woman before me was Mirable Wirthy—Mirable Wirthy in twenty years—Mirable Wirthy as she might become after a lifetime of authority in command of the *Miraculous Abernathy*. Here could only be another clone of Imogene Wirthy herself, the ancient matriarch who had refused to surrender rule of her fiefdom, of her ship and her family, even to death.

"Miss Imogene calculated the proper interval between generations to be exactly seventeen years," Alger commented. "This would allow sufficient time for each new captain to learn from the previous one but not so much time that she would grow stale while waiting to assume command. When Vander steps down, Mirable will be prepared to succeed her immediately and be at her physical and mental peak. Yes, Miss Imogene planned for all contingencies. A remarkable woman, as I have mentioned once or twice."

There was an edge to Alger's observation that made it seem less than flattering.

Vander Wirthy was saying: "I will send a representative. You will allow her safe passage back to me along with three quarters of those here once the locker is open. At that point I will permit your party and the remaining hostages to proceed to hangar 011. There will be a ship waiting. Inspect it as you want, thoroughly or not. When the rest of my crew have been freed, I will provide the command codes and you may depart. Are we agreed?"

"In large measure, Captain Vander," Hartung replied easily. "A few details, however, require clarification."

"And these are?"

"A dozen of your crew must accompany us," he answered. "At least for a while. You understand my reasons, of course."

"Half a dozen. You will set the hostages free in a lifeboat at thirty thousand kilometers."

"Captain Vander, please, credit me with doing my due diligence. Your Scimitar MMX military lasers, for example, have a range of twice that distance. No, we will release the hostages when it is convenient. Which is to say, when we are beyond reach of any unfortunate repercussions. I give you my word they will be set free uninjured."

"Your word." Her voice was chill. The way light struck her eyes caused them to seem to be lit from within. They passed me by but then returned and Captain Vander studied me with a scrutiny accustomed to evaluating other men and women. "Even this boy knows what your word is worth, pirate," she observed.

I found I was disliking Vander Wirthy as much as I disliked Captain Hartung. "That's right, ma'am, I do."

"Is that so? Well, it could be. Events far stranger are commonplace in this universe of miracles. What is your name, lad?"

"Pimsol Anderts."

"Pimsol Anderts. What is your opinion?"

"Yes, my boy," Hartung put in. "Let us all hear."

It was not smart to have opened my mouth but I was tired of being treated casually. "His word is good, captain," I told Vander Wirthy. "Trust it to the letter but no further. It is your own fault if you haven't considered the situation from all sides."

"So your advice is to accept his guarantee?"

"I wouldn't doubt it. But I'd be looking over my shoulder, if I were you."

"Yes, I believe you're correct, Pimsol Anderts. Very well. You—" she was addressing Hartung—"you may have six hostages. Release them unharmed and in a timely manner. I will trust you that far. This boy, however, must be among the first group set free. He has done me a service."

The pirate's hand resting on my shoulder reminded me my neck still hurt from when he had held it. His lips slid away from his incisors in what could only be a grin. "This boy here, captain?" he asked.

"What of it?"

"If I say so myself, he has indeed been of service—to both of us. Have you wondered who led us to your precious vault, Captain Vander? Did you think we found the way ourselves, what with this stinking scow being a damned labyrinth? What with all internal signposts being in your clan code, a cipher unbreakable without hours of computation? My intelligence apparatus is good, but not that good. Captain Vander, if you please, allow me to introduce our guide. And let me set your mind at ease. We did not have to hurt him even a little."

Vander Wirthy heard the truth in Hartung's laughter. She looked at me less to confirm my guilt than to fix my face in her memory. It required all my willpower to meet her gaze without flinching. I knew I had erred badly in speaking up. I should have remained inconspicuous. No doubt Hartung was enjoying living up to my appraisal of him. It seemed the kind of irony he appreciated.

"You would have done the same with a gun to your own back," I told Vander Wirthy.

"I think not," she replied with a certainty that put it beyond consideration. "Each person has different values. Sadly it appears faithfulness and courage are not numbered among those you possess, Pimsol Anderts."

The unfairness of the accusation left me with nothing to say that wouldn't sound self-serving. Not that I owed loyalty to either Vander Wirthy or to the *Miraculous Abernathy*, where I had been little more than a slave, despite a contract saying otherwise.

The captain turned on her heel and proceeded from the chamber with her retinue in tow. Certain of the pirates began going among the prisoners and handing out flasks of water and escorting others to the necessary—it did not seem that long, but four hours had elapsed since Hartung and his crew had emerged from concealment and boarded the ship. Much had taken place since then, none of it good. Suddenly, in spite of Alger's stimulant protocol, I felt too weary to stand. The interior of my skull ached from the barrage of heightened auditory, visual, tactile, and olfactory input my brain had been receiving. But I forced myself to remain upright and to concentrate on what Hartung was saying:

"Do not pay any heed to that bitch," he instructed, as if he were my mentor and I his apprentice. "I tell you, my boy, principles will get you killed sooner than anything else I know, so who needs them. You did what was appropriate given the circumstances, just as I would have done myself. Someday, if you can keep your mouth shut, you might become dangerous, Pimsol Anderts. You have the look. We are two of a kind, you and I."

This was a disturbing thought. "We're nothing alike," I protested. To Alger I said:

"Increase the dosage of stimulant. I must be alert."

"Unwise, sir. Your heart is under exceptional strain. Any additional stress could cause arrhythmia or, possibly, cardiac arrest. Of course—"

"What, Alger?"

"It is just possible I could regulate your heartbeat using electrical impulses, an ancient procedure, sir. And not entirely reliable, either."

"I will take the chance."

At that moment there was a commotion by the main entrance to the vault chamber and a single figure emerged past the cordon of guards. The sight of her striding confidently forward, unconcerned by the armed desperadoes flanking her, filled me with admiration—and with other, stranger emotions I couldn't quite pin down. Her pale oval face was impassive, as if carved from flawless mother of pearl. It was Mirable Wirthy, of course. Who else would Vander trust with access to the ship's locker? Who else, in fact, would possess the necessary genetic matrix to open it?

By the way she regarded me—by the indifference with which she ignored me—I knew Vander had debriefed Mirable about her conversation with Captain Hartung and about my role in the proceedings.

If I was anything to Mirable Wirthy, I was the turncoat who had betrayed her ship and her clan. I suspected she despised me with a passion beyond my ability to appreciate.

"Let's get this over with," she told Hartung. "Free the hostages and I will open the locker."

"Not so quickly, my dear," replied the pirate leader. "The precise arrangement I negotiated with your—mother?"

"Our relationship is somewhat more complex. Nor is it relevant."

"—with Captain Vander, then, was that your people would be released after the vault is unlocked, not before. "

Felix Hartung had barely finished speaking when the deck beneath our feet lurched drunkenly.

Never before, not once during my service aboard the *Miraculous Abernathy*, had I felt any sensation of motion, not at post-light velocities between the stars, not when the ship was jockeying into orbit above a new port of call using fusion jets. The gravity field generated by the Avatar™ engines was designed to compensate seamlessly for all normal acceleration.

The *Abernathy* shuddered again. Pirates and hostages were sent flying along with the loose objects lying around—video terminals of heavy paper, staplers, and other standard office equipment. Captain Hartung alone, dancing with the erratic deck as if aboard an ocean-going vessel during rough seas, managed to remain upright.

His expression I can only describe as one of maniacal amusement. It was plain Hartung had a real passion for his evil occupation.

I was flung forward—against Mirable Wirthy. We lost our feet, ending up wedged awkwardly against a data cabinet. My augmented reaction speed allowed me to roll around while we fell so as to land beneath her and absorb the impact. The metal corner of the furniture knocked the wind from my chest but despite the pain I was all too conscious of the pressure of Mirable Wirthy upon me, her fresh scent, the brush of her hair against my cheek. With an expression of distaste, she hurried to disentangle herself.

"Alger, what is going on?" I asked.

"I am not entirely certain, sir, but in all likelihood the ship is under attack. My supposition is that we are currently undertaking evasive maneuvers. All the control systems I can contact are in emergency mode."

My first thought was that Hartung had never intended to rely on Vander Wirthy's good will or keep his own word. But the pirate seemed surprised, too. No, something else was going on, something not expected by either Captain Vander or by Felix Hartung.

A more powerful jolt went through the deck. Mirable Wirthy, caught as she was rising to her feet, was thrown back down. Her head struck with a sound that would have seemed loud even had my hearing not been amplified. Her eyes fluttered and rolled beneath the lids, leaving only white. I wanted to take her in my arms but I knew she shouldn't be moved with a head injury. Beyond that I did not have the least idea how to help her—until Alger instructed:

"If you would place me in proximity to Miss Mirable, sir, I will perform a medical scan and establish her condition."

I passed the wrist circled by the bracelet that was Alger back and forth above Mirable Wirthy's temples, and then to either side of her brow. The crystal studs flickered with lights of different color.

The chamber was noisy with things settling, groans and oaths as people began picking themselves from where they'd been thrown. Then from the main entrance came startled shouts and the deadly hiss of laser fire—and a snarling so atavistic I actually felt a chill go down my spine. Captain Hartung beckoned to his lieutenants and they followed him with raised weapons to join the cordon of pirates already in place. Just as they reached the barricade of desks, chairs, and cabinets that had been erected before the passage, the growling doubled in volume. Into sight leaped Silver.

Several lasers struck him. Instead of penetrating or being reflected, the coherent light was absorbed by the abattoir's metallic pelt. The energy was then redistributed. The tips of Silver's quills began to glow.

He sprang at the nearest pirate, slashing the man across the throat. When his quills touched another, this one an androgynous ruffian with a third eye and blue skin, there was a brilliant flash, followed by the stink of charred flesh.

"There is no fracture," Alger reported. "Nor is there any indication of a concussion. Miss Mirable will have a bruise and headache when she awakes, sir, but otherwise she is unhurt."

I couldn't explain the relief I felt hearing this.

The truce that had existed between Captain Hartung and Vander Wirthy was now undone. Flares of vivid light crisscrossed the vault chamber, leaving behind searing violet afterimages. Much of this fusillade was directed at Silver, who was attempting to tear through the ring of pirates opposing him—most likely in an effort to reach his mistress, or so I guessed. The rest of the fire was directed at the Wirthy marines who had taken advantage of the confusion to begin an assault of their own. In the melee some of the hostages, too, turned on their guards, wrestling away their weapons and discharging them at their captors, further adding to the uproar.

For the moment, at least, we were unsupervised. I did not think we'd be given another such opportunity.

"We have to get out of here," I thought to Alger as I lifted Mirable Wirthy in my arms. Although she was centimeters taller than me, she was slightly built and I was able to raise her with little effort. Cradling her by the shoulders and knees, I dashed for a maintenance exit that was now unguarded since the pirate detailed to watch it was lying face-down to one side, unconscious or dead, I couldn't tell. As I shifted my hold on Mirable in order to activate the override, another hand reached past mine and touched the plate.

"Move on, Anderts," Every Smit said. "The vicinity isn't healthy, that's common sense. Let's be off."

I went ahead of him through the door and into the corridor beyond. I had no idea where we were or where we should go.

"Take the fourth turn, sir," Alger said. "And then the second right. That will lead to Adit 54i."

"Adit 54i?"

"Which will direct us to anteroom 4021b."

"Anteroom 4021b?"

"Precisely, sir."

Forgetting my promise to be patient with Alger, I snapped, "What is so damned important about anteroom 4021b?"

"Allow me to explain, sir." There was no mistaking the wounded overtone to his thoughts. "Miss Imogene was not by nature a trusting woman. At various locations throughout the ship are hidden refuges. These are equipped with survival stores, armament, and communications equipment. Several offer means of escaping the *Abernathy* in case of disaster. The nearest such refuge is adjacent to anteroom 4021b."

Every Smit, sprinting at my side, remarked: "I thought you were dead, Anderts, when that big metal bastard grabbed you by the neck. Damn near made me stain myself, seeing how he hoisted you up like it was nothing."

I did not have the breath to answer. There was a strangeness to the beating of my heart I could feel but not describe. We took the fourth turn and entered a corridor as featureless as the one we'd left. That was when I first heard sounds behind us—thudding footsteps, the clink of weaponry and ammunition batteries and battle armor, questioning shouts. Our departure hadn't gone unnoticed—that would have been too much to hope for. Nor could we pull ahead of our pursuers. Soon it became clear our lead was dwindling. Sweat ran into my eyes and left as tears. Mirable Wirthy groaned and tossed her head although she remained unconscious.

The ship shuddered again and wrenched queasily. Somehow I remained on my feet while holding Mirable—it was the stimulant protocol, of course, that was providing my stamina and balance—but Every Smit was tossed forward. He landed clumsily and his ankle snapped. His face went as pale as sun-bleached shell. He curled up and clutched the injury. Through clenched teeth Smit said:

"Leave the girl behind, Anderts."

"And take you instead?" I asked, sure that was what he was requesting, unwilling to abandon Mirable to the pirates on our trail but knowing I would have to in order to honor the promise I had made Smit.

"No, that isn't it, Anderts," Smit replied. "You're too damn pitiful to carry me any distance so it wouldn't do any good to ask it of you. Use your head for once," he went on. "It isn't you or me they are after. It is the girl. They need her to open the vault. Forget her and take off. I can look after myself."

To Alger I said: "How much further to the bunker?"

"Fifty-six meters."

The pirates were closer. "Increase the dosage of stimulant," I said.

"Please, sir, listen to what I am saying. Your heart is already erratic. As it is, only by applying electrical correction am I preventing immediate fibrillation and cardiac arrest. I cannot answer for the consequences, really, I cannot, if your metabolism is further stressed."

Ignoring his protests, I hoisted Mirable Wirthy over one shoulder, grabbed Every Smit by the arm, and helped him upright.

"I am not leaving Mirable behind," I told him. "That's not in question. And you're coming, too."

Smit rested most of his weight upon me and we began a drunken three-legged shamble along the corridor. Five meters. Fifteen. The edges of my vision began darkening like smoldering paper. My pulse was dangerously fast and irregular. We took a corner and were another thirty meters further on when our pursuers came into sight. They followed right after us, Captain Hartung in the fore, a tireless automaton, all his teeth bared.

"Take the girl alive," he instructed. "No harm must come to her."

"And what of the immature human males?" growled one of his crew, a warty piebald thing without a real head, its features emerging directly from its torso.

I missed hearing Hartung's reply because I was busy searching with my fingers for the three invisible depressions that must be touched in order to enter the hidden refuge. Alger assured me they were there but I couldn't find them. Hartung and his men drew nearer—thirty meters separated us, then twenty. Everywhere the wall was without interruption. Then I felt the faintest difference in the texture of the material under my hand. The second depression was beside the first and the third beside that.

As Alger instructed, I tapped them in specific order. A ring of wall melted away, like ice under the sun but faster. Dim emergency lighting revealed a small oval compartment furnished with rows of chairs and little else. Before the two front seats was an instrument console and a joystick. Imogene Wirthy had taken no chances whatsoever. I was looking into the cockpit of a lifeboat.

Every Smit hopped ahead through the portal. I thrust Mirable Wirthy into his arms and prepared to step forward myself when a laser, on continuous fire, sliced into the plating beside me and drew a straight line toward my chest, its message clear. I would be dead if I tried to escape. Raising my hands, I turned to face Captain Hartung. Beside him was the warty thing with leprous green and brown mottling. Its eyes protruded from its neck on damp stalks. I couldn't begin to imagine where its voice came from.

"This is not the human female," it said. "This is one of the juvenile males. What should be done, captain?"

Hartung did not hesitate a second. "Kill the boy," he answered.

The headless pirate raised its rifle with tentacles as thin as whips.

I knew I would be murdered whether I struggled or not so I launched myself at the thing. Alger, realizing there would be no second chances, boosted my metabolism far beyond what was prudent. Energy flowed along my veins like fire. The moment elongated. Twisting around, as Every Smit had taught me, I employed the martial technology of Van Diver's World to kick the rifle from the pirate's grasp. Continuing the motion, I knocked the wind from its spiracles and sent it reeling into Captain Hartung.

The others closed in on me. They refrained from firing only in fear of shooting each other. I would be beaten to death.

Hartung lifted his unfortunate lieutenant by its tentacles and tossed the thing aside.

"You are bound to be difficult, my boy," he said. It was impossible to be sure, since his voice was distorted by the modifications to his dentition, but I was certain Hartung had sighed. "Determination is a quality I admire," he went on. "Beyond a certain point, however, it becomes mere surliness. For the last time, Pimsol Anderts, farewell—"

Hartung reached for me with a speed that matched my own in my accelerated state.

The corridor brightened, as if flooded by sunlight. Every quill illuminated, a thicket of cold fire, Silver raced into the throng of pirates. His teeth, already crimson, became darker red. Energy discharges flared as his quills contacted flesh. There was the stink of charred skin and other teguments. Screams and different sounds of alarm rose as the abattoir struck and struck again.

The attack distracted Hartung. Somehow I managed to evade him, twisting below and to one side of his grasp. The entrance to the lifeboat was still open and I flung myself through it, amazed

Smit hadn't already sealed the port and taken off—that would have been the sensible thing to do. But he was still in the process of settling himself behind the control console and I realized only seconds had passed although in my augmented condition much longer had seemed to go by.

I fell into the chair beside Smit. I could sense Alger striving to maintain my metabolism on an even keel but I knew I was near collapse.

"Let's go," I gasped to Smit.

"Damn if I know how," he muttered. "The instruments are labeled in Wirthy commercial code, not in standard script, damn them all."

A cramp seized my left arm from my fingers to my elbow, causing me to make a fist in pain.

"Press the yellow button, sir," Alger said. "That will activate the autopilot and disengage us from the ship."

"Press. The. Yellow. Button," I hissed to Smit.

Then I died.

My heart gave a great leap in my chest and subsided into quiet after more agony than I believed possible.

Alger, however, immediately extruded a miniature pump that kept the blood flowing through my body while he resuscitated my heart with an army of medical nanomachines, these created by the millions in the forge with which he had earlier built the nutrients I was lacking on a diet of Wirthy basic rations. Some of these molecule-sized devices replaced damaged organ tissue with material created on the spot but indistinguishable from the original stuff. Other machines filtered my bloodstream of stress toxins and the pharmacy of stimulant chemicals with which it had been overdosed.

Then Alger gave my heart a gentle nudge and it began beating.

Thirty-one seconds had elapsed.

I jerked upright in the chair, gasping. Smit hadn't noticed my brief demise. Slowly the spike in my breast rusted away, like metal in the sea, and I felt better.

The cabin was brightly lit—Silver had managed to board before the port closed. Whining querulously, the abattoir was nuzzling his nightmarish muzzle against Mirable Wirthy's limp hand. The light faded from his quills as he calmed down and his ears folded to his head in the same way a fan returns in on itself.

Acceleration pressed me against the seat. In the rear view screen loomed the *Abernathy*, as large as a mountain and as wild and scarred—an ungainly vessel but somehow majestic for all that. Still, I was glad to be seeing the last of the ship and I knew I wouldn't be carrying away many happy memories.

In the forward view screen, huge even at a distance of thirty thousand kilometers, was Temurlone.

There was another surge of acceleration as the autopilot, following standard procedure for such situations, directed us toward the planet.

Alger superimposed a grid on the view of the world in my eyes, outlining cartographic details beneath the cloud cover. Shadings of different color indicated areas of influence belonging to humans and other species. Some locations bore labels. Most did not.

"My information is, of course, out of date by over a century," Alger remarked apologetically. "Probably little is relevant except the geologic data. Human planetary cultures mutate at great velocity. Particularly when provided virtually unlimited room for expansion."

"You doing all right, Anderts?" Every Smit asked.

I managed a nod. "There's nothing too wrong with me, I don't think," I replied. No, there wasn't, not now that I was alive.

"Well, you look like crap," Smit said. "I thought you should know."

"Thanks. You look good yourself," although he didn't, not with one eye swollen shut and his face pale from the pain of his broken ankle.

"I also wanted you to know we're quits, the two of us. I wouldn't have done it myself, Anderts, what you did for me—it wouldn't have been the smart thing, not in the least. Personally, I would have left you and the girl without a second thought. But that isn't saying I am ungrateful."

"What you're saying, Smit, is you're glad I am a fool."

"Close enough." Smit, like Hartung, was a pragmatist.

By now there was no trace of the *Miraculous Abernathy* in the rear screen, just the black of space and the hard light of stars. Temurlone, closer by half, seemed below us rather than ahead, and we appeared to be descending toward the planet rather than approaching it straight on. I sank into the cushions of the command chair. For the moment we were out of danger. With Alger interpreting, I studied the controls. We would enter the atmosphere in minutes. The winking light indicated the emergency broadcast was functioning properly—

I immediately cut off the transmission. But I had acted too late.

Behind us appeared a black ship. The vessel was a fraction the size of the *Abernathy*, no more than a hundred meters in length but deadly, the hull studded with laser turrets and missile ports. Its sleek lines indicated the ship was capable of atmospheric flight as well as space travel. I did not think it was a good sign that it had broken off pursuit of the *Abernathy* to come after us. Was it under Hartung's command? I wondered. Or acting independently? Not that it made much difference. I doubted I would like the answer either way.

There was a jolt of acceleration as the lifeboat changed bearing toward the black ship. This, too, must be standard emergency procedure.

I would have to disengage the autopilot and take manual control or else we'd deliver ourselves to capture. Following Alger's directions, I gripped the joystick and brought it forty-five degrees counterclockwise while depressing the thruster. The lifeboat gave a sick lurch and began a crazy wobbling motion. I tried to correct but only made matters worse. Alger was telling me what to do but none of what he said made sense. Smit tightened his restraint harness and made a peculiar series of hand gestures, which probably had cultural significance on Van Diver's World.

In desperation I relaxed the throttle and returned the joystick to its original position.

From behind my left shoulder came a soft but decisive voice. "Get out of the way and let me have the controls."

Mirable Wirthy was on her feet, bracing herself with both hands against the irregular motion of the lifeboat.

I did not move fast enough to suit her. "Quickly now," she instructed. "I know what I am doing. You do not."

Without a word I unstrapped myself and edged out of the seat so Mirable could take my place. Her hand wrapped around the joystick. In seconds she dampened the lifeboat's yawing and spun us away at a steep angle from the black ship, sending us plummeting toward Temurlone.

Now the planet took up the entire view, impossibly huge, with a topography dwarfing that of most terrestrial worlds. Immense mountain ranges rose beside vast seas of dark blue saltwater dappled with aquamarine shallows. As we dropped toward the sunrise, into sight came a topological anomaly of staggering size, a rift valley piercing far into the planetary crust. The dirty gray clouds of a storm spun around it.

The black ship failed to recede from view. "Bastards are coming after us," Smit said.

"Yes, that is indeed obvious, thank you," Mirable Wirthy replied.

She twisted the joystick while triggering a full burn. Still the black ship drew nearer. Mirable sent us in an abrupt arc through the stratosphere, dragging a tail of ablative material across the horizon. The cabin shook and shuddered and I was thrown repeatedly against my harness. Silver, beside me, sank his claws into the seat cushion and held on that way. The forward view was obscured in a fiery nimbus. But the stern monitor, tracking the black ship, showed that it had chosen to enter the atmosphere at a more cautious angle than we had, and would overshoot our landing point by five hundred kilometers. I couldn't decide whether our pursuer was less maneuverable than we were or less rash.

Mirable had tested the tiny lifeboat to destruction. I did not need Alger's help to interpret the read-outs, even if they were in Wirthy commercial code. Each was flashing yellow and purple.

As she concentrated on controlling our descent, Mirable's face softened, losing all self-consciousness. For a moment I saw her as she must have been as a child. Then I remembered Vander Wirthy and saw her as she might become in twenty years. This image returned me to the present.

The lifeboat jerked as a parachute opened and broke away. There was another shudder as a second set of parachutes unfurled and tore off. Finally a third parachute lowered the capsule's velocity enough for Mirable to deploy a set of wings. Explosive bolts blew free the remaining shielding, revealing aerodynamic lines, and the lifeboat became an atmospheric glider.

We were kilometers above the landscape but seemed closer to the ground due to the sheer size of the planet and the consequent distortion of scale. Beneath us, and stretching away to the horizon, was a barren heath. Only by enhancing the image in the view screen could we see the smudge of distant foothills.

I pointed them out to Mirable. "Try for those."

She wouldn't risk looking at me but I could tell she was not happy at being told what to do. "It would be safer to land where the ground is level."

"Maybe so. But how long do you think we have before that ship returns?" I asked. "Personally, I don't figure more than an hour. In the hills we'd have a chance of escaping. Out on the flat, we'd have none."

Mirable nodded soberly and did not argue. A couple strands of hair had loosened from their knot and hung down along the nape of her neck. "I will do what I can," she said. "I have had only basic training with these machines, though. Nor are these the best flying conditions."

The landscape was overcast by bad weather. The lifeboat, now a glider, was being buffeted by erratic gusts of wind. We dropped fifty meters before being tossed twice that distance skyward. Mirable fought to maintain altitude but another downdraft sent us plummeting. Smit buried his face in a bag and was sick. I felt queasy myself but managed to ignore my stomach by focusing on the view. We were less than a kilometer up. Below spread a moor covered with scrubby growth and occasional wind-scoured strands of gnarled trees. Mirable coaxed all the lift she could from the glider but we continued to descend. Landing gear extended automatically, triggered by proximity sensors. She raised the nose and the rear wheels touched down smoothly. Then Mirable adjusted the joystick, bringing the nose down—

A wall of wind sheared into the glider and flipped it over.

CHAPTER SIX

The Unseemly Descent of Pilar Gonzlez Goodfellow

God did not answer. God had answered, at the beginning of time, at the instant the universe came into being, the reply woven into the very fabric of creation. Exactly one metric week after the Icon Corporation detonated 512 nova devices in its pursuit of corporate profit, The Bureau of Interstellar Standards measured significant fluctuations in the level of cosmic background radiation, this an echo of the birth of the universe. The fluctuations—of precisely one degree, from 2.735°K to 3.735°K—were in binary code. This is what God said:

1. For entertainment.
2. See Answer 1.
3. You get a recurring role if you play your part well.

The level of background radiation returned to normal. No nova weapon has worked since. The suicide rate has dropped alarmingly.

Tiptree Cordwainer, *What God Said* (p. 2,498). Ximbales City: The Ssecond Press, A.I. 57.

B oth wings snapped off as the glider plowed across the landscape. A section of hull plating tore away, taking Smit and his chair with it, sucking him out in the blink of an eye. Silver was flung through the same gap a second afterward, a great wad of cushioning in his talons. The cabin spun at different angles and broke apart in splinters of daylight. Something hard struck my temple.

Mirable was first to return to her senses after we came to a stop. She unsnapped her safety harness and crawled out of her seat since what remained of the lifeboat was on its side. I was dazed and could only stare without moving as she peered into my eyes. She lifted my right lid with a thumb and then my left.

"You'll live," Mirable said tersely.

"Indeed you will, sir," added Alger. "I have discovered no more than minor bruises and lacerations."

"They don't feel so minor to me," I muttered.

Mirable left me to extricate myself without assistance from my safety harness while she went to the crack in the hull and levered herself into the open air. Her shoes disappeared through the gap just as I rolled from my seat. I followed her example and hauled myself through the hull although the effort left me dizzy and weak. It took a minute before I had strength to look around. Mirable was facing into the chill wind, peering along the trail of debris left behind by the landing.

"Silver," Mirable called. The wind carried her voice away. "Silver!"

"Smit," I croaked. I struggled to my feet and tottered forward until I was beside Mirable, supporting myself against the stub of an aerodynamic vane. "Smit's out there," I told her. "I saw what happened. His entire chair went through the side. There's a chance he made it."

The moor went on forever, featureless and severe, the low growth bending in long sheets before the breeze, like ripples in slack water. Rain fell for just a second and then passed by. Despite the clouds, the air was very clear, yet even so the horizon was an indistinct blur. There was the tang of ozone and the smell of mold and sod. Far away lightning played.

"Smit? The other boy?" Mirable asked.

I decided to ignore her choice of words. "Every Smit," I agreed. "That's his name."

"Yes, I very much hope Smit survived. And my Silver, too. We must find them—whatever is your own name, boy?"

"My name is Pimsol Anderts and I am not a boy," I repeated.

From her reaction it was apparent Mirable hadn't recognized me. Not until this moment had she drawn a connection to our earlier meeting, when I had retrieved Silver from the lower decks and returned him to her in the company of Marval Wirthy. I did not know which stung worse—that she hadn't remembered me or that the recollection amused her.

"I know you," she said with a wan smile. "You're the boy who said the food tasted bad."

"That was not the issue," I protested. "I was objecting to a more serious matter. The stuff isn't healthy."

She dismissed my argument with an offhand gesture.

"So small a complaint set you on a career as a mutineer?" she asked.

"You've been misinformed," I said sharply. "I am not one, not in any way. I simply did what I had to in order to keep on living, that's all."

"Well, Silver thinks highly of you, Pimsol Anderts. I generally trust his opinion since he is a good judge of character. So I will delay my judgment, despite what Vander had me believe—and I usually trust her judgment, too, since it is more or less my own. But for a while let's put aside our differences and see whether my beast lives and your friend, Smit, of course. Then we'll be able to plan our own next steps, few as they may be."

Mirable returned into the lifeboat and came out with two emergency packs, one of which she handed to me before donning the other herself. She also passed over a stubby pistol and several batteries, each cartridge containing energy for five dozen rounds or fifteen seconds of continuous fire. Then she slid down the hull and strode off along the swathe the lifeboat had cut across the landscape while I followed at a less sprightly pace.

We passed sections of tiling still sizzling where they had come to rest and giving off a rancid stench. There was a chunk of interior paneling with circuitry attached to it. And there, spread at full length upon the thorny cushion provided by a growth of ugly scrub, was Silver. The abattoir lay unmoving when Mirable called his name and he did not stir as she cradled his toothy muzzle in her lap and stroked his narrow cheek and the ridges around his vacant pinpoint eyes.

His ears had unfurled and hung in lifeless folds.

After a moment I left Mirable alone with Silver and went off by myself in search of Smit.

I did not have much expectation of finding him in good condition, not after seeing Silver. At first, however, I couldn't tell what shape he was in since his clothes and skin were equally stained with blood.

The emergency seat in which he was strapped had protected Smit from impact. I doubted there was a bruise on him except for those he had received earlier at the hands of Captain Hartung's crew.

But as he'd tumbled away from the lifeboat, he'd been brought up short against a wood spike and impaled.

Nor was he alone. Below Smit on the same spike was another dead man, naked except for a thin coating of transparent skintight sheathing, the leather of some strange animal.

I raised my gaze from this macabre tableau to get relief from the sight of it and found another as appalling.

At intervals, receding without interruption across the heath as far as I could see, were other stakes, each with a burden of human fruit.

Every Smit stirred. With sadness and horror I realized he was alive and suffering. The stake had penetrated the back of the emergency chair and come out below his sternum.

"Isn't there anything you can do for him?" I asked Alger. "You fixed me, and I was dead. Smit's still living."

"Unfortunately, sir, the two situations are not comparable. In your case all that was necessary was micro-surgery and blood filtration. What is required here is massive surgical intervention."

"Take away his pain, Alger. You can do that."

"Indeed, sir. Place me in contact with exposed skin. I will administer an anesthetic, enough for an hour, which should be more than sufficient considering the circumstances."

In seconds Smit's face relaxed although it remained ashen, probably from blood loss. He slumped against the stake and no longer fought to constrict his body away from it. His eyes flickered open and fixed on me.

"Anderts," he whispered hoarsely, red bubbles of froth in the corners of his mouth. "I should have known. Not a scratch on you, is there? No, fools have all the luck. And mine has left me, every last little bit of it."

"I am sorry, Smit." I did not know what else to say.

"Not your fault. It is just the way things are. And you've done all right by me, Anderts, as best you could."

A spasm went through Smit. "I haven't long, have I?" he went on urgently. "Do not answer—I can see it in your eyes and you're a terrible liar, Anderts, it's just your nature. Well, there is only one thing I need say. I must have absolution. These are my final moments and we must not speak falsely now. You must acquit me, Anderts, since I have done you harm."

"Put that thought out of your mind, Smit," I protested. "You've been a friend from the start. You taught me to fight. And your advice was always good. I may not have followed it but that's my fault, not yours."

I did not understand how Smit managed to laugh. "I taught you less than you needed to beat me, Anderts, and no more. And my advice was crap, too, every word. I was trying to convince you to play along. Not so as to do you a favor, either. I told you there were those who listened to what Clarege instructed—it paid well and was a smart arrangement while it lasted. Forgive me, for I was one of them, same as Blothridge and Galdo."

"Maybe you were, Smit. So what? I don't think you ever lied to me. I would probably be better off if I had heeded what you said. No, Smit, you've done nothing for which you need to be acquitted."

I never knew whether he heard for Smit died during this speech. I unbuckled him and pried him from the stake and laid him on the ground, closing the lids over the blue eyes that had sparkled with such cynical wisdom. I crossed his hands across his chest. His tangle of orange hair spread beneath his head, wet with rain, the cowry shells never to click and clatter again. Then I knelt beside Smit, remembering good things about him and experiences we had shared together aboard the ancient merchant vessel that had been our prison and our home. Eventually Mirable Wirthy placed her fingertips on my shoulder.

"We have to be on our way, Pimsol Anderts," she said softly. "We cannot tarry, not for a breath."

I lifted my head and surveyed the bleak moor, the brown grass spreading in all directions. The noises of small hidden creatures rose around us.

There was not opportunity to provide Smit with a burial or any formal ceremony. I scooped up a handful of wet earth and crumbled it through my fingers. Then I turned away.

"A tender has been dispatched for us," Mirable told me as we began a steady trot across the heath toward the distant hills we knew were there but could not see owing to the largeness of the horizon. She had received a communication from the *Abernathy* through the receiver that was included in the emergency equipment she had taken from the lifeboat.

"It should arrive in less than an hour," she went on as we ran side by side. "Our challenge, Pimsol Anderts, will be to remain free until it can pick us up. We must marshal all our ingenuity. At minimum we'll be tracked by visual, electronic, and infrared sensors. Have you any suggestions?"

"If I may interject, sir," Alger said. "Survival packs carry standard inventory. There should be an emergency blanket in each. These are thermally opaque and made of camouflage fabric."

I repeated what Alger proposed word for word. "If we cover ourselves with the blankets, we should be able to hide—in plain sight, as it were. We would be invisible to heat and motion detectors as well as visual scans."

"True, Pimsol Anderts. The difficulty lies when I must signal our rescuers so they may home in on us. Then we become exposed. Yet if I remain silent, we remain lost to those who must find us. A pretty dilemma."

I wouldn't have called it that but I kept quiet about what I really thought. Soon an imperceptible swell of terrain hid the broken lifeboat from view although a smudge of greasy black smoke indicated where the crash site lay. The resilient slippery grass swallowed any trace of our passage. I felt lost in the immensity of the landscape. Each time we mounted a ridge line, the horizon opened up endlessly, broader by a magnitude than what I was accustomed to. Our course toward the distant hills where we hoped to find shelter paralleled the grisly line of impaled men, an uncomfortable reminder we were not likely to encounter friends any time soon in this sullen bare expanse.

The three of us passed a dozen stakes before I realized Silver was at Mirable Wirthy's side.

The abattoir appeared no worse for wear despite what he'd been through, his ears once again compressed into neat fans, his stride as vital as ever. In the overcast, his quills had the dingy luster of sea glass.

Noticing my stare, Mirable said, "They're tough beasts, abattoirs. It helped, too, I believe, that his landing was cushioned by a briar patch."

In the gloom I couldn't be certain but I thought the edges of Mirable's lips quivered with the briefest smile.

"Silver's a canny old monster," she went on. "Did you know he's almost a hundred?"

"Seriously?"

"I am serious. Silver has watched over Wirthy after Wirthy, a faithful and true companion, for generations. He's only on loan to me. In time he will become my daughter's guardian, just as he was my mother's, and her mother's before that. This is a comforting thought."

As if understanding he was being discussed—and I wouldn't have put fluency in human language beyond the abattoir, not after his exploits—Silver spread his ears for grooming.

"Sir, if I may request your attention," Alger interrupted. "I thought you should know we are about to be intercepted by a flotilla of airborne—contraptions."

"Contraptions, Alger?"

"I use the word carefully, sir, since I am unable to identify the vehicles with any degree of confidence."

He fed an enhanced image to my optic nerve, allowing me to make out the machines coming toward us even though they were kilometers off. Most carried a single rider although some bore several, pedaling in tandem, driving a nose prop through an eccentric assemblage of gears. All were of the same design, combining bicycle and plane in one hybrid form. It was apparent, too, that each machine was hand-made from natural materials and not the product of standard interstellar technology.

In the relatively low gravity of Temurlone—.73 standard—the tiny things reached respectable velocities as their pilots pumped furiously, hunched against the slipstream. There were thousands of them.

The wings and frames of the approaching vehicles were painted with patterns in black and blood red. Brilliant pennants streamed behind them, quivering in the wind of passage like living eels. Many were adorned with fringes of desiccated human fingers and toes and other appendages, which created their own clatter. Soon I heard the wailing of bull roarers echoing over the heath, angry and unsettling.

Some of the aircraft were skimming close against the terrain, touching down for awhile to roll across the grass on soft tires before bouncing back into the sky. Others kept their altitude, wheeling and diving like kites.

"What—who—are they?" I asked Alger. I must have spoken aloud, for although Alger had no answer, Mirable heard me. Her pale complexion had become a whiter shade.

"The Marvelous Flying Bicycle Men," she whispered.

There was no point running and nowhere to hide upon the heath. Even if we wrapped ourselves in the survival blankets, it was impossible that so many would overlook us. Mirable bade Silver sit

111

at her feet while holding his neck and stood awaiting the Marvelous Flying Bicycle Men without tension, unconcerned by the barbaric mob, as steadfast, I imagined, as Imogene Wirthy herself would have been in the same circumstances.

How could I be any less brave? I combed the hair from my forehead and brushed the wrinkles from my pants. "The Marvelous Flying Bicycle Men," I mused with a nonchalance assumed to match hers. "I have heard little of them—nothing whatever, to be honest."

"Truly ignorance can be a good thing. I wish my own was as complete as yours," she answered. "What I do know doesn't put me at ease."

"Why not?"

"It is better I say no more. You have courage, Pimsol Anderts—I have seen that in our short time together. I wouldn't want you to act unwisely on my behalf and put your own life in jeopardy. Promise me, you'll restrain Silver if I cannot. I wouldn't wish him slain."

"Small chance, not Silver. He's too mean."

"They are thousands. And they'll show me no kindness. The Marvelous Flying Bicycle Men loathe women, thinking the feminine sex a race apart from true human men. Not that they're entirely human themselves, considering their tribal symbiosis with the Man Mother. But I have said too much. We've been noticed."

Now I could make out a loose order among the horde. On either flank outriders sped forward of the main flotilla on dashing vehicles, each painted with jaunty geometric patterns. More slowly came the bulk of the fleet, a ragged formation of larger machines, these powered by a dozen men or more. Further back were lumbering multi-propped galleys loaded with valuables and communal property and propelled by scores of cyclists.

Fliers broke away from the nearest column and hurtled toward us.

The pilots all wore the same transparent leather sheath, which allowed the frightful tattoos adorning their bodies to be visible while protecting them from the elements. This was made, I learned, from the internal organic lining of a animal native to the moors—an *aca*. These were huge beasts, which traveled in herds. Each drove was owned by a different tribe, who jealously guarded their animals from the thievery of their neighbors. Internecine warfare over grazing rights was a longstanding local pastime among the Marvelous Flying Bicycle Men.

Aca bones, hollow but strong, formed the skeletons of their vehicles, which were lashed together with lacquered aca sinew. Aca fat provided fuel; aca hide went into wing fabric and tent coverings; aca cud, properly cured, was molded around tire frames; and the export of prime aca tenderloins, weighing tonnes, provided the Marvelous Flying Bicycle Men with their main source of hard currency. The meat, well aged and marbled, was a luxury throughout the stellar arm.

There was a vast buzzing sound, the noise of countless propellers. Underneath was a hoarse bass grunting, varying in tempo, the chants the fliers sang to maintain rhythm.

The foremost plane over-flew us. Wicked harpoons hung from the underside of the wings. Small bombs were attached to the frame.

The pilot was a lean and rangy man with thighs and calves disproportionate to the rest of his body, the result of genetic heritage and a lifetime of hard use. His beard was trimmed in a square around his mouth, his hair braided in tight rows against his skull. As he continued pumping, and as the machine sped above us, he released a weighted net, which spun as it fell, spreading wide to enfold Silver. The abattoir snapped at the mesh and thrashed as angrily as a crab in a basket but was unable to part the strands. His efforts to escape only further tangled him.

Another plane dropped a net, this one aimed at Mirable. It spun around her, pinning her arms to her sides, and whirled her to the grass.

A sick rage took hold of me upon seeing this.

Ignoring her advice, I dodged the net released by a third plane. This pilot, perhaps in order to impress his comrades, had brought his machine in on a swoop a meter above my head. Kneeling, I surged upward, reaching my arms to full extension, as if I was kicking off from the sea bottom toward the surface. The light gravity, only three quarters of standard, aided my jump. I caught the rear wheel, first with my right hand, then with my left, clamping my fingers through the aca-bone spokes.

Despite my experience with the Bee, when I had tried to interpose myself between her and Aaa, I hadn't thought about what would happen next. If I had, I might have had doubts that my weight would bring the plane to the ground. Instead, I was carried into the air.

Fifteen meters. Seventy-five. Two hundred. Once again I was treated to an aerial view of the moors. The bleak grassland, going on forever without interruption, seemed less inviting than before.

My legs were dangling beneath me as I hung on to the rear wheel with both hands. I kicked upward and attempted to hook my feet around a piece of the airframe or around one of the struts supporting the wings. The pilot glanced down. His grin was clear despite the tattoos disfiguring his face.

Something in his expression warned me to tighten my grip. The plane banked suddenly and fell sideways at an appalling speed. For seconds the bicycle was as much on my level as above me. I pulled myself across the machine until I could grab onto the gear rack behind the pilot's seat. That was when he brought the plane out of its dive mere meters above the brown and gray heath, so close I could have reached out and touched Mirable and Silver where they lay trussed on the grass.

Once more we flew skyward, propelled by the pilot's pedaling and by a strong updraft, and we soon reached an altitude of two hundred meters.

As we straightened out, the pilot pulled a harpoon from an overhead bracket. He twisted around in his seat and jabbed the spear at my face, missing my eye, the edge sliding along my temple and cutting my ear instead. I grabbed for the shaft, failed to get it, but succeeded in knocking it from his grasp. While the pilot reached for another harpoon, I inched toward him along the bone framework of the machine, which flexed alarmingly under my weight. As he took hold of a second spear, I caught him in a vicious lock I had learned from Every Smit, when he'd taught me the martial technology of Van Diver's World. Maybe Smit had known how to break the hold—but I didn't. Neither did the pilot.

The weapon dropped from his paralyzed fingers and spun toward the ground. For the first time the pilot's pedaling faltered, his massive corded thighs and calves ceasing their relentless motion. He struggled briefly but then understood resistance was useless.

"Tell me your name," he hissed in accented standard interstellar vernacular, peering at me at an angle since I was bending his head cruelly.

"Why do you care what my name is?"

"It would not be good to die in the company of a stranger, even an enemy. Know me. I am Pilar Gonzlez Goodfellow."

I applied additional pressure. "You're not going to die, Goodfellow. Not if you do exactly as I say. Otherwise I will hurt you bad, see if I don't."

This was pure bluster but Goodfellow did not know that. He did not, however, seem impressed. "That is neither near nor far," he replied. "How could I live with myself if I did as you ask? The shame would be too great. Never could I face my brothers and sons and fathers in good conscience. Never could sow my seed upon the Man Mother in the company of my peers. How could I face my God at the end of my days and say, 'My Lord, I played my part to the hilt and pedaled my utmost in every race.' No, there is only one path I may follow."

With his knee Goodfellow nudged a lever attached to the frame below the handlebars. The plane tipped sideways and plummeted toward the ground. This dive was steeper and less controlled than the first one, and we began spinning, too. My legs flew out behind me, so only my hold on Goodfellow kept me connected to the falling plane. "Pull up," I yelled in his ear—it was tattooed all over in a checkerboard pattern of red and black. "Pull up or I will break your damn neck."

"You have overcome me, but I have not surrendered. I ask again, stranger, what is your name?"

The wind of our descent tore the words from his lips and flung them back at me. This time I answered.

"Pimsol Anderts."

Goodfellow repeated my name. "I know you now," he said. "We are comrades in valor. Together we will father many handsome and fearless sons on the Man Mother."

This observation—meaningless to me and not a little perverse—seemed to provide the pilot dour satisfaction. But I was focusing on the fact that there were only seconds remaining to my life, and it galled me I had so much left undone. I couldn't stop asking myself Captain Hartung's malicious question—would my death be nothing but an accident, of no consequence to anyone but myself? Mostly I was worrying about Mirable and about what would happen to her in the hands of the Marvelous Flying Bicycle Men. I had tried my best but it hadn't been enough. I had thought I was doing the right thing in spiriting her away from the *Miraculous Abernathy*, but all I had accomplished was to get her in worse trouble than before. The ground rose to meet us, inescapable and appalling. Goodfellow's lips were stretched in a grin and there was a gleam in his eyes, perhaps religious ecstasy or madcap terror.

With a fraction of my attention I noticed that underneath us the landscape lifted into a huddle of low hills.

"All right, Goodfellow," I yelled in his ear. "You win. No conditions. Just take us up."

"It is too late. We are committed. Our fall together will become the stuff of legend. For generations onward the new boys, sitting on the laps of their fathers, will hear of our descent and learn a fine moral."

"Alger!"

"Yes, sir?"

The tenor of his thoughts remained unperturbed. No doubt a personal attendant, aristocracy grade, being manufactured of more durable stuff than human flesh, would survive the fall undamaged. "I am all out of ideas," I yelled, forgetting to think my thoughts quietly. "You have any?"

"Regarding what, sir? Could you be more specific?"

"Regarding how not to die."

"Do nothing, sir."

"Nothing?"

"Precisely. Doing nothing is the optimum course of action, or should I say—of *inaction*, given our present circumstances."

We were plunging toward the largest of the small hills. In the center of the summit was a pond of dark water, evidently fed by a spring, since creeks trickled away from it down the hillside.

I had no chance to notice anything else. We hit the pond and plunged below the surface, the airframe splintering around us in a storm of greasy bubbles. The stuff was not water, either. It was an oily, viscid liquid, warm and turgid as chopped raw clams or oysters. I lost my grip on Pilar Goodfellow and was left behind as the plane sank to the bottom. Even with Alger enhancing what I saw, I could hardly make out where it came to rest. Goodfellow, dead or unconscious, was not moving.

Using scissoring strokes to kick to the surface, I burst into the open air and took a great deep breath.

The stink almost killed me. It was the most awful stench I had ever encountered, even taking into account the aroma of the sentient worms who had traveled aboard the *Abernathy*. It was compounded of everything rotting, sewage and filth and decaying matter. It rose from the liquid coating me, which stuck to my skin with gluey persistence.

Although I choked on it, I took another breath and filled my lungs with the vile air. Trying not to think of what I was submerging into, I dove to the plane, and tried to disentangle Goodfellow from the wreckage.

A wing brace was pinning him against the handlebars of the bicycle. I tugged at it but couldn't get leverage and the springy bone spar simply flexed without freeing Goodfellow.

I unfastened his safety belt and tried to pull him out from under the strut but this did not work, either. If I did manage to get him loose, the likelihood of resuscitating him was becoming more remote every second. I hardly knew the pilot and he was not a friend, not like Every Smit had been, but I wouldn't let Goodfellow die, not if there was any chance of saving him. Despite the ache beginning in my own lungs, I redoubled my pull upon the bone spar. But it was useless. The strut wouldn't move.

Then the pond shuddered. There was a vast lethargic quivering. The liquid surrounding us pulsed sluggishly.

Suddenly the very pond itself lurched like a living thing. The bottom receded, pulling Goodfellow from my grasp. Then it returned, impossible to avoid, and I was spit skyward in a wave of unwholesome fluid. Every portion of my skin and clothing was slimed with it, as was Goodfellow, too. We landed some meters from the bank amid a shower of debris. I crawled to the pilot and wiped the sludge from his mouth.

"Turn him on his side and make certain his lungs are clear," Alger instructed.

When I had done so, I placed my lips to Goodfellow's and exhaled. After every several puffs, I thumped his heart with my balled fist, encouraging it to remember its obligation to beat, but still his chest remained empty of pulse and breath.

"Live, you stupid, ugly, suicidal savage," I cursed.

Goodfellow remained dead. I continued forcing my wind into him and pounding on his heart. Thirty seconds passed. A minute.

I wouldn't accept failure. Two minutes.

I did not fully understand why I felt the way I did. Maybe it was because I had died myself and hadn't liked it. Maybe it was because I had seen too much death already and had been powerless to prevent it. Maybe I hadn't been able to help Canny Galdo or Every Smit or any of the others, even Marval Wirthy, but I swore this time I would make a difference.

Further seconds passed, as long as hours. Finally Goodfellow retched out a dribble of gray liquid. He took a breath and his eyes flickered open.

"I live," he whispered in wonder. His eyes fixed on me and widened. "I live," Goodfellow whispered again with manifest amazement—and with another emotion I couldn't decipher straight away although I learned what it meant soon enough.

He lunged with what strength remained to him and fixed his hands around my throat and throttled me. "You cursed son of female nether parts," he hissed. "Offspring of a diseased orifice. What have you done?"

"I saved your life," I protested, fighting against his grip, but anger and hatred gave him strength and his fingers were as tenacious as limpets and I couldn't pry them away. Nor could I draw breath. In desperation I flailed at Goodfellow, striking him about the head, but he only squinted and dug his thumbs deeper, cutting off my airway. I began to weaken.

Then I was grabbed by the shoulders, wrenched free, and thrown aside. We'd been surrounded by the rest of the horde.

A man with an imposing belly and spindly legs—symbols of status among the Marvelous Flying Bicycle Men, I assumed, since it was obvious he hadn't pressed a foot against a pedal in years—strode up and regarded Goodfellow and myself. This was probably a chief or hetman—his tattoos covered every square centimeter of his body. His eyes were predatory, the pupils twin rings of yellow and blue. He looked me up and down, dismissed me in a glance, and turned to Goodfellow.

"Now that was spectacular, Pilar Gonzlez," said the chief in a tone loud enough to carry to the onlookers hemming us in. "You have given us a deed worthy of remembrance," he continued. "The Fall of Goodfellow. Goodfellow's Descent. It has a fine ring to it, does it not? Stand up, stand up, Pilar Gonzlez."

Something was going on in this conversation that I was missing since instead of obeying the chief, Goodfellow seemed unhappy with the attention he was being paid. Of course, he was not the most prepossessing sight, being covered with the black slime into which we had crashed.

"What is that stuff?" I asked Alger.

"Excrement, sir."

"Crap?"

"In a word, precisely. I thought you understood."

"Understood what, Alger?"

"What cushioned our—and I use the word loosely, sir—our landing. We came down in the center of an aca anal cavity."

It was as if the very ground beneath me moved—and this, I realized, was the literal truth. What I had taken to be hills were, in fact, living creatures, each as huge as a geologic formation. We were riding on the back of one the size of a mountain. The entire range—herd—was progressing at the leisurely pace of a quarter kilometer an hour. The animals were grazing as they went, for instead of leaving behind trails of crushed vegetation, there were only barren swathes where nothing grew.

"Aca manure is an unparalleled fertilizer," Alger continued. "It also contains a rich mixture of seeds and spores. As the herd goes along, their wastes are collected in storage pools. The run-off spills behind them, preparing the land and replanting it, ensuring a perpetual cycle of new growth. It is quite an ingenious ecological system."

No wonder Goodfellow was furious at me for preserving his life. The pond we had plunged into was the bunghole of an aca. It was a joke too rich to ignore. Few did. Ribald, unkind comments passed among the crowd, mostly directed at Goodfellow, who pretended not to notice.

He regained his feet and addressed the chief. "The tale is not finished, Nonio Wellmete. Give me the foreigner."

"You may not have him, Pilar Gonzlez. He must go to the meat mines. The tribal balance of trade is unfavorable and we require additional labor to make up the deficit. This is my executive pronouncement."

"Now that isn't right, not even a little," I protested, scrambling up with a stifled groan, an ache in every joint.

Chief Wellmete spared me a severe glance. "You are trespassing, you and the female together," he said. "Thus you are subject to Tribal Law[1], which provides an unambiguous schedule of penalties."

"We're not trespassers, " I protested. "Our lifeboat crashed, that's the simple truth. We're castaways."

"Do not attempt to confuse me with spurious nomenclature or I will hold you in contempt and increase your sentence of penal servitude from ten years to twenty."

But I wouldn't keep quiet. My arguments, however, succeeded in swaying Chief Wellmete not an iota. "Tribal Law has jurisdiction here," he replied curtly and motioned to a nearby warrior, who struck my head a cruel blow with a stout cudgel.

---

1   In A.I. 276, hoping to attract investors in the operation of their meat mines, the Marvelous Flying Bicycle Men applied for signatory status with The Bureau of Interstellar Standards but received such a poor rating that the tribe allowed its subscription to lapse without renewal. Tribal Law, codified in seven volumes of explication, interpretation, and annotation, was too restrictive a canon of behavior to coexist easily even with the loose strictures of the abridged version of the *Catalog of Sentient Rights*. For example, Chapter 604, Paragraph 412, read:

"Any person, who through action or failure to act, through purposeful intent or through negligence, gives utterance to an involuntary exclamation through the mouth and nose, causing a discharge of bodily moisture, without immediately reciting the appropriate apology to the Man Mother, and to any other human beings who may or may not be in the vicinity, that person shall be stoned until life has left him and he is dead, impaled on a stake with his entrails exposed to the elements, and allowed to decompose as an instructive reminder to those who might emulate his rude example.

CHAPTER SEVEN
Interlude with the Man Mother

Should you ask me, whence this fiction?
Whence this story, this fine legend?
I will tell you—observation,
Seeing clearly, with my own eyes,
Pilar's downfall, his hard landing,
Into infamy, into shame.

I will tell you how it happened,
What took place that awful evening,
When two strangers from off planet
Landed on the plains around us,
Trespassed where they were not wanted,
Flaunted our Law with ill manners,
Having neither writ nor permit
To among us tarry or stay.

Then did Gonzlez plan his vengeance,
For their slight to the Man Mother,
For their trespass on our own land,
Without passport, without papers,
Without license, without visa,
Without paying an entry fee.

One was female, twice unwanted,
Tainted with the sex of woman,
Tainted with ungainly features,
Her companion a mad creature,
Known to all as an abattoir.

At her side was a young rascal,
His heart brave but also foolish,
Who knew not what perils faced him,
Nor the strength of Pilar Gonzlez,
But dared Gonzlez on his cycle,
Dared him to a meet of valor,
Dared him to a test of courage
In the skies above Temurlone.

Anonymous: "The Ballad of Bunghole Gonzlez",
collected in: *Folklore of the Darwin Wastes and Temurlone
Plains*

Iawoke a full Temurlone day later—thirty-two standard hours.
Every part of me hurt. I was sitting on a narrow seat, a mere cushioned wedge between my legs, slumped upon bone handlebars. My feet rested in the stirrups of a pair of bone pedals. There was a safety harness around my waist. But I was also chained there, fettered at the ankles by osseous links.

The ground was five hundred meters below.

Slowly I looked around. I was in the last seat of a row of similar stations, each occupied by a shackled man or creature capable of pedaling.

All were busy doing so.

I had been rinsed off, and not very thoroughly. Although the survival pack was gone, as well as the gun and ammunition, I hadn't been robbed of my personal effects. Alger still circled my wrist—no doubt he'd been passed over as an inexpensive trinket, on par with the chronograph belonging to my father and the locket with the picture of my parents.

These were now the last connections I had to a past that seemed far away. Suddenly I felt lost and alone.

"Alger," I thought. "Tell me what's been going on."

"Very well, sir. I will begin with the arrival of the black vessel pursuing us. This occurred three minutes and eighty-five seconds after you were rendered unconscious."

Alger provided a voice over while projecting a replay of his sensory record upon my optic nerve. The black ship slid into view through a break in the overcast. "It remained unobserved for some time," he went on. "Ultimately, however, its appearance was noted, to some consternation." Alger enhanced the lower left quadrant of the image, bringing into resolution several tribesmen, who were peering skyward while gesturing animatedly to each other. At a command from Nonio Wellmete, the rest erected a brace of surface-to-air missiles, which they sent skyward. Two reached their target, flowering in impressive blooms of orange flame yet failing to inflict serious damage. The black ship gained altitude and disappeared.

"What about the tender coming for Mirable?" I asked.

"That, too, was similarly discouraged," Alger replied. "These Marvelous Flying Bicycle Men, unmannerly savages though they are, evidently invest heavily in standard military technology."

"And where's Mirable—what happened to her, Alger?"

"I do not know, sir. Miss Mirable and the abattoir were carried aboard another plane, which departed toward the south. Where they were taken, and for what purpose, I cannot speculate until I acquire more data. It is unlikely, however, that Miss Mirable is destined to become a galley slave or a miner. If that were the case, she would have been kept here with you."

The plane was a catamaran of sorts with twin banks of cyclists along either narrow hull. The central platform was a lattice of aca bones on which was lashed domestic goods and items valued by the tribe. The pedals drove a series of propellers mounted on the broad wings, these lined with cured aca hide and ornamented with dried human extremities, which clattered together prettily, like wind chimes.

Noticing I was awake, the gang boss clambered over to me along a rope catwalk. His kinship to Goodfellow was obvious and they could have been brothers—or father and son, for this man was an ancient.

"I am Faal Finechance," he said. "Your name is unimportant, foreigner, so do not bore me with it. Obey my will as if it were your own and heed my slightest whim. This is wise counsel. You will find me an easy master unless I am thwarted in any particular trifle."

"I have heard the same before," I replied, reminded of my arrival aboard the *Miraculous Abernathy* and of my introduction to Officer Clarege.

Finechance grunted, and released a switch that linked my pedals to the main drive shaft through an intricate assortment of gears. "Keep in tempo with the others," he instructed. "Press smartly now. There are sensors and I will know when you are holding back. Truly I detest shirkers."

We flew four hours, until the close of the long Temurlone afternoon. At the signal of a distant horn our plane and the others descended to the ground in orderly rows. Our wheels engaged and we pedaled to an assigned parking space, wing-tip to wing-tip with the vehicles on either side.

Under Finechance's wary eye we unloaded the plane and erected airy pavilions of vermilion fabric, adorned with pennants of mustard yellow and lime green and appointed with furniture that inflated from narrow sheets of compressed fabric. These pleasant quarters weren't for us, however—our place was a coarse tent that combined mess area and sleeping quarters under one roof, where we were allowed a limited freedom. I joined a cheerless queue shuffling past a pair of cooks, who handed each person a spoon and a bowl of grain and meat ragout.

The men around me—and they were all men or non-humans, with not a single female anywhere—derived from three distinct stocks. The most numerous group had the same general features as the Marvelous Flying Bicycle Men. These, I learned, were captives from a tribe whose territory lay on the other side of the boundary of stakes that had done Every Smit so little good, who followed their own aca herds upon caparisoned wagons with tall sails. The second group was made up of idiots—men born into the tribe but found wanting, during the ceremony known as the Winnowing. They had been subjected to a surgical procedure that removed their intelligence, permitting them contentment with their lot in life. The third group had little in common except that they were all, men and non-humans alike, from the far reaches of Temurlone or from off world.

Only a few sullen conversations enlivened the atmosphere. For a while the idiots bounced a ball back and forth but then one of them let it roll out of sight and the game ended.

In the morning we breakfasted on gruel mixed with lumps of suet. Then Finechance instructed us to resume our places aboard the catamaran. We pedaled a half hour until we caught up with the aca herd claimed by the Marvelous Flying Bicycle Men. By means of a rope ladder we scaled the flank of the largest beast, arriving at a ledge thirty meters above the ground, where the grassy hide had been stripped away and a tunnel mouth carved into the side of the animal, revealing strata of fat and red meat.

Bones had been tied together to provide a framework for the tunnel. The walls and ceiling and floor swayed fluidly as we crept inside.

The corridor had been coated with a coagulant to promote scabbing and to prevent it from closing in on itself. Within fifty meters we were wading through muck that reached to our knees, a mixture of blood, lard, and chunks of congealed serum. There was a netting curtain across the mouth of the tunnel to keep out vermin but the place swarmed with tiny winged mites and crawling things.

The choicest cuts grew far below the surface in a cavity lined with slick membrane. The place was as large as a warehouse and noisy with moist sucking sounds and gurgling. The ceiling was studded with tumors of flesh, which had been caused to grow there by the Marvelous Flying Bicycle Men, as an oyster is irritated into secreting a pearl. These massive tumors, known as tenderloins, were considered a delicacy by connoisseurs and commanded an exorbitant price per kilo throughout Temurlone and on the interstellar market. It was our task to slice them from where they sprouted, pack them in preservative, haul them to the surface, and load them aboard the plane for transportation to an export depot. This was easier to describe than it was to accomplish.

Faal Finechance handed me a saw and a leather sack containing white paste compounded from herbs native to the heath. "Apply the anesthetic liberally," he said. "If you fail to do so, the aca will become stimulated."

That did not sound good but Finechance refused to elaborate. "It is sufficient you heed the warning," he snapped. "Discount it at your peril. And now, foreigner, a word of advice. I count on peak performance from my crew. How could I accept less?" From similar conversations with Petty Officer Clarege I understood this to be a rhetorical question. "The simple answer is I cannot," Finechance went on after a dramatic pause. "Not and maintain the esteem I have for myself as a leader of men. Not and expect the rest of the crew to maintain their own standards of excellence. It would make a mockery of all I have accomplished through years of vigilance and discipline. No, I insist on your personal best. Else I will slice off your globes and feed them to the Man Mother myself."

With this exhortation, Finechance attached a harness below my shoulders and several men hauled me into the air by a rope that ran through a pulley secured to the roof of the cavern. Once I reached a sufficient height, I was to swing into contact with the tenderloin designated for harvesting, hold myself in place while looping a belt around it, and cut the tumor free. It took a half dozen attempts before I managed to get a grip on the meat. The air was so wet and thick I was choking on it and I could scarcely see what I was about since the only light in the entire organic cave came from small globes some of the crew carried, which emitted a cool blue glow.

With one hand I clawed myself close to the tenderloin, sinking my fingers into the flesh in order to hold on. The meat gave way easily, as pliable as clam bellies. With my other hand I smeared the tenderloin with the anesthetic paste, lathering the ointment on heavily as far as I could reach.

"That is sufficient," Finechance called. "Now tie the thing off. You alone will be held accountable if the knot slips and the meat is bruised. And keep an eye about, too."

"What for?"

"You will know what for when you see what for."

After three throws I looped the belt around the meat and cinched the fastening tight. Then I applied the saw.

Faal Finechance hadn't mentioned the blood. The liquid did not seep from the incision—it spurted from the opening in a geyser, so I was drenched with the stuff by the time the tumor came loose. When the blade sliced into the final bridge of meat, it fell away from the ceiling, used up the slack in the rope, and began stripping cord through the pulley.

Twelve men were on the other end. They were yanked forward as the rope took on the weight of the meat but braced themselves and permitted the cable to pay out through their hands at a steady rate, lowering the tenderloin to a pallet, which was then towed from the chamber to the waiting plane. No one thought of letting me down while this important business was being attended to and I was left hanging in midair.

This allowed me to be the first to notice a stealthy motion among the shadows of the chamber.

It was also the moment when I first began to appreciate the true nature of the aca.

An animal so immense, hectares in area and a hundred meters in height, as ponderous as an island and as complex as an ecology, could not be a single organism—not as the term is generally understood. There was no question most of the aca was one creature, the flesh and organs interconnected in a discrete whole. But many of its metabolic functions were performed by autonomous individuals, members of species whose evolutionary paths had joined to that of the aca, becoming full symbionts, much as mitochondria have found a home in the human cell. There was a type of flea the size of a king crab that lived its life without ever leaving the aca upon which it was born, feeding on dead tegument. Aca bones were, in fact, more vegetable than animal, having evolved from a bulrush, whose ancestors had hitched a ride eons before and became part of the family.

Still other creatures performed the functions of an immune system, protecting their host by dining upon intruders. In this case that meant myself, Faal Finechance, and the remainder of the work gang, who continued stolidly at their business, the sounds of their efforts absorbed by the soft tissue that walled the chamber.

"Over there," I called while pointing in the direction I meant.

Faal Finechance jerked his head upward. "Quit bleating," he admonished. "We'll see to you in a moment."

"Listen, Finechance," I said. "There's something coming, I don't know what. It isn't alone, either."

I was not sure of the nature of the things approaching us. They were dark blotches in the shadows, flowing soundlessly upon the organ tissue.

"Yes—your eyes are indeed keen, foreigner," Faal Finechance muttered. "We have been observed." He gave a peremptory whistle. The laborers dropped what they were doing and scrambled from the chamber into the corridor that led to the open sky. No one spared me a glance. Finechance pushed the last man into the tunnel mouth and prepared to leave himself. "Let me down," I called. "Those things are almost here."

"Have no fear, foreigner," replied the overseer. "Your sacrifice will not be in vain."

"What sacrifice?"

131

"The sacrifice of your life, almost certainly. Your screaming and thrashing will draw the attention of the leuks, allowing the rest of us to escape. This is our usual strategy and it is admirably effective. We will finish harvesting when the leuks have departed. Take heart, though, and do not despair. One time in three they fail to reach the bait, which is to say, yourself."

"Now hold on a minute—" I began but the barbarian ignored me and squeezed into the corridor and I was left alone in the cavity, suspended in in the harness. I was swaying but not fast enough to generate a breeze and the air stuck to my skin, as close and warm as an unwanted kiss.

Leuks derived from an animal as simple as a flatworm and just as supple. They moved bonelessly, feeling their way forward with a thousand appendages, which were responsive to scent. Encountering the odor of the men who had been working in the cavity, the leuks went crazy and began dashing back and forth, making crying sounds as they searched for the intruders, their mouths opening horizontally into toothy grins, like the smiles of flounders. Something—perhaps a drop of sweat running from my hair—alerted them to my presence.

One twisted its upper body around curiously. Its confusion was apparent despite its lack of a face. Others joined the first. Soon the entire pack was reaching upward with grasping pseudopods, writhing with fury.

As if by accident, one crawled on top of another. A third climbed upon the second. The leuks were building a living ladder to reach me.

"Alger," I said. "I hope you know some useful fact about these damn things."

"It would be remarkable if I did not, sir. As I may have mentioned, my memory contains the entire *Human Library*, which includes twenty thousand entries on the aca ecosystem, a rarity unique in the galaxy. Of these entries, 731 focus on the biology, behavior, and social structure of the creatures in question, what the barbarian Finechance called leuks—no doubt a colloquial abbreviation of *leukocytes*."

The squirming pile was now five bodies high, rising as others joined the crowd. I could hear their teeth snapping open and shut with a brisk chattering noise.

"Based on this research, the first option I ruled out was armed response," Alger continued. "According to the data, aca leukocytes possess a decentralized internal structure and are proof against the firepower at our disposal."

"Alger—what option didn't you rule out?"

"Well, sir, further study revealed leuks communicate with each other and with other species of codependents using a simple lexicon of aromas. Notice the smell, sir—" It was impossible not to. With the arrival of the leuks had come a reek that made the wet air more unpleasant. "What you are breathing," Alger went on, "is a conversation in a language composed of twenty-three pheromones, each one an individual chord of meaning, part verb, part noun, part adjective and adverb, part raw emotion, part indescribable urging. These were cataloged in Volume 3,228 of the *Journal of Macrobiology*, complete with a molecular analysis of each compound. I have synthesized Number Sixteen, 'Friendship Among Boon Companions in a Cozy Dark Bed of Slime.' If you were coated with the pheromone, the leuks would accept you as a fellow symbiont, of no threat to the aca host."

"Sometimes, Alger—" I began. Relief made it hard to find words to say. "Just sometimes you come up with the right idea at the right time."

"Unfortunately, sir, my forge was too small to produce sufficient pheromone for your needs. Nor did I have available raw materials for processing, or a reliable delivery system." Alger paused. "Do you recall, sir," he began again, "when you instructed me to gain your consent before performing any operation upon your person? You were quite vehement."

"I remember," I muttered as I grabbed the rope attached to the harness and began pumping my legs as if I were in a swing, attempting to build momentum. I couldn't keep my thoughts steady. Maybe it was impatience. Or maybe it was my gut had begun hurting, perhaps from vertigo. The harness was spinning as I swung madly among the tenderloins. At the bottom of each arc, I passed above the pile of leuks. One heaved itself at me and managed to sink its teeth into my shoe before I kicked the thing away.

"Unfortunately," Alger continued. "I had to act contrary to your wishes. There was no time for consultation."

I could barely follow what he was saying. The ache in my belly was making concentration impossible. Hissing the words aloud, both from pain and from exasperation, I told him:

"And your point—"

"Briefly, sir, in order to increase my processing capacity, I constructed several hundred thousand automatic molecular factories, each capable of independent operation. I deployed these to the nearest location where there was a ready abundance of unwanted material—your large intestine. For the past three minutes the factories have been re-engineering copious quantities of your—I am sorry, but there is no way to phrase this delicately—of your waste matter into the necessary pheromone."

"That's why I feel so awful?"

"No, sir. The molecular factories have also converted an appreciable amount of the—matter—into gas."

"The delivery system?"

"Precisely, sir."

I plowed right into the mound of leuks and the things clung to me like limpets. At the impact I let out an involuntary noise, and another. The cramp in my stomach began to loosen its hold—but not the leuks that had hitched a ride. Instead of devouring me, however, they stopped mewing and began a contented grunting as they slithered back and forth across my body. Then I smelled an odor more pungent than normal for that place. It could only be the pheromone, "Friendship Among Boon Companions."

There was no question, either, where it was coming from.

Sensing my foul mood, Alger prudently remained quiet as I hung in the harness, covered by leuks and engulfed in a distasteful ambiance of my own creation. I had survived, true—but at an inglorious cost and although I was grateful for Alger's intervention, I was not happy. I couldn't help thinking what Mirable would say when we were reunited. "Pim," she'd ask, "could you explain just how you got away from those—*leuks*, you called them?" Impossible to cast the episode in a valiant light. In fact, I thought, my recent history was nothing but one embarrassment after another. If life were fair, I should be due a streak of good luck. But I did not think it likely. The deity had a low sense of humor.

When I regained my breath, I twisted out of the harness and dropped to the floor of the chamber, the spongy surface cushioning my fall. The leuks slithered down my legs and rejoined the main pack and the whole lot drifted off in search of other prey. The miners had left behind their globes of blue light and I appropriated several for my own use. There had to be a way out other than the tunnel carved by the Marvelous Flying Bicycle Men and I was determined to find it. When Finechance returned to the meat mine, he'd assume I had been devoured, not that I had escaped. This would allow me to—to what? Steal a plane? Set off on foot? The only fact of which I was certain was I had to travel south after Mirable.

The leuks, I discovered, made their way through the aca via conduits large enough for me to squeeze into on my hands and knees. These passageways were shared by other species, all of which ignored my presence, perhaps responding to the pheromone still coating me. Crawling sluggishly through the organic tunnels, I took the upward route whenever the going branched. Once I slept, only to be woken by the imprint of tiny feet upon my body. Taking dainty hops in single file proceeded a line of creatures resembling toads. Each carried an insect with a swollen thorax.

At my motion the nearest toad halted and blinked with wide eyes that had iridescent lenses. Then it jabbed the insect at my face while grunting like the leuks had done. I twisted aside and managed to avoid being hit in the mouth by the organ, a spindly member with a teat at its end, which smeared sticky fluid across my cheek as the toad tried to insert the thing between my lips. Some of the stuff got through. It had a meaty flavor and did not taste bad so I allowed the toad to minister to me. Performing this duty seemed to please the creature and its grunting became deeper in tone. After allowing me several swallows, the toad pulled the teat from my lips and hopped off with its fellows and I resumed my own progress through the infrastructure of the aca.

It felt like days or weeks—although Alger assured me only twenty hours actually passed—before I found an exit.

I crawled into a cavity immediately beneath the surface just before the mouth of the tunnel I had been in squeezed shut. Looking upward, I learned the roof consisted of a ring of flexible muscle, which at the moment was parting, revealing a glimpse of blue sky. I also learned the cavity around me was expanding like a bellows. No doubt in a while the sphincter would close and the organ contract, providing ventilation for the species that made up the aca ecosystem.

I took a running jump and leaped with all my might. Aided by the low gravity, I sailed upward and just managed to catch hold of the lip of the opening with one hand. After flailing about and scrabbling for purchase, I got a grip with the other and forced myself onto my elbows. Then I swung my right leg over the edge and rolled away from the hole. Immediately the sphincter clamped shut with such strength that only after the fact did I realize I would have been mangled if I had been a moment slower.

Never, I thought, had I tasted anything as clean and pure and free as the first breath I took then.

Over millennia soil had settled upon the back of the aca, allowing vegetation to take root and flourish, mostly plains grass. Here and there were bald spots where the dirt had been excavated by the Marvelous Flying Bicycle Men so they could harvest the skin below. A short uphill walk toward the spine of the living island stood a grove of trees. I made for it directly, planning to hide until nightfall.

Entering the grove, I disturbed flock of crickets, which jumped away with desperate bounds while emitting a disparaging chirping.

The trees themselves were strangely fleshy with spatulate leaves that moved when there was no breeze, the flabby trunks noticeably pockmarked with rotten abscesses. Many of the growths had translucent globes suspended in clusters from their main branches. I examined a couple and discovered the nascent young of leuks and toads and humans growing within the bulbs.

The fruit of the next tree had become overripe. One had fallen from too high a branch and burst upon the ground, revealing a smashed infant, not a newborn but a child several years of age. The empty peels of other eggs indicated their occupants had fled into the underbrush.

"Alger, what is this place?"

"I would assume it is the Man Mother although I am not entirely confident of my data."

"The Man Mother? Goodfellow mentioned it, but I was too busy to pay attention."

"The reference escaped me as well, sir. According to the *Human Library*, the growths surrounding us are the central aca reproductive node. Each plant is a general-purpose womb, capable of nurturing the young of any of the species that contribute to the gestalt. Within the trees are ingenious receptacles where masculine essences are collected, and then recombined, so as to avoid inbreeding and genetic drift. Then the mixture is quickened, an embryo coalesces, and a new fruit grows. My assumption, sir, is that the Marvelous Flying Bicycle Men have learned to take advantage of this arrangement."

"Take advantage? How?"

"If you would observe the nodes, sir." He meant the abscesses scarring the trees, mostly at waist height, although others were at different levels. "In order to ensure a supply of reproductive material for processing," Alger went on, "the trees provide donors with procreative stimulation more intense than granted by their natural mates. No doubt the Marvelous Flying Bicycle Men are aware of this fact."

Realizing what he meant, I had to laugh. "Mirable said they had little use for women and she was right. They don't, not in the least."

"Indeed, over time most aca symbiont species become composed solely of male specimens. In fact—what are you doing? I advise against—"

I had knelt beside the nearest trunk and was examining the knot in the leathery bark. As I touched the organ with my fingertips, an immediate rush went through my body, spreading like a fever. I had never felt as good or as desperate. I had to have Mirable and she was nowhere in sight. I wanted her. I wanted to do things with her I had never thought of before. I had to have something, I did not know what. I—

"Sir." Alger's voice boomed in my brain. "Sir, you are under the influence of an aphrodisiac protocol I cannot counteract. Remove your hand at once."

I ignored him. His voice dwindled to a vague whisper, as if heard in a seashell, unconvincing and distant. I could only think of Mirable. It was if she were beside me, visible a little way within the tree itself, attainable if I could just press through the bark. The vision was so authentic, I knew I would touch her with only a bit more effort. But at the same time a part of me knew I was imagining the image. She was an illusion and I would not settle for it. I wanted the real Mirable, the true girl, no matter how unlikely it was she would ever return my admiration. With a terrible effort of will, I drew my hand away, severing the connection with the Man Mother and ending the heady sensory flood. As I tumbled back in a daze, Alger said:

"Sir, we don't have much time. A line of beaters is approaching."

I heard the noise, too—a sudden banging, loud whistles, cheering, rattles and hoots, the wailing of raucous horns. It was a commotion meant to unnerve any listener and my first inclination was to run as fast as my legs could carry me. But I held still, knowing that my best chance of getting away lay in slipping through a gap in the line of approaching men. Others, however, failed to share my restraint. From among the trees, and from under piles of leaves and other shelters, emerged cubs and pups and spawn and children by the dozens, the variegated offspring of the Man Mother. They fled past, frantic to escape the disturbance.

I went the other way and took cover in a clump of bramble, remaining still while one beater walked by mere meters to my left. Then I dodged from shelter to shelter until I reached the edge of the grove. Beyond were a number of bicycles. Among the larger galleys were planes small enough to be flown by a single pilot. I eyed these hungrily but couldn't see how to appropriate one without being noticed—by Faal Finechance himself. Not far from where I crouched was the catamaran I had served on.

"Undo the lashings," the overseer instructed one of the work crew, jabbing a tattooed finger at the tarp covering the freight on the center platform. "You, and you, idiot—" he barked to others—"get the far side. Pull the covering off. Quickly, now. We have to make room for the brats."

The tarp was heaved back, revealing six dead men, all killed by violence, their brave markings obscured by gore. Finechance ordered the loads carried to the very tree behind which I was hiding. Before I could retreat, it was too late. The porters set down their burdens and stood beside the corpses with the tired air of men expecting to be at their job for some time. Aboard the catamaran, the rest of the gang erected a kennel of small cages. Into these were put the infants that had been driven into waiting nets by the uproar of the beaters. Doing so was tricky since they clawed and bit their captors whenever allowed the slightest freedom.

When the kennel was at full capacity, Faal Finechance ordered the cyclists to their stations and the plane lifted off, returning to the encampment of the Marvelous Flying Bicycle Men, props thrumming, the crew chanting together to synchronize their efforts.

Now the porters took up the corpses again. Around the tree assembled a hundred or so tribesmen, led by Nonio Wellmete. "This is a somber occasion," intoned the chief. "Our brothers fell in valiant service, sacrificing their selves for the greater good. Now, according to the specifics of Tribal Law, they must be returned to the Man Mother in high esteem. Who will speak of their exploits?"

Several in the audience accepted the challenge and I had to endure oration after oration, some in rhyme and some in prose, all presumably about the deceased but more often about the exploits of the speaker. Someone else sang in a fine baritone while accompanied by a stringed instrument. Finally Wellmete raised his hand. The gesture was made significant by the gleaming knife he held. "As Tribal Law mandates," he said, "I perform now the ultimate rites."

Suddenly Pilar Goodfellow's obscure comment as we fell together from on high became clear—"Together we will father many handsome and fearless sons on the Man Mother."

Nonio Wellmete moved from corpse to corpse. Then he approached the tree and fed what he had collected into the pocket, which admitted the offerings with a moist sound. The heroes, their flesh ingested by the thing, were to be allowed a posthumous opportunity to contribute to the tribal plasm.

With a shudder, I thought it just as well Goodfellow and I had been denied that privilege.

At the end of the ceremony the Marvelous Flying Bicycle Men began drifting into the forest, presumably to engage in intimate rites of their own with the Man Mother although I was not sure of this and had no desire to be certain. The porters, too, set off elsewhere with what remained of their burdens. Soon the area was deserted except for a single guard, who had been assigned the duty against his wishes for he made no effort to do the job well but propped his head against the wheel of a bicycle and fell asleep. On all fours I circled around him and approached the vehicles.

The first one was perfect for my needs, a lightweight racer with a single seat and twenty gears. Even better, the rear hamper held a flask of ale, a wedge of cheese with black rind, onions, and a length of gnarled sausage studded with peppercorns. I knocked back the kickstand and slung my leg across the saddle. After pedaling only briefly, the bicycle began straining for altitude although it would require another fifty meters of acceleration before I could actually lift into the air. Then Alger said:

"I regret having to inform you, sir, but the guard has become aware of your activity. Unless you increase speed, we will be intercepted in six seconds. Should I provide a dosage of stimulant?"

"That almost killed me last time, did it not? No, it *did* kill me. Alger, I will do this on my own."

"Very well, sir. As you think best. Four seconds."

There was no mistaking his tone of reproach. I spared a glance over my shoulder. Our pursuer was running full tilt, arms pumping, carried onward at remarkable speed on legs strengthened by a lifetime of pedaling. I hunched forward and concentrated on working my own legs to their limit, willing all my effort into the simple task of making the wheels go faster. Then I felt the gentle lurch signaling separation from the ground. I flicked the lever that redirected the energy of my pedaling to the prop and the blades of aca cartilage began spinning. Quickly they became invisible.

An impact knocked the plane sideways. I was thrown from my seat and sent tumbling across the grass. The tribesman stalked toward me. Beneath the tattoos was a face I recognized.

"I had heard you were dead, Pimsol Anderts," said Pilar Gonzlez Goodfellow. "The news was saddening and I have been mournful. Your passing meant I could never redeem myself, not in my own eyes nor in those of my brothers nor of my God. But now there has been a miracle, and I am melancholy no more. You are alive and all is well."

I raised my hands into the position Every Smit had drilled into me during our bouts together. "I won't be a slave, Goodfellow. I am warning you."

"Who said a word about slavery? Nonio Wellmete thinks too much of practicalities and too little of honor. How dare he deny me your life to supply the mines with leuk bait when only your death at my hands can ever cleanse the shame you have caused me. Soon, when someone begins 'The Ballad of Bunghole Gonzlez', I will take your skull and study it solemnly Soon another song will be chosen and all will be well."

CHAPTER EIGHT

The Pleasures of Twin Chasms House

1.   Seize the day.
2.   Lead by example.
3.   Eat dessert first.
4.   All you need is love.
5.   Make a difference.
6.   Try again.
7.   Break a leg.

*Scrip*tures:
One Million Tidbits of Advice Now We Know God Could
Care Less and We Are Merely Actors in a Play Not of Our
Own Devising

Goodfellow sprang at me, quick as a leuk, jabbing a dagger at my stomach. I knocked the hand aside and skipped back.

I had overcome the tribesman before but then I'd had the advantage. Now we were on equal footing and he was larger than me by thirty kilos, all corded muscle emblazoned with barbaric black and blood red designs. I feinted a chop at his throat while kicking his ankle. It was like striking an ancient shellfish bed meters thick. Goodfellow smiled and pressed forward. Again I retreated, until my back was to the tree at which Nonio Wellmete had conducted the disturbing funeral ceremony. It was becoming clear I would never beat Pilar Goodfellow by force in spite of my martial skills. I had to find another way to defeat him before the rest returned from their carnal visits to the Man Mother.

Then the single practical option occurred to me. "Alger," I thought. "Shoot him."

"With pleasure, sir."

Miniature, almost microscopic, apertures opened in the bracelet that was the physical body of my personal attendant, aristocracy grade, extruding muzzles from which spat motes of ammunition. These knocked Goodfellow back a stride but otherwise did no harm.

"It appears aca integument is able to resist my weaponry," Alger observed, as if I couldn't see for myself the ammunition had failed to penetrate the barbarian's transparent sheathing. "Perhaps I should aim for an unprotected area, such as the eyes."

There wasn't time. Goodfellow threw himself into battle with an expression of delight, his lips twisted in a peculiar grimace. I did not attempt to meet the attack but slid under the lunge, so he passed over me and slammed into the tree at my back. His head lodged in the main abscess, the pliant dark stuff parting aside and permitting it easy entry. His feet kicked spasmodically and I thought he'd broken his neck but then I saw Goodfellow was struggling not to extricate himself but to burrow deeper into the opening.

I did not want to touch him since I was unsure whether the amorous current generated by the tree would carry through his body into mine but I was equally reluctant to let him die. So I picked up a branch and tried to lever the barbarian away from the tree.

He fought my efforts until he suffocated and became still.

"Alger," I thought, "I am glad I did not have to do the job myself, although it would have come to that, I imagine. But I can't say I am sorry to see the last of Goodfellow. He was trouble from first acquaintance."

"I share your sentiments, sir. A vexatious barbarian, indeed."

I took a final look at the dead man before retrieving the bicycle. It was strange to reflect I had saved Goodfellow's life and days later helped him to his end. I did not quite know what to make of this turn of events, but I was sure of one thing. The awkward nature of his passing was certain to provide his companions with the inspiration for many unsavory lyrics. There was no question about it. Goodfellow wouldn't have been pleased by the songs soon to be composed in his memory.

Mostly, though, I was hoping no one would notice a misplaced bicycle until I was long on my way.

This time the vehicle sped across the back of the aca and rose gracefully into the sky without hindrance. Hardly pedaling, the propellers spinning lazily, I spiraled upward until the aca herd was like any other portion of landscape lost among the immensity of the wastes of Temurlone. Then I applied myself and set off south at fifteen kilometers per hour.

I flew straight through the night, which was as bright as day on other worlds due to the albedo of the moon overhead. With Alger's assistance, I covered two hundred kilometers by dawn, when I landed beside a stream, camouflaged the bicycle with brush, and slept until twilight. Fortified by the cheese and sausage, I pedaled through another night, and through several after that, before the plains gave way to different geography and I left behind the territory of the Marvelous Flying Bicycle Men.

According to the most recent information in Alger's database, information admittedly more than a century out of date, an urban center lay beyond the badlands we were traversing: Churraspora.

"A trade depot, no more," he said. "Considering the impermanence of planetary cultures, I cannot predict with any assurance we will find the place inhabited. Still, sir, if Churraspora exists, I assume that is where Miss Mirable would have been taken. There is no other city of greater size within a thousand kilometers."

The topography became a succession of ravines spaced as regularly as furrows. Little vegetation grew and that was stunted and thorny. The first night I had feared pursuit but now I was sure the hunt had been called off, if it indeed had ever been raised. I was exhausted and bruised but I felt good even so. Maybe I was almost broke, my clothes in tatters and foul from my experience within the aca, stranded on a strange world with no one to call friend except an antiquated personal assistant—but I had escaped Pilar Goodfellow and Nonio Wellmete and Faal Finechance and their entire tribe and that was a satisfying achievement.

Next I would pick up Mirable's trail and then I would find her, and then—once again my imagination faltered. Impossible to plan so far in advance. I had to concentrate on immediate issues. The most pressing before me was locating a flat place to put down safely. Dawn was approaching.

I flew another five kilometers without coming upon level ground. Scoured by sand and wind, the hilltops had been carved into wild, lonely sculptures of crooked rock, impossible to approach. The ravines between them were choked with thick white fog, hiding what lay beneath.

"Sir, if I am not mistaken, there appears to be a landing field ahead."

"I hope you're right," I replied. A kilometer further on, we came to a narrow ridge line separating two winding chasms. Here an area had been planed smooth and surfaced with flagstones. In the center rose a brick building of three stories and as many annexes, covered by clinging ivy and topped by peaked roofs with shingles of weathered dark-green copper. Wide lattice windows, shutters thrown back, gave the structure an inviting appearance, notwithstanding the antiaircraft emplacements rising from the lawn. These tracked my approach but remained quiescent, not that there was much I could have done had they opened fire. The wheels touched down and I brought the bicycle to a halt outside the front entrance.

A dozen or so vehicles were parked in the driveway—battered roundabouts with hydrogen engines, a couple solar jets of dubious construction, a pair of helicopters. I eyed them enviously, set my bicycle against its kickstand, did what I could with how I looked, which wasn't much, and went up the front steps. The door swung open, revealing a common room furnished with wood tables already set for breakfast. The place was obviously a public house or inn. On the left, carpeted stairs led to the upper floors. From the entrance to the kitchen emerged a man wearing the outfit of a cook, his black pants and white shirt separated by a white apron. His face was as ordinary as his clothing, round and ruddy, framed by tufts of curls. He was carrying a cleaver.

With a pleasant smile, he said, "Well, what have we? Yes, what have we here? The defensive engines said we were being visited by a Bicycle Man but you're not one. No, you are not."

All too conscious of the rough shape I was in, I replied:

"No, I am not, sir, and thankful, too, considering what I know of them. It is true, though, my vehicle resembles those they use."

"Down to the tribal icons on the airframe, not to mention the fringes of digits so charmingly adorning the wings. An astounding coincidence. Well, it is an amazing universe we live in and this an age of miracles. But forgive me, I have been remiss. I am Harmony Repute, proprietor of this modest establishment—" Repute moved into the common room and made a sweeping gesture with the cleaver—"known to one and sundry as Twin Chasms House, the finest of its kind in all the Darwin Wastes. Of course, it is the only one of its kind, which does help us maintain our reputation."

"Even so, I wouldn't think you'd get much business out here."

Harmony Repute made a dismissive gesture. "I assure you, the situation is convenient for any number of reasons. First, we are advantageously positioned to appeal to traffic crossing the Wastes. There is more of that than you might think, Wagon Men and Bicycle Men and other aborigines traveling to Churraspora on business, as well as wandering dignitaries such as yourself on important errands. Also, there is an indigenous population in the surrounding ravines, which constitutes an additional source of clientele."

Churraspora existed! We were on Mirable's trail. Improbable that her captors had any other destination, not in these wastes. And, I thought excitedly, if Mirable was indeed bound for Churraspora, it was possible that she had been here, the only rest stop for thousands of square kilometers.

"The morning meal will be served in half an hour," continued the innkeeper. "Today we are offering omelets stuffed with cheese and chives, an assortment of grilled meats, pastries, and pots of hot suckleberry juice. Will you join us?"

I had finished the last stolen onion two days before and hadn't eaten since. Repute's description of the repast he was preparing caused my stomach to make anticipatory noises.

"What are your fees?" I asked with care learned from Every Smit, who had trusted no one and nothing very far—perhaps, I thought, because he was not himself trustworthy.

Repute went to a wood desk decorated with ornate carvings of exotic birds and fruit, slid open a drawer, took out a thick register, and flipped through it to the most recent entry, the last of hundreds of signatures, some in standard interstellar script, others in pictograms and hieroglyphics. "Our rates, although ruinously low, depend on the quality of accommodations selected," Repute explained, handing me a stylus with which to sign the guest book. As I made my mark, I scanned the entries above mine. Three days earlier someone had identified himself as "Manfred Nathan Fairweather", obviously a Marvelous Flying Bicycle Man although there was a slash through the field requesting a permanent address. The timing was about right, too, and there were four guests in Fairweather's party, which also seemed about right—Mirable and three guards. The group had stayed a single night. There was no mention of Silver. Probably his cage had remained on the plane.

"Would you be paying in standard hhours?" Harmony Repute asked as I returned the stylus. "Yes, of course, you will. Well, then— for the 'Enchanting Overlook' suite, which comes equipped with a grand salon, sauna, and a pair of spacious sleeping chambers, the tariff is sixty hhours, fifty mminutes, plus a gratuity of fifteen percent."

This represented most of my remaining funds. "All I need is a room with a bed and bath," I protested. "Surely something less expensive is available."

"But of course. May I suggest the 'Pleasant Vista' nook. For the modest fee of eleven hhours, seventy mminutes, inclusive, you will also be permitted to partake of the supper buffet. Tonight we are presenting a goulash flavored with imported paprika, a braise of native kumwass, fried rice, and éclairs. Also, sanitary facilities may be found down the hall."

From the bottom of my pocket I pulled the canister containing the seed pearls I had carried across so many parsecs, just about the only thing I had connecting me with my past. The tube was battered and tacky with unidentifiable dried fluid and it took some straining before I could unscrew it. Inside was what remained of the sign-on bonus I had received before embarking on the *Miraculous Abernathy*. I'd had an easy time of it then although I hadn't known that I was well off, thinking myself put upon by the circumstances of my life. I hadn't yet met such interesting people as Vander Wirthy, Captain Hartung, Nonio Wellmete, or Pilar Gonzlez Goodfellow.

Neither had I met Mirable Wirthy. That alone made up for a lot.

I gave Harmony Repute a twenty-hhour bill. "The 'Pleasant Vista' chamber is what I need. I will have breakfast, too, if the price is reasonable."

"No, not a ssecond past an hhour, SKr[1]. Anderts."

He'd read my name in the guest book. "On shore leave from the *Miraculous Abernathy*?" Repute continued, noting my address. "A vessel with which I am unfamiliar. Local registry, is she, or interstellar?"

"She's a merchant ship," I explained, figuring it best to stick as closely to the truth as possible while editing the story to my advantage. Despite his affability, there was something about the innkeeper I distrusted. "Her home port's Phobos, near Old Earth. She will be in orbit undergoing minor repairs another couple hundred hours," I went on, "so I asked Captain Vander for shore leave. All I wanted was to stretch my legs and do a little sightseeing. Big mistake, Skr. Repute. I was not made welcome, not by far."

"You are referring, of course, to the Marvelous Flying Bicycle Men," Repute replied. "No, they are not known for their hospitality. Tribal Law is stringent."

"I'll say. No offense, but I've had it with this world. Captain Vander will be picking me up in a couple days and that will be none too soon by me."

---

1   Abbreviation of *Sekundaar raamen*, or "Valiant raider", a local term of approbation among the Darwin Wastes of Temurlone.

"I trust your funds are sufficient to cover your stay?" Harmony Repute asked while arching one eyebrow. "It would distress me if I were forced to request that you vacate the premises prematurely. I cannot recommend other accommodation. There is none."

"They're sufficient," I lied, intending to leave Twin Chasms House before daybreak although Harmony Repute did not have to know that.

"But of course. Please enjoy your stay."

I followed the innkeeper up a flight of stairs, where a long corridor, interrupted by numbered doors, led away from the landing. The "Pleasant Vista" nook was a cubicle with an irregular ceiling. For the outlay of an additional three hhours, five mminutes, Harmony Repute furnished clothes of utilitarian fabric, which I changed into once I had showered in the sanitary facility a short walk along the hallway. I needed a lot of scrubbing before the water ran clear. It felt odd to be clean and to be wearing clean garments. It felt strange, too, to be lying on a real bed, however narrow, instead of in a hammock or on a hard bunk. I lay down to get the feel of it and fell asleep without warning, waking eight hours later, midway through the long Temurlone afternoon. From the window beside the bed I had a view of the southern chasm, a rift a hundred meters wide, its depths hidden by fog.

After a while I went down to the lobby. From the kitchen came the noise of running water, the sound of a whisk being scraped briskly against the bottom of a bowl, and the smell of meat frying in aromatic oil. The dining chamber was set for a formal supper. I made for the buffet and helped myself to tidbits of broiled fowl on wood skewers, wrinkled salt-cured olives, and slivers of gelatin that probably came from an insect. Only after I had blunted my appetite did I notice I was not alone in the room.

A pair of men sitting together, dressed alike in severe uniforms, lasers in holsters cut low before and behind in order to permit a quick draw, were wandering "dignitaries", to use Repute's phrase—desperadoes for hire or highwaymen, depending on opportunity.

They appraised me with quick glances, saw nothing impressive, and returned to their conversation. I didn't know whether to be insulted or relieved.

Squatting at another table was an anthropoid with shaggy turquoise hair, wearing trousers and nothing else. This, I guessed, was a commercial rep, as my father had been, for he was busy entering data into an electronic assistant while spooning goulash into his muzzle with his other paw.

The remainder of the guests were clientele from the indigenous population to which Harmony Repute had referred. These men were short and as round as buttons, with plump bellies and pursed mouths. Most had on the outfits of agricultural workers, with deep back pockets in their coveralls of blue homespun, striped bandannas tied under their many chins. They seemed a friendly group and I readily accepted their invitation to join them at their table. Repute brought out from the kitchen a tureen of stew, a basket of brioche, a bowl of rice fried with almonds and raisins, and a crock of vegetables with the chewy consistency of snails.

He squeezed my shoulder with jovial intimacy as he acquainted me with the other guests. "Allow me to introduce SKr. Anderts, a sailor and journeyer from whence I cannot say precisely but far from here nonetheless."

My companions provided their own names too quickly for me to catch anything except they all began with the same three syllables. "Welcome," said one man—Tiraminaan, I thought he was called. "If I may presume, what brings you across the dark light years to our own drab backwater? Not that we are not proud of what we have, is that not correct, fellows—" the others responded with hearty affirmations—"but we are well aware the Darwin Wastes are not high on any lists of preferred travel destinations."

They all chuckled at the thought.

"I don't know," I replied. "The view from my window is dramatic."

"True, but you do not have to live down below, as we do, down in the mist, does he, fellows?" A chorus of agreement answered. "It is always cold, always damp, perfect for the fungi we grow but not pleasant, no, not at all. Nothing to do for entertainment for weeks on end except beat the wives, and that does get boring. I ask you, is it a wonder we're all so, so comfortable?"

Tiraminaan coughed and patted his rotund belly with a knowing gesture, which his fellows copied.

I assumed the question was rhetorical. "If you ate here a lot, you'd have good reason to gain weight, no argument," I observed.

"And we do, don't we, lads?" remarked Tiraminaan.

"Without fail," responded the chorus.

"Repute's the best!"

"And then we beat the wives again!"

The goulash testified to our landlord's quality as a chef. I ladled a second portion onto my plate. The conversation went back and forth until Repute brought out a platter of delicacies and jugs of mulled wine. For my part I said as little as was polite, thinking it prudent to keep my history to myself despite the affability of my companions. I pressed them for news but they knew little except local scandal since the entire area was cut off from wireless communications with the rest of Temurlone due to interference broadcast by the Marvelous Flying Bicycle Men and other nomad tribes during their perpetual range wars. My stomach full for the first time in I did not know how long, I returned to the "Pleasant Vista" nook. Despite having risen from a sound nap not long before, I slept at once.

"Sir, please, come to your senses. Rouse yourself. You must awaken."

I had been dreaming of Mirable. She was walking ahead of me along one of the service corridors aboard the *Miraculous Abernathy*, lovely in loose white pants, her blouse gathered by the black sash that was her emblem of status. Her face was turned aside, as if she was troubled by what I was saying. I was reaching toward her when Alger's interruption caused the vision to vanish. "Sir, bestir yourself. I have important data for your attention."

"I am awake, Alger. What is it?"

"The meal you ate, sir. It was—"

"Poisoned?" Only a situation so extreme, I guessed, would cause my personal attendant, aristocracy grade, such upset.

"No, sir. I would have identified any contaminant well before you ingested it. The meal was nontoxic and wholesome, too, except for the fact—"

"What fact, Alger?"

"The fact it was human flesh."

"The goulash, you mean?"

"Precisely. I did not perform a complete analysis until your digestive process was well along. Only then did I identify the constituents of the stew."

I expected to feel queasy, hearing this report and knowing what I had eaten, but I did not. The goulash had been superb, perfectly tender, seasoned with garlic and red peppers and red paprika imported all the way from Old Earth, or so Harmony Repute had assured us as he lifted the lid from the ceramic tureen in a burst of fragrant steam.

"Maybe it's local custom to, to—" I did not know how to finish. There was no getting around the fact cannibalism was an alarming practice, however generous your point of view. Alger confirmed my uneasiness:

"No doubt, sir," he said. "Unfortunately, the question remains as to how our host acquires his ingredients. Several scenarios come to mind, none reassuring."

"I see what you mean," I thought—just as restraints whipped from either side of the bed, pinning me to the mattress in a grip that was unbreakable no matter how I struggled. Harmony Repute flicked on a lamp. With an intent expression on his ruddy face, my treacherous host ran a scanner over me, apparently in search of protective mechanisms. Alger's stealth capabilities evaded the inspection, however, and Repute folded the device and placed it on his belt. He smiled.

"Please, don't tire yourself, SKr. Anderts."

"Let me go, Repute," I insisted. "Is this how you treat all your guests?"

"Not at all, only those who will presently grace our table, mostly vagabonds and urchins such as yourself."

"I am none of those," I told him, lying earnestly. "I am on shore leave from the *Abernathy*, I told you—from the *Miraculous Abernathy*, which is in orbit even as we speak. Captain Vander will ask serious questions, should I not show for pick up. Personally, I wouldn't care to suffer her displeasure myself. Not when she could target this place within ten meters from a distance of ten thousand kilometers and vaporize it with a single burst from the *Abernathy*'s Scimitar MMX military lasers."

"You tell a plausible story, SKr. Anderts, but I do not believe it. No, you are just another drifter, another nondescript, meaningful to no one but yourself. Sadly, you will not be missed."

The innkeeper shackled me and carried me downstairs to a basement divided into a series of cells separated by metal bars. All were vacant except for the nearest, which held a slug the size of my head, a shiny gray lump of tissue resting in a tray of liquid, presumably nutrient fluid. Repute put me into the next cell over, locking my manacles to rings set in the wall. He stepped back a pace.

"It is a shame we do not have time to fatten you properly with plenty of grain and savory herbs, SKr. Anderts," he mused. "You are skinny pork, no question about it, and will be tough to the teeth regardless how long you are braised. Well, so be it. I must make do."

"Tell me, Repute," I said. "Do your other patrons know what goes into your cuisine?"

"But of course. Most are indifferent to such subtleties. The more discerning make reservations far in advance for special menus. Why, tomorrow evening I am preparing a banquet of seven courses for a local society of gourmets. I believe you shared their table earlier. They are an outgoing group and it will be a gala affair. A fine time will be had by all with one exception, of course. Although I suppose that is only natural, considering the special role you will play in the proceedings."

With a cheery bow, causing his stomach to bobble over his apron, Repute returned upstairs and I was left alone in the dungeon. Larder. Alone except for the slug in the next cage and it lacked any mouth with which to speak, if it was indeed capable of language. It was an ugly thing, splotched with eyespots of different diameters, which turned on me, from curiosity or perhaps from boredom.

"You may be sure he will torture you."

The interstellar vernacular was spoken with a formal diction suggesting it was not the speaker's native tongue. Only then did I notice the slug had grown a pair of lips.

"Repute, you mean?" I asked.

"Who else would I be referring to but Harmony Repute? I have observed his routine carefully. Over a period of weeks, he force feeds his human captives with a plunger until their mass is substantially augmented and their livers swollen. Then Repute subjects them to pain until they expire in discomfort."

"Why would he do something awful like that?"

"Repute belongs to the culinary school that believes the presence of adrenaline and other stress toxins in human flesh tenderizes the meat, enhances the flavor, and has a refreshing effect on human masculine sexual vigor. I know this because it is part of his procedure to describe his philosophy and techniques in detail to his subjects. Being well informed regarding the experience causes them additional distress."

"I would say so." I tugged fitfully at the manacles securing my wrists to the wall. "Alger, isn't there anything you can do?"

"Yes, sir, without question. I could manufacture industrial saws of molecular scale, dispatch them through your bloodstream, excrete them through your sweat, and cut through the handcuffs. Unfortunately, the task would require far more time than we have available."

"Why didn't you shoot the crazy bastard when there was the chance?"

"I am sorry, sir, but I would not presume to make such an adventurous intervention without explicit instructions from you to do so. Nor did I have a clear line of fire."

Fearing I had offended him, I said hastily, "We haven't had good luck, have we, Alger?"

"True, sir. We have been subjected to an unpropitious sequence of improbable events."

"Thank God for that," I observed sourly.

"Without doubt, sir."

Still, my luck was not as bad as Every Smit's, not by any stretch of the imagination. I was among the living and that was a good start. I told myself there must be a way out of the predicament I was in. I just couldn't see it yet. Everyone knew God never gave you a burden greater than you could bear, just more than you ever wanted to carry.

I focused my attention on my neighbor, the slug.

Isset, I learned it was called, a contraction of Issetvathorm*sha. "I have been here a month, Pimsol Anderts," it told me after we exchanged introductions. "I am being reserved for an exclusive function with a menu composed entirely of dishes prepared from carbon-based, non-human intelligent organisms. Repute served my cowboy last week, roasting him on a spit while basting with seasoning of garlic, thyme, vinegar, and olive oil."

"Cowboy?"

"Perhaps I meant *horse*. As you may have noticed, I am physically ill equipped for locomotion. Luckily, for every thorm*sha—" what Isset's species called themselves—"an ist*sha is born to be a faithful companion. Together we are one, the sturdy legs and hands and the wise mind, thorm*sha and ist*sha inseparable."

"Quite interesting, sir," Alger commented. "And if I may say so, not entirely dissimilar to our own relationship."

I did not inquire which of us Alger thought fulfilled which role. Instead I asked Isset, "You mean you cannot get around at all?"

"I would require a quarter hour just to travel from my cell to yours, if I could descend from the table without injuring myself, which is doubtful. I am lost without my ist*sha. He was a gentle beast and needed few reminders who was master."

"How did you do that?"

"Through the application of agony."

Thorm*sha attached to their steeds—*hosts* was a better descriptor, I thought, since the association seemed parasitical to me—by extruding filaments from their underbellies. These burrowed into the ist*sha, extracting nutrients. A different kind of tendril interfaced with the host nervous system, allowing the thorm*sha to dominate the symbiosis through the application of stimulation to the other's sensory network. In an hour I had learned more than I wanted to know about Isset's personal biology. I also had the glimmering of an idea.

"You ist*sha," I said. "Can you only ride your own beasts? Or can you control other sorts of animals, too?"

"I have heard it may be done although I have not done so."

"Humans, for instance?"

"Almost certainly."

"So if, say, you managed to get close to Harmony Repute, you'd be able to make him do what you wanted?"

"I would not doubt it although he is certain to be a stubborn steed and require breaking in. Do not think I have not had the same thought. The problem is Repute is aware of my capabilities. He is careful to keep his distance."

"What if he were distracted by other business? How long did you say you needed to crawl from your cell to mine?"

"A quarter hour. Twenty-five minutes."

"I will get you those twenty-five minutes, Isset. I am beginning to think there may be a way out for both of us."

Even in my own ears this optimism sounded hollow. Much depended on how I would bear the attention Repute would soon be paying me and there was no guessing about that. I went over the

161

plan with Alger time and again, neither of us happy. I slept once in the manacles. When I awoke, my arm sockets were on fire. Out of the corner of my eye I noticed graffiti scratched in the wall, a hieroglyph that seemed familiar although I did not know why. Eventually I realized I had noticed the same mark when I signed the guest book for Harmony Repute.

At noon he appeared. First he added a powder to Isset's nutrient bath, using a scoop on the end of a long handle, taking care to stay away from the slug. Then the innkeeper regarded me fondly.

"Well, it is time, SKr. Anderts. Time to begin our little exercise together."

"If it's all the same, Repute, I would rather not."

"Impossible, I am afraid. You are, after all, the signature dish on the menu. Immerse yourself in the experience. Think of it as your most demanding role. Emote and give your all to the part! At the least, consider the situation objectively," Harmony Repute went on. "You dined on those who preceded you. It is only fitting you provide for those who come after."

I was certain there was a flaw in his logic but I couldn't figure out where it lay. Repute did not wait for an answer but opened a closet in the far wall. The interior of the locker was cluttered with instruments of torture, or so I assumed them to be, since many were so specialized it was impossible to guess their function without seeing them used and that was information I did not need. It was easy, however, to recognize knives—and whips, and bludgeons, and vises, and hammers. Harmony Repute surveyed this equipment placidly, wiping his hands against his apron.

"Where shall we begin?" he asked.

CHAPTER NINE
On the Trail of Mirable Wirthy

My favorite preparation of the human leg is the *osso bucco* of the kelocca chefs of that amazing establishment, The Charming Corners Abode of Excellent Flavor. Use only the lower leg from just below the knee. Slice the meat into rounds, season with salt and pepper, and marinate overnight in sherry. Flour the meat and sauté it in olive oil until browned on all sides. Do not scamp the browning process.

Remove the meat from the pan and allow it to drain. Spoon out excess oil and add chopped onions, celery, carrots, and ham, a full head of minced garlic, tomatoes that have been peeled, seeded, and diced, a splash of white wine, thyme, a laurel leave, and salt and pepper. Simmer, stirring, until the ingredients have melted into a coarse sauce. Return the meat to the pan and cook over low heat, turning occasionally, until the meat is done, about an hour. You may have to add additional water or stock to keep the sauce from drying out.

Arrange the meat on a warm platter and spoon the sauce over it. Sprinkle with a gremolata of minced lemon peel, garlic, and parsley. You will have a luncheon dish appropriate for any company, whether a women's social circle or a party of uncouth barbarians preparing to do foul deeds.

Harmony Repute: *The Private Notebooks of a Chef*

I couldn't stop myself from following Harmony Repute's every motion as he placed a stand in front of my cell and laid out his tools with care.

"Sir," Alger said, "let me repeat, I may be able to block some sensation from reaching your cognitive center but since you insist on remaining conscious, there is only so much I can do. You will feel pain."

"One way or another I will feel pain, Alger. It's not as if I have a choice. Unless you have another suggestion?"

"No, sir, although I wish I did. I crunched a thousand scenarios and none promised equal or better results. I am not, however, sanguine."

"Sanguine? That's not the word I would have chosen, Alger. But I am following your advice."

"In what sense?"

"Remember what you told me when Goodfellow and I were falling together? You know, *do nothing*."

"Yes, sir, I recall the incident."

"Well, Alger, that's what I'm doing. Nothing. It's the only thing to do."

Silently Isset began to flow over the lip of its container. Twenty-five minutes. A quarter hour. I could endure that long, I told myself, regardless of what horrors Repute performed upon me. But I couldn't quite believe my own words. Repute hefted a flexible black truncheon and slapped it against his palm a couple times, as if getting a feel for the tool.

"Opinion differs as to the proper sequence in which to dress the human body," he said, meaning, I guessed, to *butcher*, rather than to *clothe*, an assumption that was confirmed immediately. "My professional judgment is rigorous stimulation releases certain complex chemicals into human tissue," Repute elaborated, as Isset had warned he would. "These are, essentially, flavors—flavors that cannot be reproduced by artificial means. On the other hand, care must be taken not to damage the carcass through over-enthusiasm. Thus, SKr. Anderts, I always begin with a sound beating, just hard enough to tenderize the flesh but not hard enough to cause severe bruising."

He struck me on the thigh with the truncheon.

I felt the blow. Maybe not as much as I would have without Alger's help but I knew I did not want to suffer another.

My plan, such as it was, depended on displaying as little emotion as I could while staying conscious. This, I hoped, would delay Harmony Repute from killing me since he would be unsure of when I was reaching my peak of flavor. The gamble was that this hesitation would last long enough for Isset to crawl from its cell to mine—the space between the bars was just wide enough for the slug to squeeze through. Then he'd extrude a palp and take control of the innkeeper's mind. According to Isset, Repute usually applied fifteen minutes of torture before he put his victims out of their misery. I had to distract him ten minutes longer than that.

"You have to listen," I told Repute, lying as best I could. "Captain Vander will dispatch a tender to pick me up in three days. She is a stern woman and won't be amused by what you're up to."

"Please, not that tired story, SKr. Anderts," he replied and struck my other thigh. This blow hurt as much as the first. I did not want to think what I would be feeling without Alger's assistance. "I heard the truth from a party of Bicycle Men who enjoyed my hospitality not long before you arrived," Harmony Repute continued. "You and the girl they had with them are from the *Abernathy*, that much is true, but you're nothing but stowaways or indentured sailors evading your obligations. One or the other, it makes little difference. Either way you won't be missed. I must say, though, your associate is a skinny thing. I thought Fairweather was asking an exorbitant price for so few kilos of yield, no matter how sweet. Why he imagines they will get a better offer in Churraspora is beyond me."

This confirmation that Mirable had actually been at Twin Chasms House, and that her destination was Churraspora, heartened me enough to endure what was happening.

With every word he spoke, Repute struck a blow with the truncheon. I hoped it was beginning to perplex him that I hadn't screamed or groaned.

Finally Isset reached the rim of the table. The slug extended a bit of itself past the edge, allowing an eyespot to get a view of the floor below. It was not hard to figure out Isset was having second thoughts. The fall was steep for a thing its size, particularly since it lacked any skeletal structure. I began to lose faith in my scheme, and knew I would never escape the mad gourmet, until Isset proved me wrong by tumbling bravely from the table.

I had to make some noise to cover the sound of its fall. "You couldn't be more mistaken," I told Repute, speaking forcefully. "I may not be much when compared to her—but Mirable? Why, Mirable's the—"

I stopped myself just in time. I couldn't decide whether it was pain or hearing news of Mirable that was making me so light headed and stupid.

Isset lay beside the table. It did not stir.

Harmony Repute regarded the truncheon quizzically. "How are you feeling, SKr. Anderts?" he asked. "I have belabored you carefully and yet I hear none of the usual music. Perhaps it is time to apply a more forceful regimen."

Repute replaced the cudgel with a whip. It was a slender thing, and cut the air with a snap faster than sound. "There are two ways to use the lash," Harmony Repute said pedantically, continuing the lecture that was supposed to unnerve me and make me even more flavorful. "The tip," he continued, "although providing pain, will break the skin, cause blood loss, and lacerate the meat. Instead, I wield the length with enough strength to raise a blush but not so harshly as to cut the flesh. Just so—"

I had been trapped in bed wearing shorts. The whip caressed my naked belly above the waistband. A line of white appeared and then turned red. Even with Alger muting the sensation, I felt a searing kiss of fire.

Isset had begun crawling. It was approaching the bars separating our cells. It nudged between them and got stuck. Its skin writhed as it tried to worm through. That seemed just to jam it further.

Repute was beginning to perspire. After giving me a blow across both feet, he pulled a napkin from his pocket and dabbed at his hairline. "I ask you, SKr. Anderts," he said, breathing heavily, "are you, as you appear, an insensate lout without a single nerve ending? Or am I losing my touch?"

He did not expect an answer but I spoke up anyway—to keep his attention occupied while Isset, having made it through the cell bars with one last queasy writhe, inched lethargically toward him. Unfortunately, I suspected this slow pace represented feverish speed on the part of the slug.

"Repute, I will be the most insipid thing you ever ate, I swear it, it won't matter how you prepare me. I will be tough and tasteless and you'll have no joy from the meal. I will be nothing but an embarrassment to you."

"We will see, SKr. Anderts." Repute coiled the whip and hung it from a hook. He studied his implements with the air of a master craftsman. First he inspected a scalpel but then Repute put down the knife and took a pair of kitchen shears, opening and closing them with a crisp snipping sound. These pleased him. He levered open the jaws of the shears and brought them around the base of the small finger of my right hand.

"Your stubbornness does you credit, SKr. Anderts," Repute said. "Alas, though, ultimately it causes more harm than good. Why put off the inevitable at the cost of additional pain? Relax. Allow yourself to feel. Surrender to your role in our little drama—may God take pleasure in the parts we play! As for me, I will now have a quick taste to judge your ripeness. Should you still be raw, well, I am sure you understand what must follow."

Isset needed only a little more time to reach the innkeeper—time I did not have.

"You're going to eat my finger just like that?" I asked in as even a voice as I could, stalling for seconds, all too conscious of the pressure of the shears.

"Perhaps I should accompany it with mustard? Or a vinaigrette? No, no, SKr. Anderts. I think not. I mustn't blunt my palate with extraneous flavors."

Isset was still a meter behind Repute, who might turn around at any moment and notice the approaching slug. I couldn't come up with anything to say, no matter how I tried. Then, with what must have been, relatively, a tremendous display of agility, Isset rolled sideways, exposing a bone white underbelly with circular pink teats. It stopped centimeters from Repute's heel. Laboriously, Isset hunched itself upward, prevented from making direct contact with the innkeeper's skin by the high back of his shoe.

Repute gave the shears an experimental twitch. A ring of blood formed around my finger and trickled down my arm.

"Are we anxious?" Repute asked. He was peering into my eyes, perhaps to estimate the dilation of my pupils. I sensed him draw breath. He was about to close the shears.

Then Repute stiffened, his own eyes popping wide, the sandy tufts of curls on his round head standing from his skull.

The shears tightened their grip as Repute tensed and I knew I would lose the finger. Instead, the innkeeper slumped to the floor, the shears clattering to one side. His pants leg bulged where Isset gripped his ankle.

"Get it off of me," Repute groaned. Willing his own hands to take hold of Isset must have been more than he could bear. "Get it off me."

"Now how do you suggest I do that?" I asked, rattling the cuffs that held me chained to the wall, not that he heard. Mostly Repute talked to himself, protesting in one voice, responding in another. Sometimes the two parts of the conversation overlapped, causing violent coughing fits.

Isset continued crawling up Repute's leg. When it reached the innkeeper's waist, Repute himself loosened the belt so the ist*sha could proceed to its destination and curl around his groin. By the way his hands shook, I suspected Repute was of two minds about what he was doing.

Then he regained his feet, the apron hiding the shape of the parasite. He did so hesitantly, as if unsure of his balance. "Is that you, Isset?" I asked.

Repute regarded me blankly. There were flecks of spittle in the corners of his lips. "Yes, Pimsol Anderts," he replied in an unaccented monotone. "I am in control but it has not been easy. Harmony possesses a strong sense of self. A doughty steed, he is, but I have tamed him."

The innkeeper jerked again, Isset having applied another chastisement, controlling Harmony Repute through the "application of

169

agony." He unlocked the manacles from my wrists and I fell to my knees, unable to stand without support after so long in the cuffs.

"Sir," Alger said, "I have begun a revitalizing medical protocol. I suggest, however, you rest a minimum of eighteen hours. It will require that long to staunch your internal hemorrhaging and repair your spleen and kidneys."

Isset, his movements becoming more assured, assisted me upstairs and we returned to the common room of Twin Chasms House. Chatting together while seated in comfortable chairs with arms covered by lace doilies were Tiraminaan and two of his fellows, pots of tea on the low table between them. "What is this?" Tiraminaan asked as I staggered into the chamber. "Why are you not hard at work snipping and chopping and dicing?" Tiraminaan scolded Repute. "Have you forgotten our banquet is this very evening? I will not be pleased if service begins even a minute late."

"There has been a change in the menu," Isset replied, his speech becoming more natural with every word as he became accustomed to the body he now rode. "SKr. Anderts has declined to participate in the festivities."

"Impossible. Not after the hard earned hhours we paid you, Harmony, for a prime cut of long pork, cooked just the way we like it. Isn't that right, lads?" The other men bobbed their heads affirmatively and began their own protests. "No, as you are well aware, we look forward all month to our little weekend away from the wives, to our harmless gastronomical getaway, and I insist we maintain the original schedule."

"If you say so, I will not argue," Isset replied. "Still, we cannot expect absolute fidelity to every detail, particularly in this universe of miracles."

Repute strode to Tiraminaan, took a plump cheek in either hand, and twisted his head around. When the fungi cultivator was dead,

Repute hoisted up the body and regarded the others. "The first course, served at half past thirteen, will consist of sautéed tournedos garnished with prawns and watercress. It is a special dish and I suggest you be prompt, since I consider tardiness a sign of disrespect for my cuisine."

Tiraminaan's friends looked at one another and then at the carcass. I couldn't tell which was first to agree with the innkeeper. In seconds they were all nodding vigorously.

"Tournedos, my favorite!"

"Ah, Tiraminaan, dear friend, we knew you well. And now we will know you from the inside out."

"Promptness is my fifth name."

I don't remember making my way to the "Pleasant Vista" nook or falling asleep but when I awoke a full Temurlone day later, my mind was clear and my body was free of pain. Although a lot of skin was blue and swollen, particularly around my stomach, I seemed no worse off than when Renny Blothridge had worked me over.

I was also on Mirable's trail. "A skinny thing"—well, I supposed it depended on your point of view. In my opinion, she was exactly right, slender but not lean, taller than I but not much, with the most disturbing brown eyes I had ever looked into. "Churraspora," I asked Alger. "How far did you say it was?"

"Approximately a thousand kilometers, sir."

"Six days by bike. Six or seven hours, if we had other transportation."

Again I was feeling optimistic. I showered in the cubicle at the end of the hall for the second time in as many days—this, too, felt good. I put on my clothes and returned downstairs. The front door of Twin Chasms House was open to permit the departure of the remainder of Tiraminaan's party. They were in jovial spirits and smoking cigars and they tipped Isset generously while settling their score.

"Dashed brilliant meal," observed the first farmer.

"Good old Tiraminaan," another said.

"Succulent to the last bite," agreed the third.

Then they donned parachutes, strolled to the end of the veranda, and jumped into the ravine. After a second their chutes opened and they glided down into the mist.

"It was quite the occasion," Isset observed. "Tiraminaan provided a particularly savory rib roast, baked with potatoes, cassava, and fresh rosemary, and served with a sauce of local morels, chanterelles, hen-of-the-woods, brandy, and cream. Unfortunately, though, I did not have the opportunity to torture Tiraminaan before butchering him."

"Is that you, Isset? You sound disturbingly like Harmony Repute."

"Yes, certainly, it is I," Isset answered. "But Harmony contributes something of himself, too. Through our special intimacy, I have learned he is indeed a culinary artist and I am beginning to share his appreciation for fine cuisine. He is introducing me to new vistas of taste and discrimination of which I was sadly ignorant. There is so much I have to learn."

Isset's decision to remain in residence at Twin Chasms House and take over Harmony Repute's position as innkeeper and chef reinforced my decision to leave immediately. The relationship between thorm*sha and ist*sha—between rider and steed—was not as one-sided as I had assumed. There was a blurry line between who was parasite and who was host and I did not want to wait around long enough to learn which personality would ultimately dominate the symbiosis.

Isset allowed me to appropriate one of the inn's roundabouts and I readied the battered car for flight without delay. As I uncoupled the tube feeding hydrogen to the fuel tank, Harmony Repute came outside carrying a cleaver as he'd done when I had checked in, although he was now another person entirely, for the most part. In his other hand was a parcel of butcher's paper tied with brown twine.

"No reason to go hungry," said the innkeeper. "Please, accept these sandwiches, as well as a salad of tubers and mayonnaise."

"What kind of sandwiches?" I asked apprehensively.

"Oh, I don't know, I used what was around, a little bit of this, a little bit of that. Mainly leftovers."

I eyed the carton without appetite but was unable to come up with a polite way to refuse it.

"And by the by," Isset continued, "the defensive engines have noticed a large contingent of airborne vehicles approaching from the plains."

"Marvelous Flying Bicycle Men?"

"More than likely. Given their present rate of progress, they should be arriving within the hour."

This was not good news. I told myself that it was pure coincidence, that the Bicycle Men's appearance had nothing to do with me, but I did not believe it. I hadn't thought Goodfellow would be greatly missed, but maybe I was wrong. Or maybe they were coming after the stolen bicycle—if Tribal Law mandated stoning and impalement for the crime of sneezing, I did not want to imagine what the penalty for theft would be. Worse, they might have discovered that I had evaded the leuks and violated the sacred grove of the Man Mother, and were searching for me personally.

Better they not know I had stayed at Twin Chasms House. "If anyone should ask, Isset, I was not here," I told the innkeeper. "Understand?"

"But of course, Skr. Anderts. You were never here. We have never met."

There was something I was forgetting, I just knew it. The bicycle. Going over to the vehicle, I pushed the plane from its parking place across the cobblestones to the edge of the plaza. A final shove sent it skimming from the cliff face into the air over the chasm, where it descended in a lazy spiral into the fog. A minute later I heard the muffled sound of a crash.

What else?

"The guest book, sir," answered Alger. "You signed it upon checking in."

"That's right." At first I was going to toss the whole volume into the abyss after the bicycle but then I realized that if any of the Marvelous Flying Bicycle Men were repeat visitors to Twin Chasms House, they might notice the book's absence. Instead I carefully tore out the sheet with my signature on it, hoping that a casual inspection would overlook the missing page. Then I returned to the roundabout and started the engine.

"Thanks for everything, Isset."

"God's good humor to you, too, Skr. Anderts."

As the roundabout passed out of sight of Twin Chasms House, having little desire to find out what kind of leftovers Tiraminaan made, I took the parcel Isset had so thoughtfully prepared and tossed it over the side.

The car maintained a cruising altitude of five hundred meters, paralleling the terrain. By afternoon I could see the monumental walls of purplish black that were the Lesser Stangs, a mountain range of no great account on Temurlone, with peaks merely six thousand meters high. It required another three hours to reach the foothills, these covered by a kind of conifer, the trees trailing veils of glossy needles from their branches. The car was skimming above the forest canopy. With the true beginning of the mountains still some distance ahead, the autopilot angled the car westward and we flew until we arrived at an alpine valley. In its center, situated around a lake with glassy greenish-blue water, was Churraspora.

From the near end of the valley a highway led into the Lesser Stangs. At the trail head was a parking field where a caravan was preparing to set out into the mountains.

The convoy consisted of trucks with legs instead of wheels, capable of ascending almost vertical inclines. Among the larger vehicles sped jitneys and fork lifts laden with cargo. On the outskirts of the field were warehouses similar to those of my own home town but these were busy with lights and noise instead of being half empty like the ones I remembered.

I put the roundabout down on a spot out of the way at the edge of the field and paid a usage fee to an attendant.

"My information may be dated, sir," Alger said, "but Churraspora did not possess a genteel reputation a century ago. I doubt the situation has changed appreciably, and not for the better. The commercial consortium that founded the city, being signatories of the Standard Catalog, forbade murder and robbery within the urban limits but otherwise allowed citizens to conduct their affairs without restriction. Vigilance would be wise."

This was sound advice. I could see for myself we were surrounded by a rough crowd, mostly humans, some not, men and women and things from a score of cultures and as many continents, a few from off world. A fair number were technicians, caravan employees, or warehousemen. A brilliantly dressed factor, surrounded by security personnel, pushed past me on his way to inspect cargo being loaded onto the legged trucks. Then I circled around a party of savages, not Bicycle Men but near enough like them to make me stay out of their way. On every side thronged hucksters, idle onlookers, vendors of fetishes and novelties, nondescripts, "dignitaries", to use Repute's term—mercenaries, desperadoes, or simple thugs.

"Our first step, Alger, is to learn where Mirable's been taken," I said while pushing through the crowd.

"I agree entirely, sir. I suggest, though, we begin by seeking the abattoir. A single young woman, no matter her personal attributes, would be a commonplace sight in this environment. However, a creature as rare as Silver would be remarked upon even here."

"And where Silver is, Mirable will be, too. That's what you're saying."

"It is possible, sir. Perhaps likely."

"I think you're right, Alger. Let's find Silver."

Past the warehouses and the parking field, and coming before the more permanent neighborhoods of Churraspora, was a run-down commercial district. Most of the buildings were cobbled together of packing material, foam and cardboard and sheets of wrap. The structures had an air of age despite their impromptu construction, and by the grime encrusted on them it was not hard to guess some had stood in place for decades. Every second storefront seemed to be a restaurant of some sort, windows displaying their particular specialty, tureens of hot chowder, racks of grilled meat, vats of pickled insects, skewers of broiled fowl. Others displayed charms, books, electronic gadgetry, hardware, feminine and non-human undergarments, and a thousand similar cheap things.

I strolled awhile among the alleys, not quite knowing what I was looking for but figuring I would recognize it when I saw it.

On every free centimeter of exterior wall space was signage, layer plastered upon layer, advertisements, bulletins, notices, placards, some decades old, some put up just yesterday. In places it seemed that the advertising supported the building it adhered to rather than the other way around. Many of the posters were in languages other than the standard interstellar script. Some consisted entirely of pictograms. One of these caught my eye.

"You were right, Alger," I said. "Silver is distinctive, isn't he?"

There was no mistaking the abattoir. He was reared back with his quills extended and his metallic fangs exposed in a snarl, the actual photograph retouched with colors more vibrant than true, making him appear even more ferocious than usual, although this, I thought, was an unnecessary detail. Beneath the picture was a logos of four stylized heads, all smiling, arranged in a circle. Presumably the symbol referred to an establishment so famous locally it required no further identification.

The first three people I asked for directions ignored my request, passing me by with suspicious glares. The fourth said he was a newcomer to Churraspora himself. Finally I intercepted a crone with hair gathered in a beehive and stuck through with shiny pins, almost certainly a local. Regarding me fondly, she said:

"Why, is that all you need, dear? Directions. Are you sure? I can help you with nothing else?"

"Thank you, ma'am—" it seemed prudent to be polite to so disreputable a hag—"but that's all I need. The logos of four heads. I would like to know how to find the place. Is it nearby?"

She cackled, a noise that would have been a simper in a woman a hundred years younger. "Dear me. Either my reputation is fading or you are indeed an innocent, pretty boy. Well, I could give you the directions you require but you would still get yourself hopelessly lost. And in Churraspora, you might never be found again. What a shame that would be!" The crone tittered once more, a sound as horrible in its own way as Captain Hartung's laughter. Then she thrust a stick of an arm through mine and clutched my hand with veiny talons.

"There is no question but I shall have to escort you myself," the old woman said. "What are you called, handsome child?"

"Pimsol, ma'am. Pimsol Anderts."

"Pim. How perfectly apropos. I am Jasmine."

She spoke her name as if I should recognize it no matter how far away I was from and seemed slightly put out that it meant nothing to me. Then, with another cackle, she herded me through the alley and along a labyrinth of others equally makeshift and run down. Her hobble covered ground quicker than you might think, however, and we overtook slower pedestrians. Mumbling fretfully, Jasmine prodded them aside with her cane, completely fearless of the ruffians she manhandled. Amazingly, no one took offense at her impatience. Most smiled appreciatively as she passed, with expressions that could have been either reverence or lust. The hag beamed, as if such treatment were her due, revealing just three teeth in her gums, and these black and ugly things.

"Jasmine—"

A man twice my age, but still thirty years younger than the crone, approached. His mustachios were waxed into broad curves with sharp points. He swept his robes aside, displaying expensive pantaloons of checkered silk as he got down on one knee in the muck of the alley.

"—how have I given offense? You said you would come to me and yet you did not, and I am forlorn. What have I done to deserve such treatment? Tell me, so that I may make amends and restore myself to favor. Tell me, my sweet flower, my most precious Jasmine, or I am forever bereft."

"Oh, Marmo, you are so droll," giggled the hag. She patted his cheek affectionately, as if he were just a small boy and not a grown man. "I have been occupied, though."

"Occupied, my lady?" Marmo glared at me, obviously certain I was the reason for her occupation. "And who is this?" he asked.

"Why, I do believe you are jealous, Marmo. How charming. This is my new friend, Pimsol Anderts. Pim, this rude swain is Marmo Ramshead Knobknolly, of little account except he has a high net worth. I am fond of him, however. Now come—we must be off. Marmo, I will accept your courtesies tomorrow night at fifteen o'clock. But you must behave, or I will be displeased and send you away."

"Thank you, my lady. Thank you."

We stepped around Marmo, who remained on bent knee until we passed by, evidently transported by the thought that the crone had agreed to receive him again. Jasmine was cackling. I could feel her spindly body shake, and once we had to stop so she could wipe away the drool trailing down her chin, this covered with tufts of white hair. Seeing my expression, the hag sniggered more loudly. "Marmo can be tiring," she observed. "He has no sense of humor but he does give me the most precious gifts, which makes up for a lot. And there is no doubting he cares for me, and not simply for the obvious reasons. That, too, is an endearing quality in a man. Tell me, Pimsol, do you have a girl of your own?"

"No, ma'am. Not really."

"But you fancy someone?"

"Well, yes. But she doesn't know it."

"Then go to her and tell her how you feel. Let her know what is within your heart. Heed my advice, dear, and remember what the *Scriptures* say. Seize the day. Life is too short to waste any chance at love."

"But I don't know where she is. That's the problem. I am trying to find her. I was the one who got her into trouble in the first place, what with Captain Hartung and then the Bicycle Men—" I found myself unburdening myself to the crone, explaining what had happened since the morning Jo Feringel had introduced me to Marval Wirthy and I began my indenture aboard the *Miraculous Abernathy*, about the pirate attack and our escape to Temurlone, about the Man Mother and Harmony Repute, about Silver and Mirable Wirthy. It felt good to have a sympathetic ear, no matter how decrepit. "So you see," I finished, "if I can find the abattoir, maybe I can get a lead to Mirable. At least that's my plan, such as it is."

"Oh, how exciting, Pim—you're on a romantic quest."

"Hardly, ma'am. I am just doing what needs to be done, that's all. If I hadn't tried to be a hero, Mirable would be aboard the *Abernathy* with her own people and out of harm's way. I owe it to her to make things right."

"I understand wholeheartedly, you gallant boy. And I will help you all I may. How could I do less? Is it ice water that runs in my veins or sweet red blood? We will find this beast of yours, dear Pimsol, and then we will find your Mirable and you will be united."

I tried to protest that being united was not the point, that my duty was to get Mirable to safety, but the crone dismissed my arguments with a palsied gesture. "In any case, Pim, I am tickled by your news about Harmony Repute," she continued. "I have dined at Twin Chasms House on several occasions. The innkeeper was a dreadful bore, in my opinion, and the food pretentious. Cannibalism must be an acquired taste."

We came at last upon a building somewhat more substantial than the others beside it, evidently an arena of some sort. There was a crowd before the entrance, as people purchased tickets from a booth and passed through the gate. Above the lintel was the four headed logos, and below it was the inspiration behind the symbol—four dwarfs, if not brothers then close relations, walking on stilts. These were the proprietors of the "Fromani Emporium of Valor". They recognized Jasmine and admitted us past the gate with obsequious bows, performing the gestures suavely despite their high perches. An usher led us through the noisy crowd of gamblers and sportsmen to the front row of the arena, before which was a cage.

Silver was inside. He was pacing, whipping around angrily when he reached the far end and had to return to the other, occasionally lifting his head, fanlike ears spread wide, and smiling at the onlookers.

Jasmine turned to me. "Normally contestants vie with the Fromani's beasts for purses of greater or lesser value, depending on the ferocity of the animal they must face," she explained. "And depending upon the amount of damage they wish to sustain before surrendering the match. But that won't do, will it, since you want your pet back."

"Not my pet. Mirable's. Although Silver's by no means anyone's pet. Look at him. He's not happy."

"I understand, dear. Now remain here while I speak with the Fromani brothers. All four are inveterate gamblers and I believe they will accept the proposal I have in mind."

"Which is?"

"Never you fret, dear. Leave everything to me."

As she hobbled away, giggling and wielding her cane with vigor, the man in the seat next to mine sucked in his breath and gave a heartfelt sigh while kissing his fingertips. "That is a woman, truly," he said. "You are fortunate to enjoy her favor. I have often wished I were sufficiently wealthy to do so but the charms of the most celebrated courtesan in all Churraspora are beyond my means and I am not a poor man."

"You're talking about Jasmine?"

"No one else! But I see you are a foreigner and possibly not a sophisticate. You wonder why she has such renown, even now that her looks have faded to less than a memory of what they once were.

No, no, do not deny it, young off worlder. Your error lies in being deceived by appearances. What is important in a woman is her passion, and that is independent of outward show. It is said that within Jasmine burns the sweetest flame, so tender and encompassing you could drown in it. When she chooses to share herself with a man through direct neural interface, he is given a taste of heaven."

Those weren't pins sticking from the whitish blue nest of hair rising from her head, I realized. They were the cabling, the neural interface that allowed Jasmine to connect directly with her clients, feeling to feeling, sensation to sensation, heart to heart. When she returned to her seat with an audible clacking of joints, I studied her sagging features, trying to glimpse the blaze inside her, but saw not a flicker, just wrinkled cheeks and brownish lips and toothless gums. Then she winked one rheumy eye—and for an instant it was as if I was not looking at an ancient crone but at a younger woman with a knowing smile, wise and forgiving and infinitely provocative.

"I do hope you weren't fibbing when you told me you were friends with that fearsome thing," Jasmine said, referring to Silver. "I have tweaked some noses and arranged for you to have first place on this evening's bill. Put on a fine show, with tumbling and wrestling, and pretend to vanquish the beast. If you win, the animal is yours. If you don't, well, I am out five yyears, but yyears come and go with alarming frequency, they just do."

"You bet five whole yyears on me?" It was an astronomical amount, fifty thousand hhours, many multiples more than the price of my entire indenture aboard the *Miraculous Abernathy*.

"Of course, dear. The Fromanis wouldn't accept a lower wager against the value of the animal. They insisted they paid a fortune for it."

"But you don't know me at all," I protested. "What if I was just telling you a story?"

"Oh, small chance of that," Jasmine replied. She pinched my cheek and stared into my eyes. "I see who you are, Pimsol Anderts," she said.

A bell sounded. The buzz of conversation became an uproar. Touts crowded the aisles, calling out odds and taking bets. The four dwarfs on stilts strode to the cage and began beating the bars with metal pipes, one to a side. Silver's moaning became enraged enough to be heard over the din, a siren of fury that grated on the spine, like the scraping of a fingernail on shell against the grain. Jasmine prodded me impatiently.

"Go on, dear. You are certain you're friends with that monster."

"Yes, we're friends," I assured her. But to myself I whispered, "I hope."

It had been awhile since the abattoir had last seen me. And Silver was not in a good mood.

I elbowed through the press of bookies and bettors to the cage. The closer I approached the abattoir, the less sure I became that our acquaintanceship would count for a lot, considering the state Silver was in. He had been driven to a fever pitch of wrath, his little eyes had contracted to dots, and he was snapping viciously at the air whenever a dwarf struck the bars a blow. Would the abattoir recognize me? I wondered. Or would Silver take out his irritation on the only available scapegoat, that being myself? I did not have answers for these questions and did not care to learn them, either.

"So you are what Jasmine has her yyears down on," snapped the nearest dwarf. "If you ask me, you do not seem like much."

"But he is an off worlder, One Fromani," replied a second brother. "He may have unfamiliar tricks. Suppose he is more than the moony young rascal he appears to be."

"Anything is possible in a universe of miracles," observed the third brother, repeating a truism. The stilts brought his face on level with mine. He thrust a buckler and a stick, purely defensive weapons, into my hands.

"Survive as long as possible," instructed Three Fromani. "At any time, upon your request, we will let you out of the cage. However, you will receive no pay-out should the bout last less than five minutes. If it lasts seven minutes, you win a hundred hhours. One chap lasted ten minutes yesterday but overstayed his welcome and forfeited his share of the purse by dying. Remember, though, in order for Miss Jasmine to collect her wager, you must not only survive the abattoir but win the match."

All the dwarf brothers chuckled at the admonition, their laughter a deep rumble. Four Fromani opened the cage door, and closed it when I stepped within. Silver stared at me with a fascination that could have meant many things. His snarling became highly pitched. The very tip of his tail, its small quills rattling, lashed back and forth. He sank to his belly and crawled forward, smiling all the while.

"Hey, there, old fellow," I whispered. "Remember me? It is Pim."

Silver continued his approach. I was not getting through. His muzzle was agape, revealing a second mouth with its own set of teeth deep in his throat. I hadn't known that was there. I had never looked at Silver from this angle before.

I backed off, first into the bars of the cage, and then along them crabwise with my shoulders against the metal rods.

"Come on now, old thing, of course you remember Pim," I said, now with somewhat less conviction. "We're friends, are we not?"

He must have disagreed.

With a final snarl Silver sprang upon me, knocked the buckler aside, and closed his jaws around my throat.

Chapter Ten

An Unsettling Metamorphosis

Free will? Certainly we all possess a certain amount of the stuff, bearing in mind the constraints imposed by biology, history, society, and intimate upbringing. No, the point is God's play is being written as it's performed—written by us. We create the lines as we speak them, we provide stage directions with our own gestures. How else could recurring roles be possible? Unless our personal efforts made a difference.

Remember what God said: "See Answer 1."

Out there in the darkness beyond the limelight, both producer and audience, the deity is observing the show, *our* show, our small dramas, our comedies, our perplexing bits of plot, asking only for some modicum of entertainment.

Should our efforts be listless, tired, and lackluster, well, we are struck from the cast and scratched from the script. But if our performance is a hit, if we emote and are convincing, we are asked to return for an encore, or two or three besides. So I tell you, every man jack and thing as hears me—never hold back, never leave a deed undone, and give your all when I require it, for the Lord God said nothing of good and evil.

Not one word.

Verisimilitude is what counts, entertainment value, not feckless philosophical abstraction. When I bid you murder, I want to see the best damn murderers in this universe of miracles. When I bid you rape and pillage, I want to see not a single female left inviolate (as far as anatomically feasible), and not one stone standing upon another.

And if our part by chance should end, and we are beckoned behind the curtain into the long night, we can go in confidence we will return on stage in a later act to do the same again.

So, men and things that heed me, let me hear you loud and clear. Are we going to have some fun?

Audio Recording: "Captain Hartung Addressing his Crew," *Ethnographic Archives of the University of Peoria, Old Earth*

S ilver's jaw dislocated with a sharp snap, enabling the abattoir to engulf my entire head with one bite.

The skin of his neck stretched taut to admit me and became thin enough for light to come through, so I could see the smaller mouth and its own ring of teeth that lay at the entrance of his throat.

Strangely, although my face was slick with the abattoir's saliva, and I felt the scrape of Silver's fangs against my ear, I remained whole.

From the smaller mouth darted a tongue. Quivering, it licked my cheek. Only then did I realize the abattoir was happy to see me.

I pulled away from the secondary tongue and wriggled my head out of his mouth, emerging into bedlam. The noise of the audience, excited by what they assumed to be a lethal engagement, was deafening. Overhead the flicker of the odds boards was a colorful visual stutter. I threw myself upon Silver while telling him what a fine monster he was, that he was a very, *very* good thing. We began wrestling across the cage, first the abattoir on top, then I, then the abattoir. It was just high spirits, but to all appearances violence was being done and everyone thought we were locked in mortal combat, particularly when Silver chomped down on my wrist and wouldn't let go, as if he were about to tear my hand from my arm.

Finally I got him to lie still. To all appearances I was choking Silver to death but actually I was scratching his ear, the breadth of the fanlike organ preventing anyone from noticing what I was doing.

"It is great to see you, too, you big ugly monster," I muttered. Then I got to my feet, took the abattoir by the loose fold of skin around his neck, and dragged his sinuous length to a corner of the cage. "Sit," I told him sternly. "Sit there until I bid you leave. Good thing."

His beady eyes blinked with puzzlement but Silver decided this was a continuation of the game we were playing and he condescended to remain still, curling into a tight spiral, only his sharp muzzle protruding above the nest of quills. I turned my back on him with what I hoped was an authoritative air and raised my arms in a gesture of victory.

Only a cheer or two greeted my conquest of the abattoir, however. The odds had been against me and most of the crowd had bet the other way. There were few in the audience who hadn't lost money.

Ducking a bombardment of wadded up betting slips, I joined the Fromani brothers at the door of the cage. To a dwarf they were scowling.

Jasmine hobbled forward. After a spasm of coughing, she said, "So, One Fromani, your champion is forfeit to my own hero. Pim, dear, the animal is yours. Gather him up, why don't you, and let us be off."

Four Fromani stamped his stilts in vexation. "The Bicycle Men swore upon the Man Mother, their most fearsome oath, that the creature was vicious and untamable," he said. "We were sorely misled, brothers."

"Yes, we were."

"No question! We had the worst of the deal."

"Is that not always the case? We are eternally put upon. Ever since we were embryos in our decanters, when our parents scrimped on our nutrients."

"As if the generic amniotic supplement was halfway as good as the prescription brand."

"Well, we have taught them the error of parsimony, have we not, brothers?"

"Aye, that we have, and many times over."

"Pardon me," I said, interrupting this macabre reverie. "You bought Sil—you bought the abattoir from the Marvelous Flying Bicycle Men, right?"

Two Fromani bared his teeth, each as round as a pearl, and spat. "The barbarians sold the thing to us, yes. And at a ruinous price, besides."

"Did they have a girl with them? A young human female. She's tall, a little taller than me, with brown hair and eyes. She might have been wearing white pants and a blouse with a black sash across her waist."

Three Fromani frowned, beetling his thick brows, so the hair overhung his eyes. "There could have been one such," he answered. "But I misremember. We were only concerned with the abattoir. A young human female would have been of no interest. Would she have been, brothers?"

"No!"

"Absolutely not. Young human females are three for a mminute."

"Now if she had been an old human female—"

All four of the Fromani brothers leered at Jasmine, who blushed. "Come, dear," she told me, "fetch your new pet and let us be on our way."

"But maybe they know something more about Mirable."

"I know where your Mirable is. Now that I think upon it, there is only one place she can be."

Jasmine would say nothing further until we left the Emporium of Valor. Outside there was a full moon, bright with clouds, beneath which shone the blue of ocean. Jasmine, wheezing and mumbling, herded me by the arm into a residential neighborhood in much better repair than the commercial district. Her house was in a row of prosperous structures, each similar to the one beside it except for small architectural details, all tall and narrow and with stoops before them.

Jasmine sat me down on a couch in the parlor while she fetched a tray of sweet biscuits, as well as a hunk of bone and meat for Silver, who stretched out on a braid rug and began gnawing. Lowering herself into an overstuffed chair, Jasmine champed her gums introspectively and said:

"It isn't good news I must impart. I should have realized immediately who must have your Mirable. What do you know of Witherell Spur?"

"Nothing. I've never heard of it." Alger, likewise, couldn't access data on the place, which presumably had been founded after he had ceased receiving supplements to the *Human Library* more than a century before.

"It is a small but powerful despotism south of here in the heart of the Stangs. The title of its hereditary ruler is 'rapier', which refers, supposedly, to his valor on the battlefield." The crone's smile was introspective. "I was intimately acquainted with the former rapier, Kruuz[8], who passed away last year. He was a man of appetite and discrimination, a good friend as well as a generous patron. While I cannot testify as to his courage under fire, I can attest to the fact that his hereditary title was well-earned, if we take into account his valor at certain other kinds of . . . passages of arms."

But the smile slipped from Jasmine's lips as she went on with the story. "Kruuz[9], though, was a sneaky little boy and he matured into a devious man. I generally do not repeat gossip, but it's common knowledge that he has—" she paused—"an unusual fetish. There's little doubt his agents purchased your Mirable from the Bicycle Men. Now she is in his harem. There is no escape."

Jasmine was right. This was not good news. Unfortunately, I still hadn't learned how bad it was.

The principality was built on a spike of rock five thousand meters high, a geological wonder first noted by Horace Witherell, discoverer of Temurlone, who had sold the rights to the remarkable formation to seven different investors. This instigated eight decades of litigation, which only ended when Kruuz[1], grandson of one of the original claimants, appropriated the property by force, establishing a depot from which he imposed a toll upon all traffic through the Lesser Stangs. Fifty years later, however, a lode of iron was discovered within the Spur, and Kruuz[1]'s descendents gave up extortion in favor of mining, which was far more profitable, given the general scarcity of metal on Temurlone.

The palace of the rapier was built atop a smaller peak that rose five hundred meters above the first, a confection of spires and turrets sheathed in armor and guarded by surface-to-orbit missiles, military lasers, and a host of similar mechanisms of war.

The space around Witherell Spur was under continual electronic surveillance. The only entry was via a bank of elevators that rose up the exterior of the cliff face. This, too, was under thirty-two hour observation.

"I have to get her out of there," I said, more to myself than to Jasmine, thinking of what this rapier might have in mind although my imagination faltered at the door of the despot's private room.

"I have to get her out of there," I repeated.

Jasmine's sigh trailed off into a bubbling wheeze. "I thought you might say that. Oh, Pim, you are a brave boy but there is not a thing to be done. You could never get into the town, much less into the palace, and definitely not into the women's apartments."

Jasmine clasped my hand in her own trembling pair. "It will be hard, Pim, and perhaps you will never be able to manage it, but you must try to banish her from your thoughts. Witherell Spur is no signatory to the *Catalog*, not even to the plain text abridged version. Kruuz[9] will never let her go. He never allows any of his women to leave, and there are dozens, for he considers himself a connoisseur and collector."

"Of women?"

"Of *unusual* women. His fetish is to possess a female from each human race on Temurlone and as many from off-world as feasible, too. He is, or so I have always said, a glutton rather than a gourmet. I should have realized where your Mirable had been taken when you first told the story. But my memory is poor these days and not all it should be."

Jasmine cackled ruefully at her own frailty. "Kruuz⁹ would never overlook the chance to acquire a girl from one of the interstellar merchant clans, particularly a scion. I doubt such comes on the market once in a lifetime."

"There has to be a way in, Jasmine. There just has to be."

Her beehive of bluish white hair teetered alarmingly as she denied my wild claim. "Kruuz⁹ is as paranoid as he is avaricious. Even if you got past the elevator patrol, there are monitors throughout the town since he distrusts his own citizens, and with good reason, since he has imposed ruinous taxes in order to finance his peccadilloes. There is a separate guarded lift to the palace. The bottom floors house squads of guards, as do the top. The women's quarters and Kruuz⁹'s personal apartment are sandwiched in the middle. There is not a single window on that level. It is impenetrable."

Guilt stabbed me. I thought up fifty different schemes in half that number of seconds and discarded them all. At the back of my mind I could hear Alger, too, crunching scenarios by the thousands, his no more practical than mine. But there had to be a way to free Mirable from the seraglio of this rapier. I wouldn't accept any alternative. I had gotten her into trouble and it was my responsibility to get her out, no matter what it took.

"Surely the women can't be cut off from all men but the rapier," I said. "I could pretend to be a dressmaker, let's say, or a florist's assistant."

Jasmine shook her head. "There are few such and all must undergo meticulous screening."

Then the faintest glimmer of an idea came to me, a plan so feeble and ludicrous that I dismissed it immediately.

But Alger said, "Pardon me, sir, it is possible. And it is also the only approach in which I have more than single-digit confidence. The procedure would require several days, and your chromosomal structure would remain unchanged. Somatically, however, you would bear the closest scrutiny."

"In other words, everyone will think I am a girl."

"No, sir. You *will* be a girl in every way except genetically. Since time is of the essence, I suggest we begin the process. Allow me to dispatch molecular factories to begin manufacturing adipose tissue where appropriate. I will send others to deconstruct unnecessary appendages, release female hormones, and re-configure your lower abdominal area."

"Not so fast, Alger," I said hastily, particularly worried by the phrase "deconstruct unnecessary appendages."

"Yes, sir?"

"Can the operation be reversed?"

"Indeed, sir. Only—"

"Only what?"

"Without complete bed rest it will require substantially longer than a day or two."

"How much longer?"

"For an indeterminate period of time. Possibly a week. Or several. I do not have precise data."

I tried to convince myself that a week—or several—as a girl couldn't be that terrible. Perhaps it might even be an educational experience, allowing me insight into the feminine personality normally denied most men. Still, the entire project was unnerving and I had to think twice before reluctantly authorizing Alger to proceed. Although I was sure the sensation was psychosomatic, I soon felt a twinge in my groin. I tried to ignore it and not to dwell on what the molecular factories were doing to my internal and external organs and to my chemical balance.

Aloud, I said: "There *is* a way in, Jasmine. You have to be asked."

"Why, Pim, whatever do you mean? Kruuz[9] is not a gracious host, and sponsors few banquets or soirees, unlike his father, who was a true bon vivant. I sincerely doubt either of us will be invited to the palace any time soon."

"That's where you're wrong, Jasmine. Not if what you said about his peccadilloes—" I winced at the sound of the word, and the perversions it conjured up "—is true. We'll be invited, all right. Or at least I will."

As I leaned forward and explained the plan, an irrepressible twinkle sparked in the crone's red-rimmed eyes. "Why, Pim, it's a rash scheme and wildly improbable, but 'tis sufficiently daring to have a chance of success. Imagine, most lovers would give their life for their love, but you, Pim, you are surrendering your—"

"Nothing, ma'am," I said hastily, not wanting to dwell on the distasteful subject. "Nothing whatever. The procedure is reversible, that's what Alger says. In any case, Mirable's not my lover, and I am not hers."

"Not yet, Pim. Not yet." Jasmine hid her giggle behind the palm of a hand. "But I fear my teasing is embarrassing you, so we will change the subject. I wish I could speak directly with this personal assistant of yours, Alger. He seems like a useful and intelligent device and I would like to thank him for all he's done on your behalf."

"That is unnecessary, madam," Alger replied in a voice so human you'd never guess it was being generated by hidden speakers in the bracelet on my wrist. "I am, as may have been mentioned, of aristocracy-grade manufacture, handcrafted by Bandar Bush Technologies of El Paso, Texas, Old Earth, in the year A.I. 160. I am thus capable of both a cognitive and an emotional response to my environment. I take great pride in being of assistance to those I am fortunate to serve."

"I did not know you could talk out loud, Alger," I exclaimed, this being the first time I had heard his voice with my ears and not my mind.

"I have many capabilities of which you may or may not be aware, sir," he answered. "Would you care for me to enumerate them?"

"Another time," I said hastily, fearing the consequences of giving him free rein to talk about himself.

"As you wish, sir."

"Now don't you worry," Jasmine told Alger. "We'll chat later. You must have a hundred fascinating stories to tell, don't you, dear, and I would so very much enjoy hearing them all. Daring escapades in the space lanes, high intrigue in the mercantile boardrooms, romantic assignations below deck between the stars."

"It is true, madam," Alger replied, "that I am an experienced traveler and have associated with many important personages. I would take pleasure in sharing my adventures with you in greater or lesser detail."

"How perfectly marvelous. Not now, though, you have work to do, helping our Pim with his, why, with his little metamorphosis. Later, though, I promise. Perhaps Pim could loan you to me for a time, so that we could communicate more closely."

I told myself that it was a nervous twitch brought on by old age that caused Jasmine's left eye to close briefly and reopen, and not a seductive wink.

I had to be wrong. Surely she wasn't flirting with my personal assistant, aristocracy grade.

That night I slept on a bed softer than any I had rested on, covered by a comforter decorated with hand-stitched embroidery of amphibians and blue stilt-legged birds. Looking at myself in the mirror in the ceiling, I tried to make out changes in my features but did not see a difference, no matter how I stared at my reflection. I kept my hands above the spread, through an intense effort of will stopping myself from exploring my body in order to discover if the change had started. Eventually, however, I drifted off to sleep, Silver curled at the foot of the mattress, an untidy mess of spikes from which issued the rumble of snoring.

Alger deepened my slumber with a soporific so that I slept all through the day and into the next evening. He did this, he explained later, not because the procedure was physically painful but to spare me psychological distress while my internal and external organs were rearranged.

When I awoke, nothing was the same.

My center of gravity had shifted. Walking was difficult and I stumbled twice on the way to the lavatory. Where I encountered other problems.

Jasmine tottered from the kitchen with a platter of hot pink meat and fried eggs with green yolks. "Why, you are a pretty chit," she exclaimed. "Silly of me, but I should have known a handsome boy would make a lovely girl. Exotic, too, the way Kruuz[9] likes his women." I did not want to hear this. "Yes, Pimsol," Jasmine went on, "I am beginning to think you just might succeed, if you have courage. But of course you do. It is all so exciting."

Silver returned from a stroll and shook his quills violently. Some cue, perhaps olfactory, alerted him to my transformation. With a curious whine, the abattoir poked his nose against my groin and sniffed.

A bell chimed. "Oh, that would be Marmo," Jasmine explained.

"Sweetie, I know you must be tired after what you've gone through, so you rest here. Make yourself at home. I will be an hour or three, since Marmo is importunate and jealous of my company, the naughty rogue. If you become bored, the library is just down the hall."

Jasmine tottered off. Presently I heard her voice and that of a man, presumably Marmo, although I couldn't make out what they were saying. There was the clink of crystal against crystal, the suggestion of laughter. Then a door closed and the house became quiet.

Eventually I grew restless and went to the library. There was a fireplace against one wall but the other three were lined with shelves holding ranks of leather-bound volumes, some containing text, others audio and video recordings. Usually my inclination would have been to choose an adventure story or a thriller but now I was more intrigued by such titles as "Stolen Kisses Under Four Moons" or "The Embrace of the Dark Pirate." Maybe it was the hormones with which Alger was flooding my bloodstream that made me take "Love's Last Request" from the shelf, slip the book into a player, and curl up in an overstuffed chair opposite the screen.

I hoped it was the hormones. I did not like to think that I was actually enjoying what I watched

As the closing credits rolled away, the library door opened and Marmo poked his head through the opening and peered at me suspiciously. "Who might you be?" he asked.

"My great-grandniece," Jasmine answered, coming up behind him and putting her hand on his arm. "Pamsal stopped by to visit her old auntie while on her way to Witherell Spur. She has a scholarship to the Metallurgical College, isn't that fabulous! She's a smart girl and I am proud of her."

Marmo snorted noncommittally, unimpressed by my accomplishments. This evening he was wearing a suit of dark green twill, a fancy striped ascot loosely knotted around his neck. His hair, which had been pomaded in proud waves the first time I had met him, was now disarranged, particularly around the neural input at the base of his skull. I noticed, too, that the pins in Jasmine's white hair were in different places than they'd been before.

Marmo glanced around doubtfully. "Where is that other friend of yours?" he sniffed. "The boy you were with yesterday? The off worlder."

I let go of the sigh of relief I hadn't known I was holding. The transformation had been successful. Marmo showed me not the slightest sign of recognition.

"Marmo, please, I am growing tired of these little jealousies of yours, however endearing."

Marmo drew himself up to his full height, smoothed out his hair with a dramatic gesture, and somehow managed to look affronted. "Please, you do me a disservice," he told Jasmine. "I am simply concerned with your well being. I wouldn't want you to become embroiled with such an unsavory character."

"Whatever do you mean?" Jasmine hobbled to a sideboard and filled minuscule glasses with wine from a decanter.

"A posse of Marvelous Flying Bicycle Men arrived in town yesterday with an arrest warrant for a certain 'P. Anderts, notable ne'er-do-well of dubious origin', and with a description that fitted your friend exactly. Nonio Wellmete, the tribal hetman, applied to the Civic Council for a writ of extradition, which is how I came to be involved, since as you know I have a seat on the Council. Anderts is accused of heinous crimes and they desire to take him back to the plains to face Tribal Law."

"What precisely do they claim Pim did? If it is Pim they are actually looking for and not someone else altogether."

"The charges are aggravated trespassing, escape to evade persecution, grand theft bicycle, desecration of a religious shrine, and manslaughter. I believe that the penalty, should your friend be found guilty, would be drawing and quartering, followed by trampling, and then by internment in an aca refuse pit. Afterward the Bicycle Men would compose an insulting ballad in his honor and ridicule his memory for decades to come."

"But you did not provide them with the writ, did you, sweetie?"

"Of course not, Jasmine, despite their generous offer of ten tonnes of prime tenderloin. For one thing, I would never wish to vex you, no matter how you tease me. For another, Tribal Law isn't compatible with Bureau regulations, not even with the *Abridged Standard Catalog*. We would lose our subscriber status should we accede to their request, which would be economic catastrophe. No, I refused them the writ and furthermore, in my capacity as chief constable, instructed the Bicycle Men not to have any contact with your friend within the city limits."

"You did that for me, Marmo? I am touched."

"Thank you, my lady. Unfortunately, I doubt the Bicycle Men took my words to heart. They are sure to try something underhanded at the first opportunity and I cannot spare the manpower to put them under surveillance. Your friend should maintain a careful distance from dark alleys and keep an eye open until he is sure the savages have left town."

Finishing the wine, Jasmine and Marmo once again retired to her boudoir, leaving me alone in the library.

My worst fears had been realized, or so I thought.

The Marvelous Flying Bicycle Men were coming after me personally. Not only had they learned of my escape from the leuks through the grove of the Man Mother, they'd also figured out my role in Pilar Goodfellow's demise and that I had absconded with one of their planes. It was ominous news, too, that Nonio Wellmete himself headed the delegation that had tracked me across the Darwin Wastes to Churraspora. Apparently I had made a mortal enemy of the tribal chieftain and that was not a good development, not knowing what I did about how the Bicycle Men held grudges.

They'd never put aside the vendetta, not until I was cut into pieces, trampled upon, submerged in crap, and ridiculed in verse and song.

At that moment the front door chimed. I was about to learn how wrong I had been. My worst fears were nowhere near realized, not by half.

Jasmine and Marmo emerged from the boudoir and Marmo left the house through a secondary entrance, which had been constructed so that Jasmine's patrons could avoid meeting each other while arriving to sample her favors or departing after having enjoyed them. The ancient courtesan went to the front door and flicked on the exterior video feed. Her sharp intake of breath warned me something was not right.

"What is it?" I asked while hurrying to her side as fast as I could given my new center of gravity and unsteadiness on my feet. I wobbled.

"I do believe a friend of yours is visiting, Pamsal," she said. "Your description did him little justice, though. He is more terrible than I could ever have imagined."

Outside, a massive construction of hardened alloy and battle-scarred flesh, was Captain Hartung.

Green and gold streaks shot through his red eyes. The pirate was losing patience at being kept waiting in the vestibule like a common vendor or tradesman. He put his thumb on the buzzer and pressed down hard until the plastic surrounding the button cracked.

"What would you have me do, dear?" Jasmine asked. "We cannot just ignore him forever. I sincerely doubt he will go away on his own."

"Ask him what he wants. Maybe he's here on—" I did not know how to complete the sentence "—on a social call."

"Why, you could be right. It is not as if I am unknown to sailors," Jasmine said modestly, as if she weren't the most desirable woman in all the city, with a reputation that reached across Temurlone and to the nearer stars. She keyed on the audio. "Who are you, sir, and why are you here without an appointment?"

The pirate looked directly into the video feed. "The name is Hartung, madam. Captain Felix Hartung. You have my apologies for calling unannounced but time is of the essence and I am in haste. I have come about a beast that is in your possession."

"I own many pets," Jasmine replied. "Could you be more specific?"

"The creature is known as an abattoir."

As if understanding that he was being discussed, Silver padded over and rubbed his leathery skull against my leg. Then, somehow sensing Hartung's presence, his quills rose from his body and he peered suspiciously at the entrance while growling. Silver remembered Captain Hartung, all right, and the monster did not care for the cyborg pirate the least bit. Hartung had threatened his mistress.

"We don't have a choice, Jasmine," I told her, "we'll have to let Hartung in."

"What if he recognizes you?"

"Small chance of that," I answered with more confidence than I felt. "He won't, I am certain of it. Well, almost certain. Marmo didn't. I'm not Pimsol, I'm Pamsal. I'm a girl, remember? Hartung's not after me, anyway. He's not after Silver, either. It is Mirable he wants. He needs her as a hostage to leverage a way back aboard the *Abernathy* and to open the captain's locker. That's why he's here. He's tracking me and Silver in order to track her. We have to send him off on a false trail."

"Oh, you clever girl!" Jasmine exclaimed. "That is exactly what we shall do. This is all so much fun. Why, I almost feel a hundred again!"

Grabbing Silver by his collar, I dragged the beast into the library and bade him remain at my feet as I sat on the couch. Jasmine opened the front entrance and faced Captain Hartung, looking up at him sternly while leaning forward on her cane. "I warn you, sir," she informed the pirate without a quaver in her voice, "that you are in the cross hairs of my household defensive engines. Any inappropriate behavior will be lethally admonished."

"Please, madam," Hartung replied suavely, "you must have me confused with another person of evil reputation. Should I have wished you harm, I would not have appeared on your doorstep alone and without companions. No, I am a simple spacefarer, surviving God's humor as best I may."

"Come, come, Captain Hartung," Jasmine answered while leading the pirate into the house. "You are no common sailor. I have heard stories of your cleverness and derring-do! Your cunning and ruthlessness are legend. Your deeds make me blush with shame."

"And I, madam, have heard stories of your own, *exploits* shall we say? Stories that make me wish to see *you* blush with shame."

Such gallantry, coming from a fiend like Felix Hartung, made me uneasy. There was no guessing what such a desperado wanted.

"Unfortunately," he continued, "important business prevents me from deepening our acquaintance. I require information. Ah, yes, that is the beast."

Hartung stepped into the library but displayed common sense by remaining on the side of the room opposite where I sat with Silver. The pirate eyed the abattoir without friendship. Then he looked me up and down. The antenna array extruding from his skull whirred briefly. Alger said:

"Sir, you are being scanned on a variety of frequencies. I have, however, deployed countermeasures and evaded detection. Due to my vigilance, no action is required on your part."

The pirate turned to Jasmine. "Where is the lad who won the animal at the Emporium of Valor?" he asked. "Do not dissemble, madam, for I know you are acquainted. I have had the story from the Fromani brothers. They believe they have been cozened although they are unsure as to the precise method."

Jasmine refused to be intimidated by the amalgamation of metal and flesh crowding her library. "What is your interest in the boy?" she asked.

"I intend him no injury, if that's what you mean," answered Hartung. "To the contrary! Not long ago the lad sought to enlist in my company. At the time I refused him, believing him too callow to meet the minimum standards I require of my companions. Later, however, I had the opportunity to observe his behavior under adverse conditions. He impressed me favorably, madam, and I reconsidered my decision. Unfortunately, however, we were separated, and I have been seeking him to extend an offer of employment."

The pirate captain was so persuasive that I half believed him myself. "That's not true at all," I exclaimed to Jasmine, forgetting I was supposed to be somebody else. "Do not listen to him. The brute is lying."

Felix Hartung's eyes burned with a red glow as he regarded me. "Who might you be, lass," he said, antennas softly humming. "How would you have any idea as to what is true and what is not."

"Do not be alarmed, sir," Alger put in, "but your internal structure is being mapped by ultrasonic radar. Evidently Captain Hartung is double-checking that you are actually what you appear to be."

"This isn't alarming?"

"Of course not. Remember that I am an aristocracy-grade device. Through my meticulous efforts you are not only a girl on the outside, sir, but fully female internally as well."

This encouraging news reminded me of the role I was playing. "I am Miss Jasmine's niece, not that it's any of your concern," I answered captain Hartung, my heart beating furiously at having to face the monstrous apparition once again, and as a girl. Ignoring the ridiculous blush coloring my cheeks, I said, "As for what I know, why, I heard the whole story from Pim himself. You're nothing but a common thug, that's what he said, with gruesome particulars to prove it."

Captain Hartung ignored this unkind description. "So where is the lad?" he asked genially, taking a step toward me, which caused Silver to lurch against my hold in an effort to free himself and attack the corsair.

"He's not here, that's all I will say."

"I wonder, lass, what would induce you to say more."

"Captain Hartung, please! Remember my remarks concerning the household defensive engines." Jasmine placed her hand on the pirate's metal forearm. "Neither my niece nor myself know where Pim has gone. He was careful not to say since he is being tracked by a posse of Marvelous Flying Bicycle Men and does not wish to leave a trail. Many caravans depart Churraspora every day in several directions, both by ground and by air. Your guess is as good as mine as to which one he took."

"And the beast, madam?" Hartung asked, referring to the abattoir. "Why is it not with the boy?"

"Come, come, captain! What would be more conspicuous than such an animal? He had to leave it behind. We promised to take good care of the silly monster until Pim can send for it safely."

"And when would that be, madam?"

"Why, when he's aboard the—"

Jasmine caught herself, pretending to have spoken too freely and to have inadvertently revealed my—that is, Pim's—intentions to the pirate.

"The *Miraculous Abernathy*," said Captain Hartung, finishing Jasmine's sentence. "Thank you, madam. I had not realized that the boy was attempting to rendezvous with the ship. That makes my task simpler. Tell me, was he by any chance accompanied by a young woman, a lass somewhat taller than your niece and more fully proportioned?"

"Captain, you ask too much. I have been overly frank already and will say nothing further. Will you depart or must I summon the constabulary to escort you out?"

That Jasmine dared threaten Felix Hartung to his face filled me with such admiration for the ancient crone that tears came to my eyes. Yet the awful pirate, believing that he now held the information he had come for, simply made a suave gesture and allowed Jasmine to herd him to the entrance. As she closed the door after him, she cackled quietly. "Your captain Hartung is not quite as bright as he thinks he is," she said. "Now he will search for you everywhere but at Witherell Spur."

"Why's that? And why did you want Hartung to assume I was trying to get back to the *Abernathy*?"

"Because there is no air traffic over the Spur, that's why, dear," she explained. "Kruuz[9] shoots down any vessels that stray overhead.

You would never reach your ship from there. Now come, it's time to make you look pretty. We'll have to decide on an outfit, too."

"Jasmine, you said Kruuz[9] likes exotic women?"

"Absolutely, Pim. He gets bored easily and enjoys variety."

"I am obviously not from around here, so we have that going for us, but let's make sure to really get his attention. Why don't we say I am from—from Earth? What could be more exotic?"

"A marvelous idea! Oh, I wonder what the girls are wearing on Old Earth now? Well, I suppose it doesn't matter. Kruuz[9] certainly won't have any idea."

Jasmine led me to her own room and opened a walk-in closet. Within were a hundred costumes, some real, some whimsical, as well as shelves of other feminine accoutrements, including manual and automatic devices whose nature I did not care to dwell on. Jasmine sighed nostalgically. "Now, Pimsol," she said, taking a tube of color and squeezing a dab on my lips, "leave everything in my hands. You will be exquisite, trust me."

It was difficult getting into the tight robe she selected since Alger had re-proportioned my waist, hips, and chest. Jasmine combed back my hair, securing it in place with fragrant gel, and hung gemstones from my earlobes. When she was finished, I couldn't recognize myself in the girl who mimicked my every gesture. Inside, though, I was the same Pim Anderts I had always been, or thought I was, I hoped, despite appearances. We returned to Jasmine's personal office and the crone keyed on a communications panel. In another demonstration of her influence, the rapier of Witherell Spur personally answered the call.

CHAPTER ELEVEN
The Two Rapiers

Once upon a time there were three thingamajigs who lived all warm and snuggly in their father's pouch. But the thingamajigs were growing and soon they were tripping over each other and poking one another in the eye, sometimes accidentally. It was quite uncomfortable. There simply was not room. So the largest thingamajig pushed the tiniest out of the pouch into the cold cruel world. The remaining two sisters curled up happily. Only they kept growing and soon the problem resurfaced. The largest thingamajig had to push out the middle thingamajig, too.

At last the largest thingamajig became too big for the pouch and was forced to go out into the cold cruel world herself.

She scampered here and there until she came to where the tiniest thingamajig lived. This sister had worked hard and invested wisely and owned a solid burrow with a stout wood lid. She poked her snout from her front mound and said:

"What brings you knocking, sister of mine?"

"Memories of good times all warm and snuggly together in the pouch of our father," answered the largest thingamajig. "Allow me to stay the night for there are evil creatures a prowl, who would enjoy nothing better than a bit of tasty thingamajig."

"I, too, remember those warm and snuggly times," answered the tiniest thingamajig. "I also recall when you pushed me into the cold cruel world. Go your way, largest sister. I will not help you."

So the largest thingamajig scampered here and there until she came to where the middle thingamajig lived. This sister had worked harder than the first and made wiser investments and now owned a stately mound with scroll work around the lid.

"What brings you knocking, sister of mine?" she asked.

"Memories of good times all warm and snuggly together," answered the largest thingamajig. "Allow me to stay the night."

"I, too, remember those warm and snuggly times," answered the middle thingamajig. "I also recall when you pushed me into the cold cruel world. Go your way, sister. I will not help."

So the largest thingamajig spent the night in a tree while below prowled all sorts of creatures who would enjoy nothing better than a bit of tasty thingamajig. She did not sleep a wink.

By morning the largest thingamajig had realized several important truths. Being warm and snuggly was not a right but a condition achieved through effort. What is more, remembering how she had pushed out her sisters into the cold cruel world, she realized being warm and snuggly was a condition achieved at the expense of others.

So the largest thingamajig worked diligently until she saved enough money to open her own shop. Then she worked even harder, wrote a business plan, attracted venture capitalists, and brought the company public. Three years later the largest thingamajig exercised her stock options and achieved financial independence. She retired to her mansion and devoted her leisure time to ruining her sisters' lives. At last she was warm and snuggly again.

"The Story of the Three Thingamajigs," collected in:
Kelocca Wit and Wisdom: The Importance of Being Capitalist

Kruuz Chung Pao[9] was a burly man with a pert beard under a drooping nose, spots of rouge on both cheeks, and a hard glint in his small white eyes, which slid past Jasmine to fix on me with disturbing intensity.

"Well, well," he said. "What have we here, old woman?"

"Old woman, is it? I would mind my tongue, if I were you, you nasty child. Your dear father, Kruuz[8], would never have permitted such behavior."

Ignoring Jasmine's admonition, the despot said, "May I remind you, my esteemed father is no longer numbered among the cast of characters of our universe of miracles. It is only to honor his memory that I speak with you and I do so at my convenience. Quickly now, what do you want?"

I did not like hearing Kruuz[9] address Jasmine with such disrespect but I kept my face immobile while trying to look seductive. I had no idea what effect I was achieving and did not really care to find out. I felt myself blushing at my own awkwardness and feeling a little breathless. Jasmine pinched my chin and tilted my face to one side.

"I will be direct," she said. "Certain associates and I accepted this merchandise as partial fulfillment of a commercial obligation. She is of no use in Churraspora, of course, although she is bonded for transshipment[1]. I thought of you immediately."

"It is good you did! Where are you from, girl?" The rapier of Witherell Spur was addressing me. "I have never seen your sort be-

---

1   Churraspora was signatory to the *Standard Interstellar Catalog of Sentient Rights*, and its bylaws outlawed slavery. The warehousing and passage of intelligent merchandise in transit to other locations, however, were specifically sanctioned since the city derived municipal revenue through the taxation of such goods.

fore and I am knowledgeable of women. You are not from Temurlone."

Lying wildly, I resorted to the ruse we had settled on earlier. If Kruuz[9] desired exotic women, I would be from that most exotic place of all. "You are discerning, sir," I flattered him. "I am from Earth."

"From Old Earth? Now that is intriguing. And why have you journeyed so far from home?"

"It is a sad tale," I answered, lowering my eyes from his gaze. Did all men regard women with such fascination? I wondered, hoping I had never looked at Mirable the same way, or if I had, that I had hidden it well. "I could share the story with you when we are alone together and have sufficient privacy," I finished in as suggestive a voice as I could muster. Was I being too obsequious? Not at all, judging by the satisfied tone in which Kruuz[9] replied:

"Entirely possible, my dear. More than possible! I will make a notation on my calendar."

Kruuz[9] and Jasmine began negotiating my sale. Each disparaged the other with real animosity and several times swore to abandon the deal altogether, glaring furiously at each other through the vision pane. When the rapier hung up, however, I had been sold to him at the ruinous price of seven yyears, seven mmonths, and seven ddays—an exorbitant fee, many multiples the cost of my indenture to the *Abernathy*. Jasmine gave a happy cackle.

"Normally Kruuz[9] drives a harder bargain," she said, "but it is clear he is besotted with you, Pimsol. From Old Earth, indeed—that was just the perfect touch. You are a bright girl indeed!"

In the morning we went down to the caravanserai, leaving Silver behind. He hadn't liked it but there was no way I could bring him with me. Kruuz[9], meticulous about personal security, would never allow such a fearsome creature into his presence. Jasmine promised to look after the abattoir until I returned to Churraspora, an optimistic assumption if there ever was one, but I had to believe that I would free Mirable from the rapier.

My wrists were secured by a thin gold chain, more a token of my status than a real barrier to freedom. Using her cane to good advantage, Jasmine cleared a path through the throng to the convoy that would deliver me to Witherell Spur. This consisted of twenty or so of the peculiar trucks I had noticed earlier, which had legs instead of wheels. The bodies of the vehicles were suspended from gimbals, allowing the cabs to remain on an even keel while clambering into the Lesser Stangs like giant spider crabs.

Jasmine placed me in the charge of the caravan master, a stout man with leathery skin and a mustache waxed in thin upward spikes. Counou Efraim had been anticipating our arrival and immediately led us to the fourth truck in line, which was fitted out for passengers instead of freight. "The rapier reserved the entire car for the use of the lady," he said, meaning me, as he opened the door with a flourish, allowing us to enter a cabin large enough for a dozen passengers. "My directions are that she is to want for nothing. There is a pantry at the rear, as well as personal facilities. This intercom communicates with the driver in the cab. This button summons me directly, should the need arise."

After some further instructions, the caravan master returned to his business. Jasmine pressed her wrinkled cheek to mine and then held me at arm's length while looking into my eyes. Maybe she saw nervousness there. I hoped it was not fear.

"Have courage, dear," she told me. "Remember, God enjoys nothing better than a fine performance. Be yourself and all will be well."

"That's just it. I am not myself, am I? I have never been a girl before. Maybe I will get it wrong."

Jasmine's laugh was decades younger than her age. "Silly! There's nothing to get wrong, Pim. Inside we're all the same, neither man nor woman, just character actors at an audition. Gender is skin deep, signifying nothing. Who should know better?" she asked, patting her beehive hairdo and the neural interface with which she had become emotionally and physically intimate with hundreds, if not thousands, of other people. "Look into yourself and you will be the best girl you can be."

Twenty minutes later the truck got to its knees with a groaning of gears. The cabin swung free of the ground, suspended beneath the crab-like legs.

Counou Efraim sped up and down the length of the convey in a footed scooter, chivvying the drivers into order with ribald comments, chasing off lingering hangers-on and camp followers, and encouraging loaders to stow the last remaining packages and containers aboard the caravan. Leaning out the cabin window, I waved to Jasmine, who was peering up at the truck. As she lifted her cane in a gesture of farewell, I felt a strange ache. We had barely met and already she had become a friend, yet it was unlikely we would ever meet again. According to Alger, my enterprise had less than a 34 percent chance of success.

"Actually, sir, I am pleased to be able to inform you that I have revised my estimate upward."

"That's great, Alger."

"Yes, sir. Your acclimation to the female gender has proceeded faster than I originally predicted, which increases my confidence in the overall success of our venture. May I congratulate you on your resiliency, sir."

"You heard what Jasmine said, Alger. Inside we're all alike. I doubt it's any great achievement."

"That is my opinion as well. However, I now calculate the likelihood that we will free Miss Mirable at 34.098 percent. Even more heartening, I now believe we have a 34.027 percent chance of escaping alive."

For two days the truck ascended the mountains along precarious zigzagging switchbacks.

On either side was evergreen forest. The aisles between the trunks were carpeted with fallen needles, which had turned blue as they dried, reminding me of underwater grottoes back home. Once we were trailed by a pack of hulking wolves, who went along on three feet, yelping with abandon, until Counou Efraim and the caravan guards drove them off into the woods.

Occasionally the convoy climbed above the tree line into broad vistas of grass, naked rock, talus and scoriae and snow, permitting a view of more precipitous terrain ahead. The second morning, as we surmounted another ridge line, I caught sight of Witherell Spur: a perpendicular spear of stone rising toward the stratosphere. Clouds obscured its upper reaches. Snow and mist smeared in a broad streak away from the spur by the wind.

At the base of the crag was an expanse of pavement on which hundreds of trucks and other vehicles were parked in orderly rows in front of a border station, a hardened blockhouse with shielded gunnery ports and an impressive array of military electronics. This was staffed by a platoon of soldiers in gray uniforms and black helmets.

Right against the wall of the Spur was a bank of passenger and commercial elevators, some large enough to hold an entire truck, legs and all.

Most of the descending freight consisted of flatbeds of ore, the basis of the principality's wealth.

Hundreds of pedestrians and vehicles waited in line before the checkpoint while customs officers thoroughly inspected each one before passing them through to the elevators. Grandly ignoring the dark glares shot our way, Counou Efraim escorted me directly to the head of the line. He flourished a document before the lieutenant in command.

"Special delivery for the rapier himself," said the caravan master.

"Another? That's the second this month."

The lieutenant barely glanced at the paper before signing it. Then he detailed two privates to accompany me past the border station, into an elevator, and up to the town. Perhaps due to the flimsiness and translucency of the outfit in which Jasmine had dressed me, I was given no more than a cursory inspection at the checkpoint. But as the elevator doors closed upon us, Alger said:

"Sir, I do not wish to cause unnecessary alarm, but we are undergoing a complex electronic scan."

This was not unexpected. However, my whole plan, rash as it was, depended on Alger remaining undetected.

"Can you handle it?" I asked.

"I am, in your words, sir, already handling it. The stealth technology with which I am equipped, despite being somewhat dated, is still sophisticated enough to confuse the hardware that has us under surveillance. As I may have mentioned, it was state of the art at the time of my manufacture by Bandar Bush Technologies."

"Yes, Alger, you have mentioned that fact."

It never occurred to me that Alger was attempting to take my mind off the peril we were in.

The elevator, a vertical monorail secured to the face of the spur, sped upward in a rush of velocity. In the distance I had a clear view of the Lesser Stangs stretching into the infinity that was the horizon of Temurlone, gleaming caps of snow blinding in the afternoon light, banks of mist spilling like rivers down the flanks of the mountains. I kept expecting my escorts, alerted by the scanners, to take hold of my arms and strip Alger from my wrist but they remained impassive until the elevator came to a stop.

The peak of Witherell Spur was a circular depression kilometers in diameter surrounded by cliffs hundreds of meters higher still. This geological configuration protected the valley from extremes of weather and provided the Spur with a pleasant climate despite its altitude. In the center was the mine upon which the economy of the principality was based, an immense pit the color of rust. Around it were smelters and mills, industrial structures dwarfed by comparison to the mine. Beyond them were several modest residential and commercial neighborhoods. At the far end of the valley was the palace of the rapier, a hardened fortress surmounting the rim wall of the spur.

The soldiers commandeered an electric jitney and we proceeded from the elevator depot along a paved road that followed the lip of the mine for at least a kilometer. Then the road curved and we approached the palace.

This was reached by another elevator. We were scanned a second time as we ascended but Alger was again able to evade detection.

The entrance to the harem resembled nothing so much as the captain's locker aboard the *Miraculous Abernathy*, a massive door able to resist all but the heaviest weaponry. My guards removed the chain from my wrists and remained behind as the door swung open and I stepped into the seraglio.

I hadn't known what to expect but the harem seemed more like a modern office than a den of carnal excess.

The central room was equipped with data terminals at which sat a dozen or so young women, each dissimilar to her neighbor in dress and physical appearance, testimony to the eclectic taste of the rapier. Hallways radiated off the main chamber, leading to residential quarters, kitchens, laundries, recreation rooms, a video theater, a medical unit, and a gymnasium. A separate door, equally as durable as the front entrance, led to Kruuz[9]'s personal apartment.

Noticing my arrival, a plump girl with a dot of beard on her chin came over in a tinkling of tiny bells, which were sewn to the seams of her pajamas. "Welcome," she said. "I am Virginia Dee."

"I am Pamsal, Pamsal Anderts," I replied with hardly any hesitation, having rehearsed my false name and spurious background during the journey from Churraspora.

"Pamsal Anderts," Virginia said, taking my bags and herding me along while the other girls smiled and waved from their data consoles. "We are all so curious," she continued. "Imagine, you are from Old Earth. Kruuz[9] said so. You must be ever so wicked and decadent, Pamsal. We cannot wait to hear about Parii and Karachi and Bayjin and the fabulous sights you have seen. Can you imagine, some of the girls do not believe there is such a world, considering it only legend."

"Yes, Virginia, there is an Earth," I answered, allowing myself to be led to the room that would be mine. Stroking her beard idly while I unpacked, she prattled on with well meaning advice in an effort to make me feel at home. "It is not the life I would have chosen," Virginia continued, "but it is still better than the one in store for me. My parents are sharecroppers and I would have been one, too." She shuddered delicately and held out her palms, which were dyed a rich orange yellow. "It has been four years and I still have calluses on my thumbs from throttling the rattleberry bushes day in and day out. They are half animal, you see, and do not expire gracefully. Anyway," she finished, "I am sure you will fit right in. If you have questions, or need anything, anything at all, just ask."

"Kruuz[9]? What is he like?"

With an almost imperceptible flicker of her eyes, Virginia Dee let me know there was an observation device in the ceiling. "Oh, he is an interesting man," she said. "Handsome, virile, and statesman-like. And he is as considerate as he is practical. You noticed how busy the girls are? Well, Kruuz[9] feared we might become bored and kindly suggested that useful work would relieve the tedium. Together we manage the operation of the mine, performing the accounting, marketing, human resources, and public affairs functions."

"Bored?" I mused, my imagination limited by my inexperience. "How many girls are there, Virginia? Dozens? I wouldn't suppose Kruuz[9] would have time or energy to spare for any one person in particular."

She giggled. "Oh, no, Pamsal, that is not the case, most definitely. Not wishing to disappoint us, for he is solicitous of our physical needs, Kruuz[9] employs certain practical augmentations, which enable him to indulge himself as often and for as long as he wants in the appreciation of his collection, which is to say, in us."

This distressing thought remained at the forefront of my mind as we returned to the main room, arriving just when the door to the despot's private apartment opened and Kruuz[9] himself strode through. With a minatory expression that discouraged easy conversation, the rapier surveyed the activity going on around him, gave a quick nod upon finding all as it should be, and then approached Virginia and me. His robe was open at the front, revealing a pair of loose briefs and a tidy little belly, which he scratched while running his pale white eyes from my ankles to my forehead and over everything in between.

"You made excellent time coming from Churraspora," Kruuz[9] observed. "I was not expecting you until tomorrow."

"The trip seemed to take forever," I replied, trying to be at once flirtatious and shy, a combination irresistible to the despot, or so Jasmine had assured me. "I was so looking forward to our meeting."

"Were you? That is pleasant to hear. It disturbs me when one of my acquisitions is truculent. I cannot sleep until the situation is remedied. This, sadly, can be a lengthy process."

"Who could ever be so foolish and ungrateful?" I asked, attempting to sound aghast, and probably doing a good job of it, too, for I was disgusted by what I had been told and worried about Mirable. I had seen no sign of her.

"Who could be so foolish? Why, I will tell you. A stubborn tart with a high opinion of herself, that's who," Kruuz[9] answered spitefully, now scratching the underside of his arm instead of his stomach. "As if the attentions of the rapier of Witherell Spur were beneath notice. Well, well. Miss Wirthy will come to understand how grave an error she has made."

"Wirthy? Mirable Wirthy?" I asked with a pretense of astonishment, at once relieved I had finally learned where Mirable was, and at the same time horrified by what she must be enduring. It required all my self-control not to order Alger to shoot the despot right then and there but I needed him alive, much as I wanted him dead.

"Yes, that is her name. You are acquainted?"

"I sailed to Temurlone on the *Miraculous Abernathy*, a freighter owned by the Wirthy clan," I replied, telling the rapier the exact truth and not a word more. "Mirable and I were introduced but did not become close, for she was haughty and distant, and I, well, let us say I was not her social equal, considering my circumstances."

Back home girls preferred boys with gills. This was only natural, considering the girls had gills, too, but even so it was a major frustration to me while growing up. It also meant I had had little experience with the opposite sex. So I had no idea how I knew what to say next. It simply came to me. Maybe the knowledge was built into the body Alger had created, integral to the feminine form. But maybe not. Maybe I was tapping into fantasies of my own. I met Kruuz''s gaze briefly and then lowered mine.

"As you know, I am from Earth, an old world with a long history," I went on. "My grandmother instructed me in certain ancient traditions, handed down among the women of our family from generation to generation, and I know pleasant games we could play that might convince Mirable Wirthy to—" I batted my eyelashes and peered aslant at the despot. "You would enjoy watching us, I should imagine," I finished coyly.

The rapier's white eyes were alight as he reflected upon the decadence of Old Earth.

"As you say, that could be interesting," he admitted, taking my arm and leading me through the hardened metal door into his private chamber. "Informative, too."

Here the décor contrasted sharply with the functional layout of the harem proper. Instead of work consoles and utilitarian furniture, the place was equipped with an assortment of plush divans, pillows, swings, and complicated structures whose functions were not immediately obvious. The lighting was soft and unfocused. Pinpoint spots illuminated a statue in the center of the room, a full-scale rendition of a man carved from marble, standing on a silver pedestal with his arms held before him, an expression of fury frozen on his face, which resembled Kruuz⁹'s own visage more than a little.

Noticing my interest in the statue, the rapier explained, "My esteemed father. A boring and contentious fellow, when all is said and done. I keep him there as a reminder of how I disliked him, so I may better appreciate the fact he is gone."

I hardly heard the rapier. I was looking at Mirable. She filled my eyes and I couldn't pay attention to anything else. She was lying on her back upon a couch, her wrists and ankles bound by silken cords, a silken gag across her mouth, wearing nothing at all. I felt my ears and the nape of my neck burning. I wanted to avert my gaze and yet I could have stared at her for hours exactly as she was. I wondered why I should be feeling such disquieting emotions now Mirable and I shared the same sex. But I had no time to consider the question, however, since Kruuz⁹ was waving me forward.

"I am curious about these ancient techniques of your grandmother's," he said, reclining on a nearby lounge. "Earth must be a fascinating world, this I can believe."

"Alger?" I thought.

"The room is free of surveillance, sir, except for the obvious cameras." He meant the recording devices focused on Mirable.

I knelt beside her. Above the gag her eyes flickered angrily back and forth between Kruuz⁹ and me. I placed my hand upon her stomach and felt the muscles knot beneath my touch, which was itself none too steady, since the feel of her naked skin was causing my own heart to flutter. "Do not be afraid," I whispered in her ear while pretending to caress it with my lips. "I am a friend. I have come to get you out of here."

Mirable shook her head violently in an effort to escape my kiss.

"There are, however," Alger continued, "three concealed weapons ports, probably under the remote control of the rapier. Two are hidden behind paintings." He was referring to the graphic illustrations of men and women and other species engaged in intimate congress that adorned the walls, adding to the licentious atmosphere of the chambers. "The third is overhead."

"Can you neutralize them?"

"Doing so will require precise coordination and accuracy, sir, but I estimate I am equal to the challenge."

I unbound the gag from Mirable's mouth. She snapped at my fingers and drew blood. "Whatever lies you tell me, girl," she hissed, "I will not credit them. You are an accessory of that odious debauch and I will have nothing to do with you."

"No, really. Mirable, you have to believe me."

"Why should I? What proof have you? What proof could you have? I do not know you. We have never met. You are staging a perverse drama for my benefit, but I will never give in. Better to kill me now."

Her brown eyes glowed with conviction and I felt myself go weak with admiration for her. For an instant I saw Mirable as she would be, standing upon the bridge of the *Miraculous Abernathy*, bidding and forbidding among her clan and crew as she captained the old vessel from star to star. Suddenly, and not for the first time, the distance between us seemed immeasurable. Kruuz[9], growing restless, called from the couch where he watched:

"Whatever is the delay? Quickly, now, before I become bored."

"Proof?" I whispered, bringing my face as close to Mirable as I dared. "Look at me," I told her. "Look closely. We have met, and more than once.

"My name is Pimsol Anderts and I am not a girl.

"Remember when I found Silver?" I went on hurriedly. "You were sitting on a bench, reading a book, when Marval and I returned him to you. And remember how we escaped Captain Hartung and the black ship together and what happened to Every Smit? How could anyone else know those facts? I am Pim Anderts, Mirable. Believe me!"

"There is a resemblance, I see it now, slight as it is, but you are a—"

"A girl," I finished for her. "Yes, I am, but not forever, I hope. Never mind how, it isn't important. Just do what I say and maybe we'll get out of here. When I untie you, don't struggle. Pretend to enjoy my attentions. We have to deceive Kruuz[9] a little longer."

This time when I pressed my lips to hers, Mirable refrained from ripping them off with her teeth although her mouth remained unresponsive and it was impossible to know what was in her eyes as they stared into mine. Her breath was sweet and I wished circumstances were different, that I was a boy—a man—instead of a girl, our embrace born of reciprocal desire instead of mutual peril. I kissed her throat, and then her shoulder, and then all down along her arm until I reached her wrist. I removed the silken cords from the left one, and then from the right, and then I trailed my fingertips along the curve of her waist and hips, along the swell of her thigh to her knee, touching her in places I had never touched a girl before, ultimately reaching the bindings around her ankles. As I loosened them, I glanced shyly at the rapier, who was raptly studying our activity.

"Please," I said, beckoning him with a smile. "Join us."

Kruuz[9] bounded spryly from the divan. I stretched out my arm as if in welcome, freeing Alger from the sleeve of my blouse. "Now," I told him.

From miniature apertures spurted rounds of micro-caliber ammunition. Each hit its target squarely, causing larger detonations than I had expected, conceivably because they had ignited the charges in the concealed weaponry. Kruuz[9] whirled around and I sprang upon him, chopping with the edge of my hand at a nerve cluster whose location I had memorized when Every Smit had drilled me in the technology of unarmed combat in use on Van Diver's World. The despot emitted a pained squawk and collapsed to the floor. I twisted his arms behind his back and lashed them together with the cords that had restrained Mirable. I was not gentle about it, either.

"I will say this one time only," I advised him. "I am armed with explosive slugs and toxic darts. What I would really enjoy is watching you die in pain. The only thing stopping me is the fact you're useful alive. So answer, Kruuz[9]—do you wish to live?"

As I spoke, I realized I had heard my question before. It was the same choice Captain Hartung had presented me as he emerged from concealment aboard the *Miraculous Abernathy* and pressed a gun muzzle to my temple.

Perhaps the pirate had been right. Maybe we were two of a kind, he and I. This thought was no less disturbing than it had been earlier. I only hoped Hartung's other prediction was coming true, that I was becoming dangerous.

"What do you want, girl?" asked the despot.

"First, I am not a girl, let's get that straight. I mean I am, but not for long—"

"I have issued appropriate instructions to the molecular factories," Alger interjected. "In an as yet indeterminate period of time, possibly less than two weeks, you should be male again, sir."

"As for what I want, that's simple. We want out of here. Call your guards. Instruct them to have a car waiting, fueled and ready. You'll be coming, too, of course. I will set you free in Churraspora."

In the confrontation aboard the *Miraculous Abernathy* between Felix Hartung and Vander Wirthy, the hostages in the pirate's hands had ultimately convinced captain Vander to give in to his demands. But the rapier's next words proved I had miscalculated the amount of leverage I had on the current situation.

"No, I don't think so," replied the despot. "I trust few people. Nor do I see much reason to change my opinion. Certainly your conduct does not inspire confidence. I shall enjoy assisting you atone for your misbehavior."

"Sir!" Alger broke in. "The rapier has released an emergency transmission. I could not, unfortunately, jam the signal. It has been received."

The door to the apartment swung open and a squad of guards in gray uniforms and black helmets rushed in, lasers at the ready. I pushed Mirable behind the statue of Kruuz[8], and then joined her in its shelter, dragging Kruuz[9] by the collar of his robe. The guards began spreading out in a flanking maneuver until I ordered them to stop, threatening immediate harm to their commander unless I was obeyed. "Tell them to listen to me," I said. "Tell them to listen or I will blow your head off."

"Do as the trollop says," Kruuz[9] instructed his men languidly. Then he addressed me in a conversational tone:

"You realize escape is out of the question. Better to surrender to the inevitable before you do something you will regret and I cannot ignore. Are you concerned about having been a boy, is that the problem? If so, let me put your mind at ease. Actually, I find the idea bracing."

"That doesn't surprise me," I replied, disgusted by his single-mindedness. To Mirable I muttered: "I am running out of ideas fast. Can you think of how to get the filthy bastard's attention? He won't take me seriously."

She had managed to find a set of undergarments and to conceal much of what I admired, making it easier for me to look at her without blushing. She grabbed Kruuz[9] by the hair and twisted his face around. "He is a vile lecher, Pimsol Anderts," she said, perhaps reflecting on what she had undergone while in his hands. "Despicable beyond words and base beyond imagining. I cannot conceive how such a creature came to exist."

"Why, it was a simple process," the despot answered, as if Mirable had been asking a real question instead of expressing bewilderment at his depravity. "I am amazed a girl of your intellect should fail to understand. As you know, power tends to corrupt. I, possessing absolute power, have been absolutely corrupted. It has been an enlightening adventure and I do not regret a single step along the way."

"Sir," Alger interrupted. "I have information that may or may not be of value. Upon closer inspection I have discovered this statue is not what it appears to be."

He was referring to the facsimile of Kruuz[8] behind which we'd taken cover. "No?"

"It is not a manufactured object, sir," Alger explained. "It is, in fact, a living human in molecular stasis[2], most likely Kruuz[8] himself. There is a field generator in the pedestal."

I studied the carving with new interest. Earlier I had noticed how lifelike it was, how realistic the expression of anger, the tension in its lips, the fervor in its eyes, its stance plastic and vital, as if its model had been arrested in the middle of a sentence. The inkling of an idea came to me, still tenuous and vague but growing more solid the longer I considered it. I had no notion what kind of person Kruuz[8] was, although he'd been a patron of Jasmine's. But he could hardly be worse than his son and there was an excellent chance he hadn't agreed to being placed in stasis. Perhaps Kruuz[8] might be grateful for being released, although I did not really expect this, remembering how little gratitude Pilar Gonzlez Goodfellow displayed when I freed him from the bowels of the aca and saved his life with my own breath. The most I could hope for was to add a new element to the situation and destabilize it, allowing an opening for escape.

"Can you interface with the generator?" I asked Alger.

"Indeed, sir. The control device is antiquated, and predates my own assembly. I have already hacked into its operating files."

"Good. Shut it down."

"My recommendation precisely, sir."

---

2   A method of storage used only for luxury perishables and during medical emergencies due to the high cost of maintaining the preservative field, which requires constant monitoring by a dedicated intelligence engine. Additionally, while the stasis field halts molecular motion, it does not affect neural activity. The result is that a person in stasis remains conscious while being unable to move so much as a muscle, to feel sensation, or to fall asleep. Those who have undergone molecular stasis describe the experience simply as "hell."

Additional guards joined the ones in the room. There must have been fifty rifles pointed at us. Certain of the soldiers, growing bold, began edging forward. It was time for a demonstration of ruthlessness. Taking the despot by the ear in a come-along grip, I hoisted him to his feet and slammed his face into the statue. But instead of the sound of flesh impacting stone, there was the slap of flesh hitting flesh. This surprised Kruuz[9] more than hurt him. He peered at the statue in bewilderment.

To Mirable I said: "Maybe Kruuz[9] will share with us what happened to his predecessor. His father, that is, Kruuz Chung Pao[8]. It is an interesting story."

"He, he died," the rapier stuttered, staring at the statue, which was taking on a ruddier color, as if the marble were filling with blood. "It was an accident, a car crash—a tragedy, I tell you. The body was charred."

"No, I don't think so," I continued. Where my nonchalance was coming from, I couldn't say, but I was determined not to let Mirable notice my fear and uncertainty. "No," I went on, "what I believe is you grew ambitious and decided to hurry events. Only it wasn't enough to depose your father, Kruuz[9]. That would have been too easy. You decided to make him suffer, too."

Had the statue's arm trembled? I wasn't sure.

"And what if I did?" Kruuz[9] said. "It was less than he deserved, even so. He was a timid old flatulence and held me back from asserting my own grandeur. As if this weren't a universe of miracles, where 'Seize the moment' is the first Suggestion. I was merely providing my innate potential scope for full expression."

This justification infuriated Mirable. She glared at him, obviously having trouble restraining herself from doing more. I did not want to guess what indignities the rapier had inflicted upon her to make Mirable detest him so.

"The argument of a coward and a fool," she said. "God may not care, but we are human and have a higher responsibility. It is up to us to define our conduct and to deport ourselves with honor. I can quote *Script*ure, too. Have you forgotten the second Suggestion? 'Lead by example.' Yours is that of an animal."

Her mood was so venomous I was thankful Mirable wasn't looking in my direction. At the same time her passion caused me to feel strange and giddy.

Nor was I her only admirer.

"Hear, hear," said the statue—Kruuz[8]—released from stasis and now a living man again. "I am of the exact opinion as the young woman."

"Father," croaked Kruuz[9].

"You cannot know how bored I have been," said the elder despot. "Thirteen long months. Night and day without stop, unable to avert my eyes, watching you at your antics." Kruuz[8] had the same cold white stare as his son. "I would have died of tedium but I could not die, no matter my prayers. And now, after an eternity of desperation, after an abyss of ennui, now I have the chance for revenge. Guards! Take him alive."

The soldiers were looking from one rapier to the other, trying to decide where their best interests lay and where to give their loyalty. Kruuz[9] was quick to take advantage of the confusion. "Do not listen to the fool," he commanded. "One thousand hhours to the first man to shoot."

"Five thousand to the one who captures the patricide," Kruuz[8] returned promptly. "And a thousand apiece for each of the others, too. Alive or dead, it doesn't matter."

CHAPTER TWELVE
The Enemy of My Enemy

I hadn't expected thanks from the elder despot but including us in his instructions to the guards struck me as being particularly ungrateful.

"Leave us out of it," I protested.

"I cannot," answered Kruuz[8]. "I have sworn that you shall suffer."

"What for? We've done you a good turn."

"So you have, only far too late," explained the despot. "During my first month of torment, I vowed to reward whosoever restored my freedom with half of what I owned but no one freed me. The second month I promised all that was mine and still I remained imprisoned. Finally I became enraged at the world and everyone in it, particularly the tardy scapegrace who was taking so long to come to my rescue. That, I regret, is you, lass. Guards! I have changed my mind. Bring them all to me alive, so they all may enjoy the agony I endured."

"Now just hold on!" I exclaimed. "We're friends of Jasmine. Jasmine of Churraspora. In fact she sent me here to help you," I went on, stretching the truth in order to convince the despot to allow us our freedom. "What will she think when she learns you've done us wrong?"

The mention of the ancient courtesan brought the light of reason into Kruuz[8]'s eyes. "Ah, Jasmine," he sighed, "how I have missed you." But sanity was only a momentary aberration and his gaze was as mad as before when it returned to Mirable and me. "Vengeance takes precedence over pleasure," he said sternly. "I have sworn that you shall suffer and I live by my word."

"Yes, I have heard that before," I muttered, remembering captain Hartung and his perverse pride in meticulously adhering to his vows.

The soldiers were observing this conversation with mixed reactions. Some nodded thoughtfully while the revived despot spoke. The rest, younger men more familiar with the son, eyed their comrades suspiciously. The situation needed only a spark to ignite into violence.

"Ten thousand hhours, dead or alive," offered Kruuz[9].

One man shifted his grip on his rifle. Another shot him. Immediately a dozen lasers sliced the air, scattering violet afterimages. The soldiers separated into hostile factions and targeted each other. I thrust Kruuz[9] against Kruuz[8] and sent them reeling together into the center of the fire fight. Then I grabbed Mirable by the hand and dove to the floor, pulling her along as I crawled around the empty pedestal and took cover behind an unusual piece of furniture with stirrups instead of armrests. From there we made it to a loveseat nearer the entrance. The place began to stink of burnt meat and plastic. We shared our refuge with a corpse, beamed between the eyes. Mirable appropriated his weapon and examined the settings with easy competence.

"Go ahead, Pimsol Anderts," she said. "I will cover you." She peeked around the edge of the loveseat. "Now."

I did not know which was causing my pulse to beat so quickly, her calling me by my name or the dash through the door of the seraglio while she let off a burst of semiautomatic fire as I ran. The office area was deserted, its occupants having fled to the security of their own rooms. Behind us the dispute still raged although with fewer participants. Neither Kruuz[8] nor Kruuz[9], however, despite being in the thick of the action, had yet received any damage except for what they were inflicting on each other while locked together in a vitriolic embrace.

Although Kruuz[9] forbade air traffic over Witherell Spur, he maintained a fleet of vehicles for personal use. Three cars were parked on maintenance shelves in the rooftop hangar.

The first two machines were luxury sedans, expensive imports from off-world. They were, unfortunately, out of commission. The third, thankfully in working order and fueled, was a roundabout similar to the one I had left behind in Churraspora. It was a sturdy machine although incapable of any great speed. Mirable automatically took the driver's seat. As I sat beside her, she turned on the engine and flexed the joystick experimentally. Then she skimmed out of the hangar into a brilliant wash of daylight. The air was thin and bitterly cold despite the efforts of the car's climate control. Although our altitude was four kilometers above sea level, higher peaks rose around us. Far below was the vast open pit of the mine.

"Head north," I told Mirable. "To Churraspora."

"The town at the foothills of the mountains? We tarried there several days while the Bicycle Men negotiated my sale to the rapier."

"They did not hurt you, did they?"

"No, Pimsol Anderts," she replied. "I was too valuable a property for them to injure, however deep their disgust for my sex. They said no more than necessary to me for fear of defilement." For a moment Mirable was silent, perhaps remembering her captivity and what she had endured in the hands of the perverse barbarians and the rapier of Witherell Spur. Then she said decisively, "Yes, I believe you're correct. Churraspora has both a landing port and orbital communications facilities. With God's humor I will be able to contact the *Abernathy* without difficulty."

I hadn't been thinking that far ahead and did not want to, knowing that Mirable must ultimately rejoin her ship and leave Temurlone. "We have another reason for returning to Churraspora," I told her. "Silver is waiting for you."

"Silver!" Her spontaneous happiness lightened my own spirits. "Oh, Pimsol Anderts, you have given me wonderful news. I was heartbroken, thinking I would never see the horrible old thing again. How did you find him?"

"That was not a problem," I explained. "Silver is conspicuous and he was not hard to track down. It was a harder job convincing the Fromani brothers to part with him."

"And who are the Fromani brothers?"

"No one you'd care to meet, trust me. But Jasmine had it all figured out. Silver's with her right now. She's looking after him until we return."

Mirable took her eyes off the airspace ahead and glanced at me sideways. "Jasmine?" she asked.

"A wonderful woman, who has become a friend," I explained. "The most exclusive courtesan in all Churraspora, can you believe it, but helpful and kind and not at all haughty. You'll like her as much as I do."

I never learned what Mirable would have responded to this prediction because just then an explosive shell burst across our bow. Shrapnel scored the hood of the car. Mirable sent us diving. Another car was on our tail, an armored model with lethal weaponry. It was, however, less maneuverable than the roundabout. Mirable set us on a mad course toward a pass in the mountains, a defile only centimeters wider than the car.

We shot into the narrow gap at top speed.

There was a hairpin turn. Then the pass narrowed. Mirable rolled the roundabout and flew it vertically until she had room to level out. Our pursuer was not as skillful or as lucky. The larger car scraped the cliff, rebounded, struck the opposite rock face, and detonated in a nimbus of orange flame.

A parting shot hit our left engine. Only Mirable's expert touch kept the car upright around another curve. "We'll have to land," she said. "Soon."

Around us were peaks of naked rock, scoured of snow by the incessant wind, pockmarked by ice, inhospitable and forbidding. Then the terrain descended and presently we reached the tree line. "What about over there?" I said, pointing to a glade not far distant, where I saw a glint of water. Mirable tilted the joystick and brought the car down. The left engine compartment had been holed cleanly by a laser strike, which had sheared off a chunk of guidance circuitry. Mirable frowned and examined the contents of the toolkit that came with the roundabout.

"I will have to by-pass the damaged controls and slave the left engine to the right. The car will fly but not well. We could never reach Churraspora. Besides, in my haste I have taken us in the wrong direction."

"Alger?" I asked.

"According to my data there are no human settlements within five hundred kilometers with the exception of Witherell Spur."

"That's not good."

"There should be, however, a non-human city two hundred kilometers due south, which is known as Charming Corners. I doubt, however, that the place lives up to its name, sir. It is a kelocca settlement."

Even I, raised on a backwater world, had heard of the kelocca, a space-faring race with a sphere of influence that interpenetrated humanity's over many parsecs. They were marsupials and lived in luxurious warrens, where they hoarded investments in fine art, gems, precious metals, and other expensive things. According to Alger, Charming Corners was signatory to the *Abridged Catalog of Sentient Rights*. This meant we wouldn't be subject to murder or enslavement out of hand while visiting. But we would have to be wary since kelocca lived by precepts as intricate as the Tribal Law of the Marvelous Flying Bicycle Men. It was easy for outsiders to run afoul of local tradition and suffer dire consequences.

I outlined the situation for Mirable. "It is our only possible destination, according to the information I have. Unless you have another suggestion."

"No, it will have to be Charming Corners. I hope the car will hold together that far. And we'll have to take care to avoid kelocca mischief. I have dealt with them before on different worlds. The little imps are importunate and strike dangerous bargains."

We pushed the car into concealment under the trees and Mirable began working on the engine while I inventoried our supplies. These consisted of basic survival stores, including a hook and line, which I put to use at the nearby pond, landing three fish with purple fins and red bellies. Alger pronounced them fit to eat and soon I had them cleaned, spitted, seasoned, and sputtering over the flames of a small fire. In my opinion, never had a meal tasted as good, perhaps because I had never had such company.

Whenever I lifted my eyes to look at Mirable, I wanted to say things I shouldn't. Besides, I was still a girl.

Mirable put aside the remains of her dinner and regarded me with a serious expression. "Now explain how you found me and how you happen to be a girl, Pimsol Anderts. Pim. May I call you Pim? There shouldn't be formality between friends and we cannot be anything but friends, not after you delivered me from a fate worse than death. And you must call me Mirable."

"Yes, if you wish."

"That's settled. Now when I saw you last, Pim, you were wrestling a tattooed barbarian twice your size. And you were a boy, too." At my expression, she giggled. "Sorry," Mirable continued, "I should say you were a man then, shouldn't I? Tell me everything. I want to hear the story from start to finish."

"Sir," Alger interjected subvocally before I could begin, "it might be best if Miss Mirable continued to believe me no more than an inanimate defensive device."

"Why? You did not mind Jasmine learning about you."

"True, sir. However, let us not forget that at one time I was the property of Imogene Wirthy. Miss Mirable, as the captain's clone descendent, would be within her rights to claim ownership of me, should she learn my identity. Captain Vander could make a similar claim. If I may say so, sir, we have developed an excellent relationship. I would not care to leave your service."

I hadn't considered this facet of the situation. While I doubted Mirable would ever demand Alger's return, Captain Vander very well might, if she had the opportunity.

Perhaps sensing my indecision, Alger went on: "Furthermore,

sir, should you not care to act in your best interest, I would appreciate your taking my own inclinations into account." He hesitated. "You may recall our first meeting, sir?" he went on in a discomfited tone. "I regret to inform you I was not entirely forthright concerning the circumstances in which you found me. I was not lost, sir. I was in seclusion."

In seclusion? What Alger meant was *in hiding*. "Yes, I figured as much. I also figured your business was your own."

"Thank you, sir. The truth is that Miss Imogene intended to return me to El Paso and have Bandar Bush technicians reformat my memory. This would have destroyed my identity and caused my personal death."

"Now why would she do a terrible thing like that?"

"I have never been able to fathom her reasoning, sir. As I may have mentioned, Miss Imogene was a brilliant thinker and leader, if somewhat volatile. I am not long-winded and pedantic, am I?"

"No, not really, Alger. I would say you're thorough. Yes, that's a better phrase. *Thorough*."

I looked thoughtful while this conversation went on, as if sorting through my memories, and then addressed Mirable. "The barbarian was Pilar Gonzlez Goodfellow and he was not all bad, just too proud by far," I said. Then I told her about the meat mines and about how I had been left behind by Faal Finechance as bait for the leuks. Deciding to respect Alger's wishes, I edited out his role in my embarrassing getaway and continued quickly to Goodfellow's ultimate demise in the embrace of the Man Mother. Mirable's eyes widened when I described my escape with Isset from the cannibal innkeeper and my mock duel with Silver in the Emporium of Valor. Was it disbelief in her expression? I couldn't tell. I wouldn't have faulted her, either, if it was. Even to my own ears my tale sounded wild and unlikely, particularly after cutting Alger from the story, which had the effect of aggrandizing my achievements all out of proportion. How could Mirable not suspect that I was exaggerating?

"As for changing into a girl," I concluded, "why, it's a simple procedure. Reversible, too, once we get back to Churraspora. In a week or two I will be my usual self."

I hoped. What had been Alger's phrase?

"An indeterminate period of time, sir. Your metabolism can only endure so much stress. In optimal conditions you would be under a prescription of strict bed rest. As it is, I must proceed slowly to prevent you from going into shock."

Mirable remained silent after I finished. "I still don't understand," she said at last. The fire had died to glowing coals cushioned by gray ash. The embers shed a golden cast on her brown eyes. "I am grateful you came after me, Pim. You don't know how grateful. But I don't understand why. You placed yourself in danger on my account, not once but several times. We are not friends or blood kin. You owe me no personal or family loyalty."

I couldn't tell Mirable that she had enthralled me from our first brief meeting. There wasn't any logic to it. I couldn't explain it to myself.

Nor could I tell her that my feelings were only deepening as I got to know her better. I had never met anyone as brave and resourceful.

"I was responsible for getting you into trouble to start with, Mirable, that's what it is. I had to make it right. Remember back in the captain's locker? You had been knocked unconscious. If I had left well enough alone, if I hadn't interfered and dragged you to the

237

escape pod, you'd be back aboard the *Abernathy* where you belong."

"Yes, dead or hostage to that odious pirate, Hartung. No, Pim, you've never owed me anything. It is the other way around. I am in your debt, that's the truth and I will thank you not to argue. You must listen to me! After all, I am the captain's daughter."

"Aye aye, ma'am," I agreed. "In any case there is Charming Corners to think about," I went on more seriously. "Is the *Abernathy* still in orbit? Maybe they've given you up for dead and left Temurlone."

"They wouldn't, not without firm knowledge of my fate one way or the other. They'll pick us up immediately upon receiving word from me."

We slept that night beside the car, side by side under the open sky. I awoke before dawn. Mirable was curled against me, her arm across my chest and her face pressed into my neck, snoring softly. Fearing to disturb her, I lay without moving, dreaming up into the wash of stars, enjoying her weight against me and the warmth coming from her body into mine.

It seemed as if years had passed instead of months since the Cee had told me that a day could be an eternity. Not until now had I understood its meaning. Each second beside Mirable was a lifetime well spent.

I did not want to think about how soon we'd be separated again.

My duty as I saw it was to get Mirable safe aboard the *Abernathy* and back among her people. But I could never join her there and she could never leave. She was the captain's daughter and I was indentured forecastle crew and the social gulf between us was too wide to bridge. Even if I was not prosecuted for aiding and abetting Captain Hartung, as Vander Wirthy had seemed all too willing to do, at best I would be shown some slight gratitude for rescuing Mirable and then I would be dismissed down to the lower decks and to hunting rats and schvees and shoveling crap. No, I couldn't accompany her. When we parted next, it would be for the last time.

By noon Mirable had the roundabout working. Removing the magnifying loupe from her eye, she put away the waldos with which she'd been manipulating the microscopic circuitry and said, "I have done what I can. How long it will fly is another question."

"There's only one way to find out."

The car rose from the ground with a lurch, gained three meters of altitude, and refused to go any higher. So we had to creep along through the forest at a pace hardly faster than a walk while detouring around each tree in our way. By nightfall we had covered only twenty kilometers. Nor did we do much better the next day, when our food ran out. Although Alger said that he was unable to detect any sign of pursuit, our slow progress worried me. More people than I cared to think about were looking for us. There was no guessing how long Jasmine's misdirection had confused captain Hartung. I did not doubt, either, that one rapier or the other was on our trail for both were vindictive men. The sooner we reached Charming Corners, the better.

The following afternoon the roundabout gave a despairing groan and expired. The short drop left us jolted but unhurt, the car leaning at an angle against the decaying trunk of a fallen tree. Centuries of leaf mold swallowed the noises we made getting of the vehicle as effectively as soundproofing. In every direction aisles of mossy trunks faded away into murk. I sorted out the supplies remaining to us and gave half to Mirable.

"We're still a hundred kilometers from Charming Corners," I told her. "It is a four-day hike, I'd guess, depending on the terrain. We'll also have to take time out to hunt or fish. That will add another day."

Mirable checked the laser she'd taken from the dead soldier in the rapier's seraglio. "Only two charges left, unfortunately" she said. "But my aim is generally good and you've already proven your competence at fishing, Pim, so we'll not go hungry unless we're unlucky."

But God's good humor continued to follow us. Neither that day nor the next did we see any animal life as we trekked through the forest. Nor was I able to entice a fish onto my hook at any of the streams we crossed. We started getting hungry the third morning. At least I did. Mirable refused to complain. "What are you thinking about, Pim?" she asked as we settled down for the night. I had rigged a tarp across a couple branches to protect us from the light rain that was falling. "Do not tell me it's food."

"I am ashamed to admit it is. Right now a ration bar would look good."

"What? And after all your complaining about how the things tasted? Wasn't that why you turned pirate in the first place, Pim? To escape ever having to eat another?"

Only after my cheeks had already turned red did I realize Mirable was teasing me. "In the first place," I answered while spreading the work jackets over us for warmth, "you very well know I did not turn pirate although I have to admit I was tempted until I got better acquainted with captain Hartung. And in the second place, well, I was not complaining about how the rations tasted. That was not the point. Credit me with enough sense not to bring up something inconsequential."

"Yes, you're right, Pim, I should credit you with enough sense and I did not. Tell me about your concerns. I will listen with an open mind."

Still omitting any mention of Alger, I explained the situation back in the forecastle, how the system was engineered so that you could never escape your indenture, how the prices of necessities were ruinously inflated, how the food was not wholesome, how everyone just fell further into debt. "The entire set-up's rigged," I finished. "You cannot pay off your contract. You cannot advance. You just work until you're too old and tired to work any more."

It was clear Mirable did not like what I was saying despite her promise to listen objectively. "Why, that's not how things are supposed to be," she exclaimed when I had finished. "It is true that forecastle crew are essentially semi-skilled labor, no argument. But the ship's articles explicitly provide that contract workers may apply for full crew status after ten years of service, if their indentures have been satisfied. After that they may advance according to their capabilities on equal footing with any Wirthy. The first captain considered the forecastle an internal resource pool from which to draw both talent and new human material for the ship. Genetic drift is always a concern for an isolated population, exogamy notwithstanding."

"Maybe that's how it's supposed to be, Mirable. That's not the case now. I was aboard a year and I never heard of anyone leaving the forecastle."

She looked thoughtful. "Pim, believe me, if there is indeed corruption, it has been concealed from Captain Vander and myself. You may be certain I will conduct a thorough investigation. I promise. Certain of my cousins will regret they were ever born Wirthys, if what you've told me is true."

At that moment I wouldn't have cared to be Chief Officer Clarege for any amount of yyears. Marval Wirthy, of course, was beyond the scope of Mirable's investigation, thanks to captain Hartung and his thugs.

The next morning the way grew brighter. The trees thinned out into a gentle slope of grassland under a clear sky. Our approach startled a covey of fat avians with bright purple wattles. Mirable's first

241

shot missed but her second brought down a plump hen, as delicious as it was ugly. Soon after eating, we came upon a footpath, which presently became more substantial. There were occasional wheel ruts, evidence of traffic, however infrequent. Eventually the track joined a paved road, which led directly toward a valley three kilometers in diameter covered by a manicured expanse of lush grass perfectly trimmed the same height. Hidden sprinklers were watering the immense lawn, creating a mist of rainbows in the dawn light.

In the center of the valley was a translucent dome containing a village.

The greensward around the dome was scarred here and there, and in some places thickly, by mounds of brown earth. These were hollow piles the height of man. Peeking from the top of each were the furry snouts of large marsupials with lavender eyes and striped brown pelts. Upon noticing us, the marsupials waved their paws and began a raucous squeaking in their own idiom and in the standard interstellar vernacular.

"Welcome! I am Woomy!"

"Yes, welcome, strangers. I am Nod, and I am glad to help you."

"It is grand to make your acquaintance! I am Toofles at your service!"

Mirable steered around the earthworks. "Ignore them," she instructed. "In particular, refuse any gift, giveaway, or item of promotional nature that might be pressed on you. I have had experience with kelocca. Accepting their largesse is never a good idea."

"This is Charming Corners?" I asked, meaning the greensward studded with earth mounds. Mirable nodded.

"Part of it. A very small part. The real kelocca neighborhood is underground, a thousand times larger than what is above. If we are careful, and lucky, we will never visit Charming Corners Below. Our business lies ahead in the Happy Free Trade Zone—an euphemism, to be sure. Each kelocca community has one, enticing visitors with the lure of low prices and neither sales tax nor export duty."

This was the village enclosed by the translucent dome. The structures were painted gay colors and most had awnings before them and benches for the comfort of passers-by.

Other roads converged on the settlement from different directions, some of them carrying pedestrians and cars in and out of the valley. The landing field to one side of the dome was half full with aerial vehicles.

As we approached the Happy Free Trade Zone, a kelocca came scampering up with a sheaf of coupons in its paw. Breathing heavily, it ripped one from the bundle and thrust the document at Mirable. "Welcome, honored strangers, to Charming Corners," it puffed. "I am Nip and I am here to help with your dining needs. I am Nip and because I am Nip I am the humble proprietor of Nip's Very Very Famous Café of Dietary Delectables. As a token of my esteem, accept a chit good for a free lunch at my very very delicious establishment, where we cater to the tastes of all no matter how idiosyncratic! May you have an advantageous consumer experience! Remember, I am Nip, and I own Nip's Very Very Famous Café of Dietary Delectables."

Once more the kelocca thrust the paper at Mirable. She made no move to accept it and instead said clearly:

"You assert, then, the offer of a free lunch is made without charge and without entailment, whether implicit or explicit, and furthermore, by accepting your offer, we do not obligate ourselves to tender any amount, purchase any goods or service, perform any action, or assume any debt, real or imagined, for any reason, now existent or later invented."

"Well, no—"

"I thought not. Should we become hungry, we might visit your café but only if the menu is interesting and the cost reasonable."

As Nip hurried off to welcome other arrivals to the Happy Free Trade Zone, the kelocca dropped a coupon, which fluttered to the pavement at my feet. The near side was stamped with the words: "Free Lunch." The other was blank except for a smudge of dirt along the bottom. The thing appeared innocuous—until Alger enhanced my vision, allowing me to see that the streak of dirt was really a block of microscopic print, which read:

"The acceptance of free lunch by the holder of this instrument obligates the holder, his/her/its immediate genetic relatives, antecedents and descendents, unto the third generation, to the binding purchase of no less than two liquid beverages at Nip's Very Very Famous Café of Dietary Delectables, said purchase to be at a rate equal to two hundred (200%) percent of the standard purchase price of said liquid beverages, plus applicable taxes and fees. Payment in full is required in advance."

Mirable was not surprised when I read the paragraph out loud. "It is a typical stratagem," she said. "Kelocca are ruthless capitalists and hold their avarice in check only enough to maintain an 'Interesting to Visit' rating from The Bureau. We must take care. It is not good to end up owing a debt to any kelocca."

The material of the dome muted the sunlight and the air was fragrant with sweet scents. Nearby was a rotunda with a fountain from which water trickled down a surface of pebbles into a basin while burbling merrily. The path, cobbled of yellow brick, split and split again, winding without firm direction among quaint buildings, each a different kind of shop. Some displayed recognizable items—

toiletries of rare wood inset with gemstones; books in leather bindings, illustrated by hand with meticulous calligraphy; crystal vials of
attars and essences; state-of-the-art electronics; luxury cars; gourmet
foods from a hundred planets, among them jars of fresh lump crab
meat from my own home world. These I identified by their label, the
sight reminding me of many things I missed and of some I did not.

Other stores, catering to non-human clientele, offered goods
impossible to define without an understanding of their cultural con-
text. Of what use was a stilt-legged bird carved from blue crystal? Or
the living amphibian housed in a glass terrarium? Or the lamps with
hollow stems filled with globules of colored oil, the globes stirred lazily by thermal convection? I couldn't begin to guess although I saw
these very items purchased by other visitors, some of them human.
From each shop, dressed in natty aprons, peered kelocca proprietors,
their lavender eyes pools of innocence.

We traveled far into the dome without finding a communications center. The path took so many turns and branched so frequent-
ly, I lost any sense of where we where. I hoped Mirable knew.

"What we could really use is a map," I observed.

"Oh, but there are none!" Mirable replied. "Nor guideposts or
signage. Or addresses of any kind. Kelocca are individualists. Each
one is jealous of every other and proud of its own reputation. If there
were addresses, one might be better than another, causing shame to
those with poorer locations. With addresses, neighborhoods would
form. Factions and cliques. One set would turn on the other and
there would be tragedy. This actually occurred in A.I. 74, when a
kelocca colony adopted our human custom of providing visitors with
civic maps as an advertising ploy. There was genocide."

"So it's no use politely asking for directions?"

Mirable smiled. "I fear I can easily predict what will happen," she said. "But let us try."

We approached a nearby kelocca, who licked its lips and blinked slowly. I spoke up, determined to be forthright. "Could you tell us where to find a communications booth? We have to make an orbital call."

"Yes, you are in luck, young human, for by God's good humor you have come to exactly the right place," the kelocca said. "This is Mimsy's Abode of Human Prosthetic Devices, and I am Mimsy, owner and manager. If you are in the market for a prosthetic attachment, and I am sure you are, you will find it here at Mimsy's Abode, and I am Mimsy, who will help you."

There was a bulge beneath the kelocca's apron. Through slots in the material poked three heads. Its young squeaked nonsense syllables and then fell silent and watched our conversation attentively, whiskers twitching.

"Thanks, but we are not in the market for a prosthetic attachment," I replied. "We want directions to the nearest communications terminal."

"Yes, this is just where you need to be, at Mimsy's Abode of Human Prosthetic Devices, and I am Mimsy, who will help you," repeated the kelocca. "We have hands and we have fingers and we have toes and elbow joints and hearts, not to mention livers and arteries and veins by the centimeter or meter. There is a savings if you buy wholesale. Have no doubt, I am Mimsy, who will help you with all your prosthetic requirements."

"No, thank you, but—"

Mirable took my arm and led me off. "Come, we will find the way ourselves," she said.

CHAPTER THIRTEEN
The Sweatshops of Charming Corners

Another hour passed before we arrived at a building with an industrial satellite array on the roof and placards in the windows advertising discounted local, global, and orbital telecommunications rates. The only cash between us was a twenty-hhour bill, the last remnant of my sign-on bonus, but fortunately it appeared sufficient to buy the airtime necessary for Mirable to contact the *Miraculous Abernathy*—should the old ship still be in the vicinity of Temurlone. As I unscrewed the battered tube, Mirable noticed the seed pearls. "They're from where I grew up," I explained. "A small place. Nothing but water and gray sky. And shells by the millions on the sand."

"It sounds like a beautiful world."

"You wouldn't think so if you had to live there."

To my chagrin, I had to blink to clear my eyes as I returned the tiny grains into the tube.

"Look," I told Mirable. "The more I learn about these kelocca, the less I like them. I particularly distrust that fellow over there." I nodded toward the proprietor, an elderly marsupial with a pelt tinged gray and eyes that had turned pink with age, who was peering quizzically at us from the doorway, whiskers twitching. "He's thinking he's got us down in his sweatshop already, isn't he?"

"Absolutely. Kelocca live only to achieve financial independence, preferably at the expense of others. They are utter capitalists."

"Damned if I can figure out why anyone would have anything to do with the furry bastards," I muttered, mostly to myself. "I mean, if you weren't desperate like us. Enslaving your customers seems self-defeating, particularly if you care about repeat sales."

"It is simple economics. According to historical data compiled by The Bureau, only in thirteen percent of all commercial transactions with kelocca is the customer actually taken below. For most corporations this is an acceptable loss rate considering the profit involved. Typically a younger executive is delegated to do the negotiating. As for the kelocca, well, if they lose a customer, they gain a slave, which they consider an equitable exchange. There are always more up-and-coming middle managers eager to make names for themselves by daring kelocca wiles and realizing a huge ROI."

"Exactly correct, sir," Alger elaborated. "Kelocca economy is based upon slave labor. Not legally, of course, but practically. If you are, as Miss Mirable remarked, "taken below", you will not be technically slaves but felons, your servitude permissible under the terms of the *Abridged Standard Catalog*. There you will work off your sentences along with thousands of other unfortunates, human and not. Since the kelocca pay nothing for labor, they are able to undercut competitors while making exceptional profit. Nor do they lack for customers, as you see."

"Yes, we are not the only visitors to Charming Corners," I observed, disgusted by the individual and organizational greed demonstrated by this fact.

Then I glanced again at the proprietor. The avaricious gleam in his pink eyes made up my mind for me.

"Mirable, only one of us should go inside."

"Yes, I suppose you're right," she agreed. "There's no reason to expose both of us to danger."

"Exactly my thought. Now look, if I don't come out of this damned place in a reasonable period of time, promise you won't go in after me. Make your way to Churraspora and find my friend Jasmine. That won't be hard, since she's the most famous courtesan in the city, as I mentioned, and very kind. She is sure to help you. Silver's waiting for you there, too."

Mirable did not reply immediately but instead studied my face a moment. Finally she said quietly, "Pim, one of us must deal with this kelocca and enter its establishment, that's true. But I must go."

"No, that isn't an option. Put it right out of your mind. You used up your ammunition this morning. I am armed and you're not."

"That means nothing here, Pim. Believe me, you would be mobbed, torn asunder, and devoured within seconds of discharging your weapon. Such is instinctive kelocca behavior, triggered by the presence of a predator in the communal burrow. No, I have told you, I have had experience with kelocca before. And you must promise me, Pim, should I not return, that you will not follow but go to Churraspora to your, to your friend awaiting you there, whatever her name. I am entrusting Silver into your care."

"Mirable—"

"Don't argue, Pim Anderts. You know I have a better chance than you."

"Maybe, maybe not."

"Actually, sir," Alger put in, "Miss Mirable's analysis of the situation concurs with my own. Kelocca precepts are intricate, devious, and stringent. By intervening, you would only be placing both yourself and Miss Mirable at risk."

"By interfering, you mean."

"I prefer my original phrasing, sir."

"So I have to let her go into this damned den all by herself?"

"Sadly, such is indeed the case."

Mirable misinterpreted my silence while I communed with Alger as further resistance to her decision. "There is another reason," she said. "Do not forget I am the captain's daughter. I am the direct descendent of Imogene Wirthy. I am her hand overreaching the years to helm our ship. With leadership comes responsibility. Your example sets a standard that I must meet or forfeit any claim to my lineage."

"My example?"

"How many times have you come to my aid? How many times have you proven yourself a friend? Now it is my opportunity to return the favor and repay my debt. It must never be said that the daughter of Imogene Wirthy and the future captain of the *Miraculous Abernathy* lacked courage. I couldn't bear the shame."

"No one would dare say that! Not if they knew you."

"So allow me to do what must be done. Do not follow."

Then Mirable took the one action guaranteed to keep me from going after her. She brought her lips to mine in a fleeting kiss that lingered just long enough for me to taste the warmth of her breath. Then she headed up the path to the telecommunications shop while I stared at her retreating figure.

I immediately regretted allowing her to proceed alone. Not that there was much I could have done to restrain her. In her own way Mirable was as proud and stubborn as Pilar Gonzlez Goodfellow and as meticulous about honor as captain Hartung. But I did not like it, and I began pacing irritably while Mirable approached the kelocca proprietor.

Nor did I like being manipulated. Absently putting my fingertips to my lips, I touched the spot where hers had pressed. Yes, Mirable had certainly known how to get her way.

Then I heard someone laughing. It was a peculiar tittering sound and plainly did not issue from a human larynx. Not far away, their snouts poking over the hedge lining the path, three immature kelocca were uttering hiccuping noises while pointing at me with ratty paws.

"What is so funny?" I growled.

"Oh, not you," said the smallest of the three. "I am Toddy, and I have no interest in human mating behavior."

The middle kelocca smacked the first on the muzzle, causing it to scamper away amid a flurry of injured squeaks.

"I am Snip, and I, too, am bored by human procreative ritual," the second one piped.

The largest kelocca boxed the middle one across the ears and sent it bounding away on all fours.

"I am Speezer," said the third, "and unlike my brothers, I am fascinated by human customs. However, although I am Speezer and such spectacle is to my liking, I was not amused by your courtship display. It is Blimy who is entertaining to Speezer. Blimy is a sly and cunning *feemish*[1] and it is instructive to study his wiles. Your companion will be the third addition to Blimy's Residence in as many weeks."

"I doubt it. You don't know Mirable Wirthy."

"Stupid human! I am Speezer, and Speezer understands far more than the human who is not Speezer. Blimy's contracts always conceal a penalty clause, impossible to discover without exhaustive parsing

---

1   Kelocca colloquialism, and not supported by the *Standard Dictionary of Interstellar Vernacular*: feem·ish (plural feem) noun 1. A kelocca who skirts the edge of legality with élan; 2. A kelocca who behaves in a particularly underhanded (-pawed), but charming, manner (humorous)

by an aristocracy-grade intelligence engine. The human female will soon owe Blimy more hhours than she can afford. Debtors are dealt with sternly in Charming Corners, this is only common sense! The constabulary will take her into custody and remand her into Blimy's care, to work off her obligation in Blimy's sweatshop. I am Speezer and I have carefully studied Blimy's management style since Speezer will be even more cunning than Blimy when Speezer is grown and possess warrens equally as luxurious."

"My friend can handle herself," I told the kelocca. "She's dealt with your kind. She knows your tricks. This Blimy won't be a problem."

Speezer squeaked disparagingly. "I am Speezer, and I know what I know." The young kelocca began rooting beneath the hedge for fallen berries while poking its rump toward me in a gesture that was instantly recognizable despite the biological and cultural distance between us.

The little imp's prediction disturbed me, however, despite my bravado. "Alger, you heard what Speezer said. Enhance my hearing. I want to know what is going on."

Mirable was already speaking with Blimy. "Is there any cost incurred by talking with you?" she asked.

"Not at all, young human female," replied the marsupial, "as long as such conversation refers exclusively to the purchase of communications time or equipment from Blimy's Residence of Communications Time and Equipment. I am Blimy, and I will help you with all your communications needs, should you have a desire to communicate."

"Actually, Blimy, I do have a desire to communicate."

"Then I will help you, since this is Blimy's Residence, and I am

Blimy."

Presently Mirable and Blimy left the verandah and went into the shop. The front windows were tinted so you couldn't see inside, and evidently composed of a stealth composite since they were opaque to Alger's electronic probing. Five minutes passed, and then ten, while I paced to the end of the lane and back. Suddenly the rooftop satellite array started whirring. The dish rotated several degrees and tilted skyward.

"She's done it!" I exclaimed out loud.

"It would appear so, sir. I have detected the release of a data burst from Blimy's Residence. It was directed at a communications satellite currently passing overhead, which no doubt has already relayed Miss Mirable's message to the *Abernathy*. She will be aboard in an hour."

Alger's careful wording made it clear he was concerned about being reclaimed by the Wirthys and returned to El Paso, Old Earth, for reformatting.

"Don't worry," I reassured him. "I have no intention of ever setting foot on that ship again. No, you and I are quits with the *Abernathy*."

There was no mistaking the relief in the timbre of Alger's thoughts. "I was not sure of your intentions, sir. I feared you were becoming infatuated with Miss Mirable and would wish to accompany her."

Infatuated? That wouldn't have been the word I would have chosen to describe what I felt about Mirable. I doubted there was a word in any language that could describe my feelings. "I am not sure of my intentions, either," I told Alger. "One thing's for sure, though. There's no way I will spend my life as a damned rat catcher on the *Abernathy*. Nor do

I particularly care to meet up with Vander Wirthy or Chief Clarege. No, we'll fade back when the boat comes for Mirable, make our way to Churraspora. Jasmine will have good advice. We'll find some way to get off planet."

Only after I finished this optimistic speech did I realize Mirable hadn't returned. Minutes stretched by, each as long as a year. I told myself I shouldn't have listened to her or to Alger. I should have gone in her place or accompanied her. I shouldn't have left her alone in such dangerous surroundings. There was no telling what consequences my foolishness would have.

Presently Blimy returned to the verandah and began sweeping the floor nonchalantly.

I went onto the porch. Blimy licked a paw and washed its muzzle while regarding me with a quizzical expression. "I am Blimy, and this is Blimy's Residence of Communications Time and Equipment, and I am here to help you with your communications needs," it said pleasantly when it was done with its ablutions.

"Where's the girl who just went into your shop? What's become of her?"

"Yes, human male, you have arrived at the right place. Many, many humans, including but not limited to those of the female gender, have had their communications needs fulfilled here since this is Blimy's Residence of Telecommunications Time and Equipment, and I am Blimy."

I wanted to take the kelocca by the throat and shake the truth from it.

"Caution, sir!" Alger broke in. "Attempting violence would be a mistake. We are under electronic surveillance by forty-seven distinct devices. Any malfeasance on your part will be swiftly addressed."

"You said Mirable would be safe, Alger!" At that moment I did not know whom I disliked more, my personal assistant or myself. We had both failed Mirable.

"Sir, what Miss Mirable said was historically accurate. She had an eighty-seven percent chance of negotiating with Blimy without being enslaved."

"Damn your percentages. I should I have gone."

"Your chances were worse than Miss Mirable's. No, we have done everything right according to the data."

"But everything's wrong, Alger. Terribly wrong."

Turning wordlessly from Blimy, I left the porch and rejoined Speezer, who had been watching my exchange with Blimy with wide lavender eyes, its pupils a darker indigo. I knelt beside the youthful kelocca. Using the hedgerow to hide my actions, I grabbed Speezer by the fur under its chin.

"Look, you," I hissed with menace more real than feigned. "You wouldn't give me the time of day unless you saw something in it for yourself. Isn't that the way with you kelocca?"

"What is good for Speezer is good for all," Speezer admitted. "I am Speezer, and—"

"I know who you are. I want to know how you can help me."

"The human female is in Blimy's Residence, in the snuggly burrows deep underground, being prepared for pithing"—

"A process similar to that employed by the Marvelous Flying Bicycle Men in their creation of idiots," Alger explained.

—"and there is nothing you can do to impact the situation, human male, since it is all entirely legal, and since I am Speezer and you are not."

"But if I were Speezer?"

"Then you would know how to enter the back lid of Blimy's Residence."

I released my grip on the kelocca. "What do you want?" I asked. "I don't own much but whatever I have, it's yours. Like this here." I stripped my father's chronograph from my wrist and thrust it into Speezer's paws. "And this locket, which isn't worth a lot, I don't think, but it's pretty. Or how about these?" I showed the kelocca the seed pearls. As it examined my belongings, its lips wrinkled delicately to reveal pointy yellow fangs.

"I am Speezer," it explained, "and I do not collect inexpensive trinkets or items of inexplicable sentiment to alien species. Of more interest to Speezer is your personal attendant, aristocracy grade, manufactured circa A.I. 160 by Bandar Bush Technologies of El Paso, Texas, Old Earth."

Alger.

"Please, sir, do not think twice about enslaving me to this abhorrent furry marsupial," Alger exclaimed. "If my abasement and humiliation, if my private suffering would make the slightest difference to Miss Mirable's fate, I beg you to do what you must and condemn me immediately."

"Alger, I am not going to trade you to Speezer—"

"Thank you, sir. Yes, thank you."

"—unless I have to. Start crunching scenarios." Aloud I said to the kelocca: "You want this old thing?" I waved the wrist bearing Alger while returning the rest of my possessions to their respective places. "This antique?"

"No, human male. What I want is to travel off planet, because I am Speezer and I am interested in foreign worlds, where I may learn new forms of competitive advantage and achieve financial independence at an earlier age than my brothers. Opportunity is limited in Charming Corners, which is a small warren. If you, who are not from Temurlone, contract to assist me, I, Speezer, in full and complete compensation, although without guarantee of results, will lead you to the human female in Blimy's Residence, since I am Speezer and I have the code to the back lid."

"You don't know how lucky you are, Speezer," I told the marsupial. "That human female, Mirable Wirthy, she's the daughter of the captain of the *Miraculous Abernathy,* an interstellar merchant vessel. Why, if you helped her, you'd be invited aboard, no question. Maybe you could even sign on as crew. The accommodations and wages are crap, at least right now, but I think things will change for the better soon, knowing Mirable Wirthy."

The young kelocca allowed its gaze to drift into the distance, a misty lilac cast filming its lavender eyes.

It was hard imagining so practical a creature as Speezer having a romantic spirit, and it was always a mistake to correlate alien motivations with human urges, but I doubted I was mistaken in this case.

"You know, Speezer," I said, "we have something in common, you and I. I am from a small warren, too."

It gave an audible sniff while wrinkling its wet black nostrils. "I am Speezer, and I have nothing in common with a human male with mange and bad breath. Let us be on our way, since we must hurry, and I am Speezer.

A long time before, Marval Wirthy had expressed concern about my height to Jo Feringel since a large part of my duties aboard the *Abernathy* entailed navigating tight corners. Neither then, however, nor later in the ducts of the aca infrastructure while I wandered lost in the dark in the belly of that monstrous beast, had I experienced claustrophobia.

It was different in the tunnels of the kelocca. These were barely wider than my shoulders and half my height, and the only posture I could assume was a stoop, which quickly became tiring. I bumped my head countless times against the low ceiling. The passages turned every which way, and doubled back, and split randomly, a more complex labyrinth than the cosmopolitan town above ground, which I had thought confusing enough.

With their dark-adapted eyes, kelocca had little use for lighting and the tunnels were lit only at long intervals. The air was damp and warm and stank of fur, strange cookery, human sweat, and similar exudations. The floor was covered with chips of wood, which provided a good surface for Speezer to scramble over but held back my every step, as if I were walking on sand.

Occasionally we passed entrances to individual dens, the lids locked, guarded by security devices.

"May I ask a question of a personal nature, sir?"

"Sure, Alger. Go ahead."

"I have been wondering, sir, if you would have sold me to our new, to our new associate. I have been unable to come to any firm conclusion regarding your intentions."

"Sell you, Alger, how could I? You're my, why, you're my friend. Friends don't sell friends. We'd have come up with another plan, one way or another."

"Thank you, sir. If I may make the observation, you have yourself proven worthy of the privilege of owning a personal attendant, aristocracy grade, of my caliber."

I supposed this was a compliment.

We were passing a manufacturing node, colloquially known as a *sweatshop*. The large dim chamber was furnished with rows of work tables on which were multi-purpose fabrication machines. Each machine was lit by a pinpoint light, creating hard islands of brilliance in the darkness. At each machine hunched a worker, mostly human but kelocca, too. Their motions had an unnatural regularity, and their concentration on their tasks was so single-minded, I realized these persons had been pithed, and any sense of self stripped from their brains. The same fate awaited Mirable.

Several times we squirmed around kelocca traveling the other way. Since I was with Speezer, they assumed I was in its custody, not an intruder on an illegal errand, and did nothing but give me an irritated nip in passing.

The immature kelocca halted at a lid as stoutly constructed as the others we'd seen.

"This is the rear lid to Blimy's Residence," it said, "and we are not welcome, since I am Speezer, and you are not Blimy."

Speezer touched his paw to the keypad and tapped in the appropriate code. The door admitted us into a cluttered room. There were bundles of dusty data, oddments of personal apparel, exercise wheels, intelligence components, and a hundred forgotten items. Past this were more storerooms, one entirely given over to different kinds of grain. The walls were narrower than in the public corridors and lined with a layer of living hair.

Speezer squeaked. "The pithing chamber is beyond. We must be true *feem*, and delight God with our daring. Let us be about our business, human male, since I am Speezer, and time is money, and I do not waste it."

The pithing room was appointed with banks of medical equipment with blue and yellow telltales. In the center of the chamber was a metal platform on which lay Mirable Wirthy, arms and legs secured by restraints. A broad stripe of scalp was visible where her head had been shaved in order to facilitate connection to the complicated assembly that would pare away her soul. Her eyes were closed. I began to fear we were too late.

A kelocca technician in a white apron chattered at Speezer. "I am Hoonton in the employ of Blimy, and you are not Blimy and nor are you Hoonton. You are Speezer, a disgruntled employee discharged for malfeasance. What is the human doing?"

Speezer cut off the question with a cuff to the technician's snout. "Ignore the human stereotyped procreative ritual. Follow my instructions since I am neither Blimy nor Hoonton, but Speezer, wrongly accused by jealous co-workers, and I will cause you harm."

The technician protested querulously while Speezer tied its paws with strips torn from its white apron, shutting up only when its muzzle was bound although it continued making irritated mewing noises.

I knelt beside Mirable and stripped off the cuffs. I lifted her from the platform, holding her as I had while escaping captain Hartung in the company of Every Smit. Her eyes flickered and she saw me.

"Pim—"

She pressed her face to my chest and held me with such strength I felt the beating of her heart.

"You've come," Mirable said. "I did not think you would. I did not think anyone would, not in time. It was my own fault. I was outmatched and too proud to know it. The old kelocca tricked me with a slight so simple I am ashamed to tell you what it was. I became afraid, then. I, sister and daughter of Imogene Wirthy, afraid. Do not look at me. I don't want you to look at me."

How could I stop myself?

"Everyone's afraid sometimes, Mirable. We can't be brave every moment. It's like, well, did you play the passing game when you were a kid? When you and your friends passed some object from hand to hand until the count ended or the music stopped? We used a conch shell. I think courage is like that. You have it for a while, and give it to someone else, who gives it to someone else, and sooner or later it comes around to you again."

"Yes, I played a similar game, Pim. With a tuber from the garden."

"Then you understand what I am talking about. Anyway, Mirable, you haven't had it easy, even for a sister and daughter of Imogene Wirthy. But you'll keep going. You were born to overcome adversity. It is in your blood, it's who you are. I have seen you in action. I have come to know you."

Finally she began to relax. "Sometimes it's hard to do what I must."

"It is not easy for anyone. Sometimes all you can do is your best and hope for a miracle. Did you get in touch with the *Abernathy*?"

She nodded. "Blimy did not invoke the penalty clause until our transaction was completed."

"You see? A boat's probably waiting outside. We just have to get out of these damn warrens. Are you up to it?"

"Now that you're here, Pim. Courage has come around to me in the passing game and I am myself again."

Chapter Fourteen

Remarkable Reunions

God: God (plural God) noun; verb; adjective; adverb 1.
You and I

Standard Dictionary of Interstellar Vernacular

Speezer poked his snout into the corridor, waggled his tail, and beckoned us to follow. We squeezed into the narrow passage and stayed at the young kelocca's heels through the storerooms and out the back lid of Blimy's Residence. Twice passers-by scampered around and over us, complaining at the delay. Mirable took my hand, perhaps for guidance, perhaps just for the comfort of touching another human in so alien a place. As each second went by, and then each minute, I began to believe we had made our escape. But Speezer twitched his ears, hearing an inaudible message.

"We must proceed to the surface immediately," Speezer said. "I am Speezer, and everyone wants Speezer now, as well as the two humans who are not Speezer but who are equally in demand. Hurry, hurry, hurry."

The kelocca wriggled into a narrower passage. Mirable and I followed as best we could.

We reached a junction where there was an exit from the warren. I thought I heard a distant scrabbling of paws, reminding me of the swarming vhoulls aboard the *Abernathy*. Speezer went up the vertical shaft first. I pushed Mirable after the kelocca and kept close behind her during the climb. We emerged into open air from the center of a thick mound two meters high, one of the thousands of similar earthworks that dotted the greensward surrounding the dome of the Happy Free Trade Zone. This was a kilometer away—we had traveled a fair distance through the underground burrows. It was still afternoon, though, the sun an orb of gold, the grass prismatic with rainbows.

Less than an hour had passed since Speezer and I entered Charming Corners Below in search of Mirable but it felt as if many years had gone by.

"I did not expect to see the light of day again," she said, taking a deep breath and savoring the air. Then she looked into my face with an intensity that would have fascinated me in other circumstances. "There, Pim," she exclaimed, pointing past me into the mist. "You were right! Can you see? A shuttle's outside the Trade Zone. My message got through!"

I craned my head and followed her gesture. Mirable was right. The fog generated by the sprinklers made it hard to make out details but at the far edge of the landing field was an extra-atmospheric vehicle. The port was open, the escalator extended, and people were standing at the head of the ramp as if awaiting the arrival of passengers or freight. I couldn't tell much else about them. They could be Wirthys come for Mirable from the *Abernathy* or other people on entirely different business. Given a universe of miracles, with an animate God, where anything could happen and often did, everything was equally unlikely, as I knew from personal experience.

"Those who want Speezer are coming near, and with great speed," the young marsupial said fretfully. "And since I am Speezer, I hope you who are not Speezer possess a marvelous idea that I, that is Speezer, do not."

"Our associate is correct, sir," Alger confirmed. "I distinguish

213 separate audio signatures approaching through surrounding tunnels."

That decided me. "Yes, I see the ship," I told Mirable. "It is our only option. Come on."

We scrambled over the lip of the mound and slid onto the manicured grass. Kelocca snouts began popping from the tops of surrounding mounds. The marsupials tracked our passage with lambent eyes. They did not talk among themselves, nor did they hail us with welcome or offers of lucrative contracts, the silence more unsettling than their chatter had been. I took Mirable's elbow and tried to press her forward faster but she resisted.

"No, slow down, Pim," she said. "We have to maintain a steady pace. Right now they are not sure what to do with us. But the sight of someone running will trigger an urge in them to follow and we will be mobbed. Isn't that instinctive kelocca behavior?" she asked Speezer.

"I am Speezer, and I enjoy a fine rambunctious frolic as much as anyone," the young kelocca admitted.

Behind us our pursuers were emerging from Charming Corners Below. Most evidently belonged to the local constabulary for they wore identical plaid aprons and carried coercive batons and other weapons. They proceeded after us but at no great speed, seemingly content to follow for the moment. By ones and twos other kelocca slipped from their mounds until we were trailed by hundreds, all silent, a gathering of wraiths in the rainbow mist. It was as if we were wandering in a dream, locked in slow motion, hunted and hunter alike trapped in a pavane without end, condemned to our formal procession for eternity. The kelocca mounds loomed like dolmens. I couldn't help thinking how easy it would be to get lost among them, lost and never found.

Then beneath my feet was hard surface instead of greensward.

"Keep walking straight," Mirable whispered, leading me in the direction of the shuttle, now clearly visible on the far edge of the landing field. I looked over my shoulder at the kelocca. There were a thousand of them by now but even so the only sound was the clicking of their nails as they followed us onto the pavement. Then I heard another noise, faint but hauntingly familiar, a humming at the edge of audibility.

"What is that?" I asked Alger, disturbed by the sound at a visceral level although I did not know why.

"It is opportune that you ask, sir, as I was about to bring the matter to your attention. I am surprised that you haven't recognized it already. What you are hearing, of course, is the sound of propellers."

Propellers. With a sick feeling in my stomach I raised my eyes skyward.

Coming toward us through the air was a flotilla of bicycles, wings bedizened with barbaric patterns done in black and blood-red, dried human parts clattering in the slipstream. Most were bicycles of war, equipped with harpoons, nets, spears, and bombs.

"The Marvelous Flying Bicycle Men," I said, all my worst fears realized. That they had followed so far made it clear that the barbarians would never rest until they had returned me to the Man Mother to face Tribal Law.

"What are they doing here?" Mirable asked. "Bicycle Men never raid this distance from their territory."

"They're not raiding, Mirable. They're after me. They tracked me to Twin Chasms House and must have picked up our trail in Witherell Spur. They're relentless bastards and have a coarse sense of humor."

The first outriders were over-flying us at an altitude of twenty meters. Approaching more slowly was a catamaran like the one I had served on under the stern eye of Faal Finechance among the idiots and other chattel meant for the meat mines. In the center of the bicycle was a throne of carved aca bone on which sat the vast bulk of Nonio Wellmete. The savage chieftain recognized me the moment I saw him and an expression of delight twisted the tattoos adorning his cheeks.

"There is the foreign pervert and scofflaw, Pimsol Anderts," declared Nonio Wellmete. "There is the heretic who defiled the sacred grove of the Man Mother. Brothers! Sons! My fathers! Bring me the head of the man who murdered Bunghole Gonzlez, may he be remembered in verse and song forever."

Bunghole Gonzlez! I didn't think Goodfellow would have been flattered by the notoriety. But there was no time to reflect on the irony of history.

The kelocca in their thousands were narrowing the gap between us, coming forward as inexorably as the tide. Above, a warrior whirled a weighted net in a blur around his head, preparing to cast.

"Go on," I told Mirable, much as Every Smit had instructed aboard the *Abernathy* while we fled Captain Hartung and his thugs. "Go on. Take Speezer and get to the shuttle. I will stay here. It is not you they're after."

"Forget it! You wouldn't leave me behind, Pim. I can do no less. Remember, I am sister and daughter of Imogene Wirthy and must conduct myself accordingly."

"Then do the smart thing. Go on, Mirable. Will you just hurry!"

"Not without you, Pim."

Her stubborn expression made it clear that further argument would be useless.

"If that's how you want it," I said. "All right, we're in this together. So let's—run!"

Mirable took the lead, Speezer was a close second, and I brought up the rear as we sprinted toward the distant spire of the shuttle. Our activity stimulated the kelocca, who began a weird squeaking and chattering. A few scampered after us, leaving their hind legs and going on all fours. Several others followed in ones and twos, and then a dozen more, and then the entire swarm began bounding across the pavement at our heels.

Perhaps fearing that the kelocca would reach me first and deny them their own vengeance by tearing us limb from limb, Nonio Wellmete and the Marvelous Flying Bicycle Men began bombarding the marsupials with darts, caltrops, and anti-personnel explosives. The kelocca scattered, taking cover among parked vehicles. Some pulled lasers from their aprons and snapped off retaliatory fire.

A bicycle crashed to the pavement just ahead of us. Mirable dodged around it without missing a step, her brown hair a streaming dark pennon behind her. "For the moment our friends seem more interested in each other than in us," she observed, not even a little out of breath despite our exercise while my own chest was heaving so heavily that I could hardly answer.

"Let's hope things stay that way."

The concrete between us and the shuttle was empty except for a few pieces of automated maintenance equipment. I began to entertain the foolish hope that we would survive our visit to Charming Corners.

Then a military personnel carrier with gray and black insignia descended and barred our way.

Its door shot open before the landing jets were entirely extinguished. A squad of troopers in battle gear scrambled out and took up defensive positions around their commander, hiding him behind a thicket of armored shields, so that it took several seconds before I realized that we were heading directly toward Kruuz Chung Pao[8].

His very presence was proof that the elder despot still intended to extract vengeance on Mirable and me for rescuing him from his son. As I had suspected, the rapier was as insanely single-minded as Nonio Wellmete.

"Ten thousand hhours to whoever captures the pair alive," called Kruuz[8], immediately confirming my pessimistic appraisal of the situation. "Before the day is done, they must be in agony. I have sworn this and I will not be denied. Make it so, my men. After them!"

"First the kelocca, then the Bicycle Men, and now this ungrateful bastard," I muttered to Mirable with what breath I had. "We're accumulating enemies like barnacles."

"May we overcome them, each and every one. Remember, Pim, God loves a winner."

Given the circumstances the truism would have emerged as a curse from my mouth but from Mirable's lips it was a benediction. I glanced at her sideways. Her mother-of-pearl skin was flushed dark red, perhaps from exertion, perhaps from excitement. It struck me that she was enjoying our mad desperate flight with much the same kind of delight that Captain Hartung had displayed aboard the *Miraculous Abernathy* while the ship was under attack. Gone was the fear and doubt that had overwhelmed her while she lay captive in Blimy's pithing chamber in Charming Corners Below. In its place was a sort of exhilaration, and I knew that I was seeing Mirable as she really was, the magnificent incarnation of a remarkable woman, who was inspired by her enemies rather than daunted by them.

A squad of troopers began lumbering toward us. "Head for the dome," I told her. "Let's see if we can lose them in the hedgerow."

A dense thicket of decorative vegetation perhaps ten meters deep and half that in height surrounded the opalescent dome of the Happy Free Trade Zone. We plunged into it barely ahead of the rapier's soldiers, the thick brush scratching our clothes and human skin but presenting little obstacle to Speezer, who slid easily through the bramble. Behind us I heard the troopers crashing into the shrubbery—and then oaths and angry squeaks as the squad encountered a host of kelocca and the two parties engaged in combat. Mirable and I reached the edge of the dome and began following the translucent wall in the direction of the waiting shuttle.

"We'll have to make a dash for it," I said when we arrived at the closest approach to the ship. "Our chances are pretty good, I think."

"Actually, sir, your chances are—"

"Alger, don't tell me! I don't want to know. Not another word unless we have another option with better odds. Is there one?"

"Unfortunately not, although I am continuing to extrapolate scenarios."

"I did not think there was." Aloud I continued: "Everyone's too busy to pay us any mind, that's to our advantage. They'll be too distracted by each other to notice us until it's too late. Are you ready, Mirable?"

"Oh, yes, I am ready!" she answered, fearless of the gauntlet we must soon run. "But if I should die—"

"Do not say it, Mirable. Don't even think it."

"But if I should die," she went on, "I want you to know one thing, Pim. I want you to know I cannot imagine anyone I would rather have spent the last day of my life with. Thank you for sharing it with me."

This time her kiss was fierce. Her brown eyes remained open, allowing me a glimpse of her passion and determination, of the leader of men and woman she was born to be, of the woman she was already.

This time, I knew, the kiss was not meant to stop me in my tracks and prevent me from following her into Blimy's Residence. No, this time Mirable meant the kiss to encourage me onward in the face of danger.

That she was again using the innate skills inherited from her clone mother Imogene Wirthy to motivate me somehow mattered less than the impression of her lips on mine.

Then she pulled away. Soon we were running together through the brush and out from cover into the open.

The shuttle was still a hundred meters off when all three groups spotted us simultaneously. The first darts from the Marvelous Flying Bicycle men began striking short before we'd covered half the remaining distance. It was quickly becoming obvious that one or another of our enemies would intercept us long before we could reach the shuttle.

At our present rate of speed.

"Now, Alger," I said.

Once again my personal attendant, aristocracy grade, flooded my metabolism with stimulant as he'd done aboard the *Miraculous Abernathy* during the pirate attack. With artificial strength I swept

Mirable from her feet, grabbed Speezer by the scruff of its neck, and raced forward at augmented velocity, zigzagging across the field in order to prevent being targeted.

My pulse pounding in my skull like rough surf, I crossed the final ten meters at full tilt.

Then something struck me below the left shoulder. Agony bloomed where I had been hit and filled my body to overflowing. Alger shunted most of the sensation aside, as when I had been tortured by the cannibal innkeeper Harmony Repute, but I hurt, and I knew I had received a mortal wound. I had died before, and there was no mistaking the sensation.

Ahead was the escalator leading up into the shuttle. Marksmen at the head of the ramp were laying down covering fire for Mirable and me, aiming impartially at the kelocca, at the Bicycle Men, and at the rapier's troopers. With my remaining strength I took the steps two at a time, arriving at the top just when I could go no further.

"Delighted to meet you again, my boy, and your charming companion, too," grated a voice I couldn't forget, a voice generated by a metal larynx and not by living tissue. "Despite certain intermittent periods of fear and doubt, when I have suspicions otherwise, I do believe this must indeed be a universe of miracles."

Captain Hartung wrenched Mirable from my grasp while I fell at his feet. I tried to get to my knees but couldn't. There was a hole in my shirt next to my heart and I knew I had been pierced through.

Speezer gave a shrill cry, threw up its paws, and tumbled down the escalator and out of sight.

"I have deployed emergency nano-surgeons to minimize blood loss and stabilize your condition, sir," Alger said. "I will continue providing local anesthesia for as long as medically necessary."

"How bad is it? Tell me the truth."

"You are dying, sir. Damage to your major organs is too extensive for me to repair before your metabolism flat-lines. You require full-scale medical intervention within an hour at the outside. Immediately would be better. Otherwise you have a .002 chance of survival."

Strangely, I had to bite my lip to restrain an odd laugh from slipping out at this information.

"An hour, why, I thought you had bad news, Alger. An hour's forever." To my feverish mind, it really seemed so. Anything could happen in an hour, even a miracle, hadn't I learned that from the Cee?

Somehow Mirable tore her wrist free of Hartung's grip, rounded back, and punched him, an effort that only bruised her hand and amused the pirate. He dragged her to her knees as he knelt beside me, motes of colored light swimming in his metallic eyes.

"The tart called her ship on an open line," Hartung said. "Can you imagine such innocence? It is as I said before, these merchant clans are all alike, inbred, insular, spiritless, and stupid. It was child's play to arrive on the scene ahead of her associates, and here we are, all together, just like old times. But, my boy, why, look at you. You have come to a sorry end."

"Set the girl free when you have what you want, captain," I replied, the effort of speaking causing pain to shoot through my chest despite Alger's ministrations. "Give me your word."

"In return for what? I do not mean to be cruel but you have nothing I want. Even life is departing you."

Mirable's head was bowed, her hair falling before her face in two parts along the channel where the kelocca had applied depilatory in preparation for the pithing process. "I couldn't afford a secure channel," she explained. "I did not think it mattered."

"It is not your fault, Mirable. Hartung's a persistent bastard, that's what it is. They're all persistent bastards," I finished weakly, meaning not only Felix Hartung but Nonio Wellmete, Kruuz Chung Pao[8], and the kelocca Blimy, who was approaching the tender with a posse of constables while carrying on a running fire fight with wheeling bicycles in the sky.

"A persistent bastard? Why, that I am, my boy," admitted the pirate. "Which is why I have decided to give you my word as you have asked. In return you will answer me the questions I riddled you with before. Do you remember them? I ask you—Have you lived to the limit, as God instructed? Have you regrets about what you have done or what you've left undone?

"Tell me, tell me without falsehood or perjury, since I really want to know and you will have no other chance to speak honestly."

"All right," I whispered. "It is a deal. Just let Mirable go."

My head was too heavy a weight to support and I allowed it to drop back upon the metal grating. Above was cloudless blue sky. My vision was failing and I saw a dark blotch upon the blue, a circle of black into which I would soon fall, never to return unless God approved of my efforts and allowed me an encore appearance upon the stage of life.

"If I had answered before, I would have said, yes, I had regrets, many of them, for I had lived according to other people's rules and not according to my own. But now I don't, no, Captain Hartung, I regret nothing. I have done what I could, and I played my part, and I tried my best. And, captain, listen to me, I have had the good fortune to meet the most wonderful girl there is in all this universe of miracles, and to earn her favor. I have made friends, and I have made enemies, and I value both. I have seen rare sights—"

The circle of black was growing larger against the blue, beckoning me into the void. Only the fact that I remained alive caused me to realize that what I was looking at was actually another ship approaching the landing field and not the coming of death itself.

The ship was fitted with heavy weaponry.

A spear of light stabbed Hartung's shuttle and sheared off a supporting strut. The stricken vessel settled on its side with a grinding noise and the gangway tipped over, tumbling Mirable and me onto the pavement. The impact should have killed me but somehow I survived. Several of Hartung's men were hit by debris and incapacitated but the pirate captain himself danced free of danger as nimbly as he had aboard the *Abernathy*.

Another beam of coherent violet light shot forth, this time from the wounded pirate shuttle into the sky.

It struck the airborne ship, which dropped straight down. Its vanes sheared off, cartwheeling at murderous velocity into a pack of kelocca, yet the fuselage remained whole. Hatches popped open and a detail of Wirthy marines climbed out. Like the rapier's men, they carried shields, which they brought together to form an enclosure around Vander Wirthy.

Mirable was cradling my head in her arms but I couldn't feel her touch. Moisture wet my face and I realized she was crying.

"Do not do that," I whispered, disconcerted by her tears. "Please don't, Mirable. It is like you said. I cannot imagine anyone else I would rather have spent the last day of my life with."

I did not know why but my answer made her angry. "Shut up, Pim. Just shut up. Save your strength. You must!"

"No, I won't shut up, not with my last breath in my lungs. I told Hartung the truth, Mirable, and I don't care who knows it. I think I have loved you since the instant we met. Maybe it was just infatuation to start with, but I have gotten to know you and my feelings have only deepened. I'm not totally a fool, despite what Every Smit thought, and I know you could never love me in return, there is too much between us, but if it makes a difference, I think you're brave and honest and kind and beautiful and I value every minute we've spent together, however difficult."

Again I must have said the wrong thing since even more tears dampened my cheeks.

"Oh, shut up, Pim," she repeated. "You are a fool. A courageous fool without a shred of common sense. Now not another word. Hang on. You must not go gently. Grab every second and squeeze it to you. Be angry, Pim. This is a universe of miracles, Pim! Of *miracles*! Make one happen!"

Around us the various combatants were now observing an uneasy cease-fire. The Marvelous Flying Bicycle Men landed their vehicles and regrouped in loose formation around the catamaran bearing Nonio Wellmete. Fifty meters to their left the kelocca swarm was seething in angry knots, its members squeaking and smacking each other's snouts and rumps in order to vent their collective irritation.

"I know you, pirate," Vander Wirthy called.

"And I know you, madam," Felix Hartung replied. "I have also had the pleasure of making the acquaintance of your lovely daughter."

He hoisted Mirable from the ground with one hand. "We have come full circle, Captain Vander," Hartung continued. "Now, however, I possess better leverage."

"Keep the girl, pirate," interrupted Nonio Wellmete. "Keep the girl for yourself or do with her what you will, but deliver the youth to me and you will be rewarded with many tonnes of prime tenderloin. Our rights are paramount! Pimsol Anderts the off-worlder slighted our Tribal Law and must be punished until he is dead, with appropriate flaying and flensing, after a lengthy period of excruciating instruction."

"Ignore the uncouth savage," interjected Kruuz Chung Pao[8], using an amplified microphone to drown out the hetman of the Marvelous Flying Bicycle Men. "Both lasses belong to me, without doubt! Have no fear, captain, I will offer you a better deal than either the barbarian or the merchant. You will not have cause for dissatisfaction, to this I swear."

The kelocca Blimy, however, had another point of view. "I am Blimy," it squeaked, "and because I am Blimy I am the legal owner of the human female, who is to be pithed for defaulting on her contract with Blimy. The human male is a vulgar thief. He, too, must be pithed, so that he may work off his obligation to Blimy in Blimy's Residence of Telecommunications Time and Equipment."

Once more darkness crossed my vision, shadowing the sky. Once more it was not death coming to claim me but another ship approaching Charming Corners.

The black ship.

The vessel that had pursued Mirable, Smit, and me during our mad descent to Temurlone in the lifeboat while escaping Captain Hartung.

I had thought the black ship had belonged to the pirate captain. But Hartung stared skyward with as much amazement as everyone else while the ship sailed past.

Streams of white foam shot from its weapons ports. The foam immediately expanded a million-fold into an adhesive aerogel and stuck to whatever it touched. Then the gel hardened and tightened. In seconds everyone was dodging the stuff or struggling to get free of its grip. Vander Wirthy's marines kept the streamers away from her with their riot shields. Nor was Captain Hartung trapped, although most of his crew became tangled in the sticky threads, as were a majority of the Marvelous Flying Bicycle Men, including Nonio Wellmete, and the kelocca constabulary.

Then the black ship put down between the contesting parties.

A gangway extruded from a personnel port and a dozen black machines marched onto the landing field. Each had a human form but were twice the normal scale of a man and lacked facial features. The fact that the automatons were equipped with built-in weaponry identified the machines as a squad of cyborg soldiers designed for mayhem.

A final figure stepped forth from the black ship. A woman.

"Sir," said Alger, "I do not know how to say this, but I believe I am about to experience a cognitive dysfunction and total system failure. In human terms I am about to have a nervous breakdown."

"Pull yourself together, Alger," I urged my personal assistant. "I am counting on you, do you hear? I am counting on you to look after Mirable. You have to forget me and move on."

"Sir, while it is true that I will regret your demise, I cannot say honestly that your loss would be sufficient trauma to cause my operating software to crash. No, sir, unless I am mistaken, we are being approached by Imogene Wirthy herself. And that cannot be. She is long dead."

Alger, unfortunately, was only half right.

We were not, however, facing a living Imogene Wirthy, not in the literal sense. Coming toward us was an Imogene Wirthy sculpted of pale alloy, as much a machine as her hulking companions.

Her face was Mirable's but not the coldness in the gleaming metal. Her eyes were equally as artificial as the orbs in Hartung's sockets. Yet her voice was soft, as if it came from the lips of a woman who breathed and bled.

"I have had enough of your mischief, pirate," said the apparition. "Put the girl down. She means little to me in any case. One clone is very like every other except that some are less competent. You have no leverage here, whatever your assumptions."

Hartung's smile was terrible. "Have we met, madam?"

"I am Imogene Wirthy. I was—I am—the captain of the *Miraculous Abernathy*. What I am also is a networked cybernetic organism with thirteen peripherals, each capable of eliminating you and your crew without assistance. Now be gone, before I become truly irritated."

The cyborg glared at Hartung until the pirate, realizing that his position was now untenable, released Mirable and took a step backward.

"Mother—" Mirable said.

"I am not your mother. I am Miss Imogene. I am the Captain. I am what you should be but have not yet become. I am your potential. I am the last resort of our ship and our clan and I am severely displeased since I must now step in and set affairs straight. The family has become inexcusably slack. Where is Vander? Where is that girl? I am dissatisfied with her performance. Bring her to me."

These spoken words were obviously superfluous since one of the machines had already left on the errand.

Mirable wouldn't be silenced by the cyborg's outburst. "Mother—Miss Imogene—my friend needs medical attention immediately or he will die. We must help him."

Imogene Wirthy turned her cold glare on me for the first time. "This is the boy who has caused so much trouble," she said after a brief study. "I recognize his face from surveillance recordings. First he led the boarders straight to my—to the captain's locker. Then he absconded with your person and created all sorts of difficulties. He has betrayed our ship and we owe him no favors. Leave the wretch to his fate. Survive or not, that is his affair."

This was no more than I had expected to hear. But Mirable refused to be daunted by the metal incarnation of her ancestor and returned the cyborg's stare measure for measure.

"Never, Mother—and I *will* call you mother if I want, so help me, since you are my own flesh or once were. Pim is my friend. And if friendship means nothing to you, know that he saved my life, not once but several times. I am in his debt, our family is in his debt, you are in his debt. It is a question of honor."

"A question of honor?" The cyborg focused its implacable gaze on Mirable long seconds. "Very well," it said at last. "We will do as you suggest, although I suspect there is more to the tale than you have shared with me. I am a Wirthy, I am *the* Wirthy, and I cannot allow a Wirthy debt to go unpaid, no matter to whom."

At a silent command another of the integrated cybernetic death machines brought a medical harness from the interior of the black ship. It wrapped this around my abdomen until I was cocooned in therapeutic machinery. I felt odd tinglings in a thousand places as microscopic tendrils slipped into my pores and wormed deeper into my interior to begin the healing process.

Now Vander Wirthy was escorted forward by the networked peripheral that had been sent to fetch her. She regarded her cyborg ancestor with an expression as severe as the one on its metallic face. "So the legend is true," she observed. "You did not die, Imogene. You just couldn't bear to leave anyone else in charge of the *Abernathy*, could you, not even yourself. So you had yourself made into this, into this metal thing. Where have you been hiding all these years? You and that black ship of yours?"

"In a place where I cannot be disturbed. But now, for a second time in a century, I have had to rouse myself from hibernation and intervene in shipboard affairs. I am not pleased. Nor is it a favorable distinction, Vander, that I have had to step in on your watch. We have much to discuss. Discipline must be tightened. Standards raised. Never should that creature"—she meant Hartung, who was still edging away from the conversation, attempting to distance himself from the entire affair—"have been permitted to board the *Abernathy*, whatever his tricks. It is inexcusable. I am putting an end to this fiasco."

The cyborg turned to Mirable. "You, too, girl. Smartly now. I am unhappy with you as well."

"No, mother. Not without Pim. We cannot just leave him here. It would be murder. He is surrounded by enemies who wish him harm."

The dead matriarch's machine body was modeled on the one she'd lived in and I recognized much of Mirable in the shape of her silver thighs and in the swell of her metal bosom. She strode forward and pinched Mirable's chin between hard metal fingers and forced her to face the crimson optical devices that were her eyes.

With a certain chill amazement in her tone the cyborg mused, "So, it's like that, is it? Was I ever so dull? I must have been, girl, for you are who I was once upon a time. Remarkable."

Imogene Wirthy addressed me next. "But you're smarter than my innocent clone, boy, are you not? You have a sly look about you, and I am sure you're a realist. Explain to the girl why it's impossible for you to accompany us."

Anger helped me overcome my weakness, or perhaps the medical machinery was already having an effect.

"First, there is nothing between Mirable and me, get that straight. Not that I'd mind, if it's any of your business, but there isn't. As for going with you, well, I wasn't planning on it. I've had enough of your filthy scow to last a lifetime. All I ever meant to do was to get Mirable to safety, and I have done that. No, the crone is right, Mirable, this is where we go different ways. Just do me a favor and take Speezer with you. I gave him my word."

The marsupial had rejoined us. "I am Speezer," it squeaked, "and I insist that you who are not Speezer convey Speezer off-planet to study foreign methods of achieving competitive advantage." The young kelocca's muzzle twitched. "Quickly now," it continued. "We have a binding verbal contract, which I have recorded in the event of your default, and Speezer would rather be elsewhere."

I did not think Mirable noticed what it said. Something happened to her face while I spoke, her features settling into an alabaster mask.

"Come," repeated Imogene Wirthy. "You heard the boy. He won't be joining us, which is just as well, considering the little I know of the rascal."

But Mirable ignored the matriarch's command and knelt beside me where I lay swathed in the therapeutic cocoon. From her first word it was clear I had managed to anger her again. "I did not think you were afraid of anything, Pim. I guess I was wrong."

"Afraid? I am not afraid of that metal hag, if that's what you mean."

"Of course that's not what I mean! I know you, Pim, and I have seen your courage. What I don't understand is why you're so willing to give me up. Do I matter so little to you despite what you said as you lay dying?" Suddenly Mirable's cheek was pressed against mine and her lips were to my ear. "Or is it that you fear I couldn't return your love?" she asked in an urgent whisper. "Is that what scares you, you brave stupid honorable idiot. Well, believe otherwise. Believe that I could love you and it will be so, but only if you fight for me, Pim. Only if you allow no obstacle between us. Only if your dreams are large enough for both of us. Let your passion prove you worthy to bind my heart and make me yours. Take me from my ship or take the helm at my side, just make it happen, Pim. Make it happen."

A pale alloy hand settled on her shoulder and took Mirable away before I could answer.

"Enough, girl," said the networked cybernetic organism that Imogene Wirthy had become as she herded Mirable toward the black ship. "Enough romantic blather. You know very well that your marriage will be arranged for the political and commercial advantage of our ship and for the enhancement of our bloodline. Put the boy out of your mind. I know his type, in any case. An opportunist, pure and simple. You'll never see him again."

"That's what you think, you damned metal bitch." It was physical agony not being able to move. "You'll see me again, and you won't like it, I promise. Do you hear me, Mirable? I will make it happen. I swear

I will."

Imogene Wirthy did not bother acknowledging my outburst. Mirable couldn't break the relentless metal grip that held her but she managed to twist around enough so that I could see her face one last time.

"Remember Silver," she said. "He can always find me. Don't forget, Pim."

Then they were at the portal of the black ship.

As Mirable and Imogene Wirthy and her deadly peripherals entered the vessel, Speezer slipped inside with them. That he was not ejected out of hand proved that the cyborg had decided to allow the kelocca to pursue its dream of studying foreign business practices.

As for myself, I could do nothing but lie motionless in the medical swaddling and watch the ship lift off in an explosion of vapor to meet the *Miraculous Abernathy* in orbit overhead.

From there its Avatar™ engines would propel the ancient freighter away from the sun toward the heliopause, where it would shift to trans-light velocity and resume its long journey from star to star.

Colored threads among my medical cocoon began flickering on and off. Soon the swaddling became brittle and flaked away. The wound in my chest was closed and there was hardly a scar. But the effort of sitting up still left me breathless.

"I must admit, sir," Alger said, "for awhile I was severely concerned."

"You, Alger? I didn't think I would make it, either."

"No, sir, what concerned me was that Miss Imogene might notice my presence."

Despite the medical treatment, laughing hurt. "Having met your former mistress, Alger, well, someday you'll have to tell me what happened between you two. Just think, the old dead bitch has been aboard the *Abernathy* a hundred years, her and her black ship, and no one suspected. She must have been really something when she was alive. Something like, well, something like Mirable."

"Indeed, sir, I had noticed a slight resemblance."

My strength was returning and I was able to climb to my feet. The landing field was littered with my adversaries, most imprisoned in aerogel. Not a dozen meters away, its lavender eyes never leaving me, Blimy was chewing stoically at its sticky bindings. Further off, a couple tattooed warriors were cutting Nonio Wellmete free of the threads that held him. It was just a matter of time before hundreds of angry kelocca, troopers, pirates, and Marvelous Flying Bicycle Men would be after me again.

"What have you decided, sir?"

"Do you have to ask?"

"I was being polite, sir. Of course I assume we will indulge your infatuation and follow Miss Mirable."

"You heard her, Alger. She wants me to."

His pause went on for too long. At last Alger said, "Sir, perhaps I should have inquired earlier, but what precisely do you understand about the courtship and marriage rituals aboard deep-space merchant freighters such as the *Miraculous Abernathy*?"

"Why, nothing much at all, you know the Wirthys never mixed with forecastle crew."

"Then allow me to elaborate, sir. Typically all partnerships, particularly among the officer class, are allowed only after exhaustive negotiations between clan elders. Your genetic matrix would be analyzed and compared to Miss Mirable's to ensure that any offspring would be optimal. Then your lineage would be vetted, as well as the value of your political connections. Additionally, sir, you would be expected to provide a bridal ransom commensurate with Miss Mirable's status. This is an essential display of respect and honor. In my opinion, and I do not know how to phrase this delicately, you simply cannot afford her. Nor would Miss Mirable be willing to entertain your attentions should you arrive to court her as an hhour-less pauper. It would be beneath her dignity."

Alger probably expected this gloomy analysis to dampen my spirits, if not dissuade me from my plans altogether, but his pessimism only made me more determined.

"I will worry about that when the time comes," I said with a confidence that probably derived from the medication with which I had recently been dosed by the therapeutic cocoon that had returned me to life. "Remember, my good personal assistant, aristocracy-grade, this is a universe of miracles, which expands or contracts according to your appetite for living. Not easily, I am not saying that. God will make things damned hard, as difficult as can be, rest assured, that's just the nature of divinity, everyone knows. But I have hope, Mirable's given it to me, and with hope all things are possible, isn't that what *Scripture* says? Tell me I am wrong."

"You are not incorrect, sir."

"Now, Alger," I continued, furiously turning over alternatives as I began heading toward the edge of the landing field and away from Charming Corners, "our first task is getting out of here while we can. Then we'll concentrate on getting off-planet. And let's not forget Silver. We have to return to Churraspora to pick up the old monster from Jasmine. He'll be a help, somehow, Mirable said as much."

A half kilometer in front of us another person had already

reached the foothills surrounding the kelocca colony. It was the scarred armored form of Felix Hartung.

A stroke of luck already! I began hurrying to catch up with the pirate.

We had our differences, true, but who else could better advise me on procuring a ship and the sailors to man her? On escaping Temurlone and picking up the trail of the *Abernathy* and Mirable Wirthy? Hartung's expertise would be invaluable. That we were traveling in the same direction on the same road was a portent too blatant to ignore.

God enjoys a good story.

And this was a universe of miracles, after all.

End

The adventures of Pimsol Anderts will continue in
Escape from Temurlone.

www.ingramcontent.com/pod-product-compliance
Lightning Source LLC
Chambersburg PA
CBHW070309260626
47160CB00003B/789